THE FIRE LINE

TREVOR FERGUSON

THE FIRE LINE

A NOVEL

HarperCollins*Publishers*Ltd

The author is grateful to the Canada Council and the University of Alberta for his stay as a Writer in Residence during the writing of this novel.

THE FIRE LINE

First edition

Canadian Cataloguing in Publication Data

Ferguson, Trevor, 1947-
The fire line : a novel

ISBN 0-00-224393-8 (bound)
ISBN 0-00-648087-X (pbk.)

I. Title.

PS8561.E759F5 1995   C813'54   C94-932375-6
PR9199.3.F47F5 1995

95 96 97 98 99 ❖ HC 10 9 8 7 6 5 4 3 2 1

Printed and bound in the United States

for the bridgemen now dispersed
&
as ever
for Lynne

The earth in its devotion
carries all things, good and evil,
without exception.

— THE I CHING

THE FIRE LINE

PROLOGUE

The
Burnt
Hills

THE MAN CAST NO SHADOW dangling in the light of the sun rising beyond the burnt hills. A squat moon set behind him. He cast no shadow upon the meadow of ash and smouldering cinders or upon the braised bark of the tree from which he hung.

He gripped the knot fastened around his neck and pulled himself up with both hands to preserve his life awhile. He wanted to say something. To die was to die but to cast no shadow at the hour of his death seemed an unwarranted indignity. He wanted to speak and have this discussed. He had been forsaken. He wanted that mentioned. He had cast no shadow. He wanted that widely known. He wished to have it explained to him. What it meant. Why it had to be.

The man was willing to die but some things needed to be said first. He wanted to talk about it but there was no one listening. Only the burnt woods. The blackened trees. The smoke. The ash. The raring sun and a disconsolate moon and his soul swinging gently forward and discreetly back between the two.

I'm awaiting on my salvation, he thought he would say. If he could speak and someone would listen those would be his first words. I'm awaiting on it now. That's how he would explain himself hanging from the last tree in the forest still standing with its limbs intact set off in a charred meadow swinging at the end of a great length of firehose.

I have come to this place in the midst of this time and here I am awaiting.

For something.

This should keep, he thought he would say. He would say that.

This should keep. *Please. Someone. Listen up.*

The moon sunk below the awning of that desolated horizon.

The sun floated above the burnt hills and beams through the remnant stalks of birch shot upon his face and he thought he would be blinded. He thought he would ascend into the sky and into the light and the man squirmed at the end of his noose and jerked so hard he kicked a boot off. The man thrashed and cried out and commenced to speak in a savage voice in a language filled with rage and sorrow and fury and complaint and abject lamentation.

He began to speak.

His rain of words fell upon the thirsty earth and gave him pleasure descending upon the ash. He almost laughed—a dangerous thing. He could lose his concentration—his strength be sapped—sootcovered bloodied sweated hands might slip. He wanted to talk about this. He wanted to go back in time and tell his friends if he had any yet alive that he had seen the future and in that future he had died laughing. They'd appreciate that sort of tale.

The man began to tell the story whether or not his friends could hear and whether or not they'd listen.

In the burnt out meadow swinging at the end of a firehose the dangling man spoke to the rising sun as if to some old friend as if this was some other beginning to a fine new day and he really ought to savour the moment.

I

The
Aforementioned
Peculiar
Puzzle
of Predicaments

1

IN THE PHYSICAL HEART of British Columbia in the Prince George railway station there a thin man with angular features wearing denim and a green peaked cap and carting about an oily old green gunnysack surveyed the substantial map of the province posted on a broad wall. The room was large and vacant with white benches and brown floors worn from the daily scuffle of feet and the ceaseless flux of human migrations. The man's name was Reed Kitchen and he traced the hatched lines of track that moved in and out of town east and west and north and south like a sketch of human arteries. He scanned whistle stops toward the Pacific coast near Prince Rupert. The name of the place where he was bound—Kwinitsa—failed to catch his eye.

He crossed the room.

Another journey to an unknown destination, he said to the stationmaster as he laid his voucher down at the narrow blackbarred wicket.

Without speaking the diminutive greyhaired liverspotted fellow seemed to agree.

Can't find this here place on your map.

It's there.

Where?

On the map.

An atmosphere of quiet persisted in the broad room with the high ceiling and the dark varnished wood trim. An atmosphere to be inhaled and gently released as though the station at this hour had adopted the forbearance of a library. No sound should rise above the gentle whir of the electric heater at the stationmaster's feet. Sound belonged to the violence of the railway yard. The pervading quiet here was taciturn—an antidote to the tramontane barbarism a step beyond the doors.

Tickets were exchanged for his voucher and methodically stamped and excess sheets were ripped away and Reed Kitchen minded his peace. The need to speak brewed inside him. He had not said much throughout an ageless night on a slow and tardy train into town. Fatigue had bloated his tongue. He had lacked the energy to gab but he could not sleep either. Thoughts like cold coffee grounds kept stirring themselves up at the base of his mind. He had detrained at dawn when there was not much to talk about and no one around with whom to share that conversation. Neither asleep nor amply awake he had passed the time on the station platform lying on a handcart in a hollow of magazine bales listening to diesels idle. He had attended to their ruminations and shivered. Reed Kitchen's gunnysack had slept alongside him like a warm contented bride and he felt himself adrift—afloat—on air—like smoke. I feel like smoke, he had told himself aloud for he sorely yearned to hear a voice. I do believe I don't smell much better.

Reed Kitchen received his tickets and before the stationmaster could pull down the blind he asked him in a notch above a whisper, Could you be a tad more specific about what certain unforeseen eventualities a fellow might be expecting to occur in this here unknown destination to where it is I'm going? I'm cautious. I'm a cautious man generally. It is my steadfast policy to keep a contingency plan handy on the side.

Excuse me? the stationmaster responded.

Kitchen had to rethink his words. He needed to pull the thought together and cull it down to its impetus. Something disorderly in his head this morning was stimulated by those cold coffee grounds still percolating at the bottom of his mind. He asked him, What's out there?

Ever been to nowhere, mister?

Plenty of times.

Enjoy those trips much?

Most times.

Then I wish you good luck this time around.

The stationmaster drew down the opaque blind.

In a trice he snapped it back up again. You're catching the noon train west. I presume you know that.

Yes I do. And I will.

Not at noon you won't. The noon train won't be here until the earliest fifteen hundred hours. Won't be out of here and gone before sixteen hundred hours. That's if you're inclined to be an optimistic sort.

Reed Kitchen continued to look at the man as though expecting him to finish and the stationmaster took that time to consider his choices.

Seeing as how you're a railway man I could put you on a westbound freight in—he looked up at the clock—eleven minutes.

The engine or the caboose? Reed Kitchen asked and his spirits ascended as rapidly as they had slumped a moment ago.

What do you think?

I think you don't want me hanging around your station six or seven more hours.

No skin off my nose. What'll it be? The freight or the wait?

There are men who are foreign in another country. I am a man foreign in my own country. That might be the same thing. It might be something different. I have worked with men who have been castaway and I have been castaway and I have cast myself away. It's who I am. It's what I do. Where I am is never where it is I've been or where I'm bound.

The stationmaster stared at him unblinkingly. He did finally say, What's that supposed to mean?

It means point me in the right direction, Kitchen told him and he hoisted his duffle onto his shoulder again. If I am headed to nowhere I would rather not get lost.

He knew enough to pass up the four locomotives—four mammoth

deities rumbling in their slumber emitting a high nasal whine—and he walked the great distance on down the track to climb aboard the caboose. This was an old caboose with whitewashed wood and varnished trim and the oil heater had been lit. The conductor and the brakemen were outside and busy so Reed Kitchen made himself at home. He chose an apple and a slice of cheese from the table and from the ice box ginger ale. He would eat and he would rest and he would reheat his caffeine thoughts and slurp them down.

This is fitting, he did believe. He had been presented with a ticket to nowhere and now he was going to get there without having to use it.

TWO BRAKEMEN STEPPED ABOARD the aft end of the caboose and entered without saying a word while the train was creaking into motion out of the yard westbound to the coast. The conductor caught hold of the grab rail and swung himself onto the boarding step as the train gained speed. He landed in the caboose through the back door and before Reed Kitchen could speak the conductor told him, You're the talker.

My reputation has preceded me.

You gab. The conductor lifted the portable radio off his shoulders.

From time to time I might feel inclined to venture an opinion on this or that subject—

You like to chat.

It's only human, Kitchen reminded him.

He was seated on one of the facing settees and feeling the need to lie upon it and get some sleep once these introductions were concluded to the conductor's satisfaction. The overnight trip had been tedious and he was stiff and weary and he continued to be disorderly in his thoughts. Reed Kitchen had worked upon the railway long enough to know that it was in his own best interests not to rile the man.

Chat separates us from the animals.

You babble.

I've been known to speak my mind—

You prattle, the conductor accused. You gossip. You argue. You pontificate.

I really don't know where you get your information—

You grouse. You gripe. You're a whiner.

Who's been saying these terrible things? The stationmaster? I only just met him. Ask him. I didn't say more'n a nickel's worth to the guy.

You blab, the conductor said. He hung up his coat and lifted back his blue conductor's cap to brush thin strands of hair. For a conductor he had a small nose. In Kitchen's experience conductors had large red bulbous misshapen noses. Men with such noses were usually jolly and kind and tolerant of him.

I'm no grouser. I don't gripe. I never complain. I've never whined about anything in my life.

What are you doing now?

Defending myself against these base charges.

I have my sources. I know you. You talk too much.

What sources? Who has said these things in this part of the country where I have never been?

Trainmen. Off the freight that brought you in here this morning.

I never heard myself talking on that train. I do believe I kept my mouth shut on that train. My lips were sealed.

The youngest of the brakemen was brewing a pot of coffee and he was the one to reveal, They slipped you a mickey.

What?

The tall and older brakeman sprawled lengthwise on the settee opposite Reed Kitchen put his feet up. He was wearing leather steel-toed boots with many gouges and nicks and scratches. His jeans were ragged at the cuffs and he wore a red eiderdown vest over his plaid lumberman's shirt with the flaps hanging out. He wiped perspiration from his temples and high above his eyes.

They gave you a sleeping pill, the conductor confirmed. He was in his railway uniform as though he had expected to be on a passenger train today and had at the last minute been reassigned. Perhaps he was commonly meticulous in his dress. He took off the jacket and donned a sweater and made himself comfortable. Trainmen said it never put you to sleep but it shut you up real good.

What? Reed Kitchen asked again.

They found a way to keep you quiet.

This is a terrible thing, Kitchen protested. This is a travesty. This is a violation inflicted upon my person. They can't do that. You know they can't do that. It's not right.

One way to make it here without killing you first, the prone brakeman told him.

Which brings us to our problem, the conductor said.

Reed Kitchen felt wounded. He felt hurt. He had been drugged by men he had trusted. He had been abused in the past for talking too much. He had had his head submerged in a toilet bowl and he had been punched unconscious and he had been forced out of a bunkhouse in the deadfall of winter to freeze his skin and have his words censored by chattering teeth. He had had his mouth shut with sticky tape. Never before had he been drugged and he was hurt again and impressed again by the bottomless pit of bottomless human iniquity.

What problem? he asked. He knew what problem.

You talk too much. I know your kind. You gab. You filibuster. I'll tell you something right now, mister, there'll be no filibustering aboard my train. None. You want to filibuster in my caboose I'll have you thrown off it. I won't ask the boys to check first if we're not out over a canyon or not out over a bridge neither.

Everybody has something to say—

How are we going to travel together today in the limited confines of this caboose? the conductor inquired.

People exaggerate. I don't talk that much really—

I know how, the conductor told him.

You do. How?

That's what I'm here to tell you. It's simple. You won't say nothing.

Can't we be reasonable—

Be quiet.

I'm not really that—

Shut up.

Listen—

Don't talk.

How did they do it? Reed Kitchen pleaded.

Spiked your coffee, the brakeman said. He was brewing a fresh pot. He smiled.

This is—

Put a cork in it, the conductor demanded.

—an outrage. They drugged me?

The brakeman on the opposite settee watched the coffee percolate and nodded in the affirmative.

Gag him, the conductor ordered.

Both brakies were aroused and willing.

Enough, Reed Kitchen said. Control yourself here. He climbed onto the settee. The spongy cushions made his feet unsteady. His head bumped the ceiling. That stuff about tossing him off a moving train he recognized as talk. What worried him more was that they might do it while the train was stationary and any number of stops convenient to their cause lay ahead. He might possibly be jettisoned into a wilderness he would rather not inhabit. What was worse— being heaved into a nowhere land or travelling to an unknown destination gagged? He saw no safe means of escape. This won't turn out right, he complained.

Kitchen raised his fists but the movement of the train and his unsteady footing foiled his balance. The brakies each grabbed an arm and yanked him off the settee and stood him up on the floor. The conductor sat down on the opposite settee and looked across at Kitchen.

Now we can stop all this nonsense, Reed Kitchen said.

The conductor reached for a pillow. He was watching Kitchen and not the pillow as he tugged off the slipcase. He held up the pillowcase first with one hand—not looking at it—then he held it taut between both hands. He made it snap. Kitchen squirmed but the brakemen were strong. He heard the steel wheels of the caboose cross a switch from the sidetrack onto the main line.

Don't you ever do this to me, mister. All I want here is to lie down and have my sleep and get to where it is I'm going wherever that may happen to be. I got no chatter on my mind. Swear to the heavens above and the earth below you won't get no conversation out of me today. Not a peep. I never caught two winks last night and I'm a tired man. No wonder I'm a tired man. No wonder I been disorderly in my thoughts this morning. I didn't sleep two winks last night and took a mickey besides. Betrayed by my own kind. By railroaders. I ask you. How could they do that to me? Don't it just break your heart? The conductor snapped the standard issue grey railway pillowcase between his hands and the sound it made was the sound of a whip upon a palm that is delicate and in disgrace. Sir, you don't have to do this to me today. I'm begging you here all right? There it is. I'm begging you. It's official. I'm telling you. I'm going to sleep. I am. I'm nodding off already. If these two boys weren't holding me up I'd be dozing on that settee this minute. I'm sure of that. I don't ever talk in my sleep much or not on a regular basis as far as I can determine—

The conductor leapt to his feet but he still did not come near him or touch him or transgress any code of railway conduct. He hollered, Shut up.

Yes, sir. I won't say a word.

You're talking right now. The conductor wrenched the pillowcase taut as though he'd forget about gagging him and go straight to strangulation. Don't you say one word, talker. Nothing. Don't answer. Not one word, gabber. You can sleep in here and when you're awake you can go outside and jabber to the wind for all I care—

Thank you—

Shut up. Don't say that. Don't speak. Not a single word. Understand? Do you get it now? Nod if you understand. If you say yes or no so help me I'll stuff the whole damn pillow down your throat. Get it?

Reed Kitchen had so much to tell him. He had so much to say. He wanted to explain. He wanted to convince the conductor that he could not possibly imagine the torture he was putting him through. He wanted the conductor to comprehend his dilemma—that to speak was to breathe and not to speak was a form of suffocation—life-threatening—that he could no more help himself than the conductor could will his lungs to hold the same air for a day or command his heart to stop beating. For Kitchen it was a great strain and a huge victory to confront the angry glower of his tormentor and at the same time quell the legitimate comments that he had a right to proffer. He nodded. A simple nod. He reduced his opinion and his thesis to a nod of concession and both brakemen as if to acknowledge his triumph released him.

He almost spoke. The conductor's finger came up to censor him as the words were about to emerge. He wanted to tell him that he was a foreign man in his own land in perpetual migration. He thought better of it. Kitchen exercised great restraint to keep mum and lay down on the settee and clamped his jaw shut for he was a man of his given word. The conductor tossed him an itchy regulation grey railway blanket. He covered himself and lay with his eyes wide open upon the wonderment of his disorderly thinking and the debacle of these days. The exercise of a great discipline allowed Reed Kitchen to subdue his voice despite it being evident to him—as obvious as the train—that what he had to say was just and vital and needing to be heard.

Threats alone did not put him to sleep. Threats alone and beatings never did. The comforting sound of the wheels clickclacking over the rail joints and the push and pull on the coupling and the rhythmic haw and sway of the caboose lulled him to sleep. Amid the welter of his dreams Reed Kitchen went rigid and finally limp. The influence of these familiar sounds and motions and the calamity of his previous night put him away and the only sound emitting from Reed Kitchen was a whistle and a sputter and the occasional impassioned irate snore.

The conductor climbed into the turret and loosened his tie. He drank coffee and read the daily paper and reported to the engineer that the next bridge had a Slow Order on it—fifteen-miserable-miles-per-hour—to be followed immediately by a whistle crossing.

The train screeched and roared and droned the sad chant of its lamentation and the obstreperous whistle blew as though to herald a destination neither unknown nor yet beheld.

REED KITCHEN BY MIDDAY CONCLUDED that he had entered the outer reaches of nowhere. He determined this by the evidence of where he had been. Seated on the rear platform of the caboose with his feet on the steps he watched the land shimmy past him—a river surge past him—whistle stops and sidings disappear behind him. An untamed woods riven with ponds. The train bore into the geography of nowhere and from his restricted vantage point at the back of the caboose he watched the world disappear. All I get to see is where I already been, he ruminated aloud. Never do I observe where it is I'm going.

For men who did not want to talk or more particularly did not want to talk to him the two brakemen and the conductor ventured out onto the back porch of the caboose frequently enough to chat. The conductor himself appeared and leaned on the back rail and smoked and conversed. He was a talker. Reed Kitchen told him so. You don't want me behaving gregarious in your caboose because you know I can talk you under the table any day of the week or night.

I never said I don't like to chew the fat, the man replied. That don't necessarily mean I am content to listen. There won't be no end-less useless gabbing aboard my caboose.

There was none. With the men either busy or napping Reed Kitchen found himself bereft of chatter. He climbed up the rear ladder to the top of the caboose to walk on down the length of train.

The conductor slid across the glass in his turret. Hey you. Motor-mouth. Get down off there.

Kitchen turned the key in the lock of his lips and tossed it over the side of the train. He turned and walked on.

Hey. Get down off my train. Don't go walking on my train. You'll get yourself killed and I don't want you doing me any favours.

Reed Kitchen scowled at that. Killed. He'd walked across the tops of more trains than all the dead hoboes of the thirties combined and usually for the same reason—to find someone with whom to share a pleasant conversation.

Reed Kitchen counted the cars as he walked across them.

Boxcars and hoppers.

Refrigerator cars.

An automobile carrier.

Flats that carried raw lumber and planed timber.

Tank cars. Grain cars.

Generator cars—a pair.

The train was one hundred and eightysix cars long.

He climbed from ladder to ladder on the boxcars. Saw himself splayed across the moving surface of the ground like the shadow of a man spreadeagled and staked to the sky. Kitchen balanced on timbers with his arms floating outward to counter the wind and he leapt between cars with his shadow on the moving surface of the ground like the silhouette of a man strolling across a darkened rumbling ridge of cloud.

The thunder of the train rolled beneath his boots.

Kitchen sauntered across the roofs of the two generator cars then down onto the diesels. He wedged himself through the narrow portal where the engineer was smoking and the brakeman cooling a coffee with his breath.

The engineer was sitting on the small operator's stool. His foot depressed the emergency brake and his right wrist lay limp upon the sliding steel throttle.

You damn fool crazy idiot, the engineer told him calmly. I told Carl. If he falls we're not stopping. We're riding on and he agreed.

I didn't fall.

How can anybody be so fool stupid? You realize the trouble you'd've made for me falling?

I'm sorry about that trouble I have not caused you yet. I thought maybe you could use a little conversation up at this end.

The engineer was a wiry scrawny guy with a lot of miles under his frown. I heard about you. You've walked on trains before.

My reputation has preceded me.

You bet your ass. Walk on a train of mine again and I'll dynamite the brakes and knock you off it.

Reed Kitchen smiled and wet his lips. He understood the jargon. He had come to the right place. He inhaled the stink of oil and brake shoes and cleared the beat of the wind and the tickle of diesel fumes from his throat and nostrils. He looked forward to the unknown land where he was bound.

Damn fool crazy idiot, the engineer mumbled to himself and Reed Kitchen accepted these words as his cue to speak.

THE ENGINEER TOLD HIM THE NAMES of the places as they passed them
by and the names of the places they had already been. Naming the
towns and the hamlets and the whistle stops and the sidings altered
Reed Kitchen's perceptions of the unknown country. Names changed
his idea of the place named. Isle Pierre. Finmoore. Vanderhoof. Fort
Fraser. Fraser Lake. No longer were the words incidental coordinates
on a map. They had become destinations. Histories and mines and
logging sites. Sawmills burning dust and scrap in fiery red cones. The
names had become the lives of the people in their homes and in their
plight. Hillside huts and churches and highway junctions. The names
had become the children to whom he faithfully waved from the window of the locomotive. They had become the places he was in and
the places he was going and the places he had been. Endako. Burns
Lake. Palling. Topley. Houston. Telkwa. Smithers. Hazelton and New
Hazelton where the late afternoon sun shone on the broad sweep of
valley away from the tracks across farmland to the high veer of mountain. The darkening green of the mountain and the coppering gold of
the fields and the speckled selvage of wildflowers and the high blue of
the sky and the blowzy disk of the sun and the burnish of the rails a
welcome. Colours worthy of an unknown destination. He had not
known a land this fair.

Kitwanga. Cedarvale. Pacific. Usk. The hulk of train an antiquated
relic. The names of the rivers. The Nechako. The Endako. Where the
mammoth train clung to the lip of a canyon and no land was visible
below save the sheer drop into the torrent—the Bulkley.

Further on—the Skeena.

This is your river, the engineer told him.

My river. All right. This is my river. When did this happen?

You're headed for Kwinitsa.

So I been told.

Kwinitsa's on the Skeena. These are the headwaters. K'shian the
Indians call it. The River of Mists.

You know things, Reed Kitchen said.

I know the Skeena River, the engineer said.

Kwinitsa's not a place I'll be staying long, Reed Kitchen said. The bridge gang there is on the move downriver one step or maybe one long stride ahead of Old Man Winter. So I have been promised and foretold.

Tyee, the engineer told him.

What's that?

Bet you. Your gang'll set up in Tyee. A Slow Order's come down on the Green River Bridge. That's how come I know.

What's that place like? I was promised subtropical climes. That's where my seniority has carried me. Out of winter's icy claw.

It rains a lot, the engineer said. If you want to call that subtropical go ahead.

Beats snow.

Tyee's on the bank of the Skeena River.

What's there?

Nothing. You will be there when you get there. Your gang will be there. I hope you like your own company because that's the best you'll keep.

A section crew lives there, the brakeman contradicted his superior. They got what? Two shacks?

A section crew, the engineer scoffed. One foreman and one worker. Tops.

Somebody to talk to.

The worker's a giant, the brakeman added. A kid. Like Paul Bunyan.

God's country, the engineer commented. You know why they call it that? All it ever does is rain.

The section foreman I heard is antisocial, the brakie said. He's not partial to people.

I am given to understand that God likes it damp in His country in a land of giants and humans opposed to their own kind.

It's people who don't like it damp. That's the ticket. Rain gives God some walking around room mostly free from trespassers. There's Indian huts down by the Green River Bridge. Can't say for sure they're occupied.

No snow though.

Only when it gets cold.

Through radio static they made out the voice of the conductor.

Hey, he hollered as though he was shouting his words down the length of the train, you still got that blabbermouth gabberyakker gabbing and yakking up there with you?

Reed Kitchen's hand reached the radio mike first and he pressed the button. I'm glad you called. I don't talk so much like people say and I want you to know something. A lot of that business is a misconception.

You're talking in my ear right now. Get off this radio and give me Henry unless you already gone and talked him to death or into some gahdarned early retirement.

Kitchen passed the mike to the engineer. The man won't listen to reason, he said. He's incorrigible.

Been on the hooter to Terrace, the conductor said. A railway dick's coming aboard we're supposed to take through to Rupert. You know what that means.

Ah, the engineer said, no. What does that mean?

Means I got to hike it back to the caboose, Reed Kitchen told him.

It means that blabbermouth gabberyakker has to get his ass back here where his friends are at.

There won't be no gagging of the mouth when a railway dick's aboard, Reed Kitchen told the engineer. Tell him.

The engineer passed along the message in his own words. Reed says you can't muzzle him with a detective watching.

Ask him if he'd like a cup of coffee, the conductor said and he stayed on the line a few seconds longer so that Reed Kitchen could listen to his robust cackle.

The train rumbled on into the deafened night. A moot sun slumped between hills that presaged the mountains. Reed Kitchen told stories about railway dicks he had known and the predicaments they had seen. I don't want you walking on my train at night, the engineer told him.

After we stop in Terrace I'll stroll on back.

That's the ticket.

You know what the saddest thing is?

What's the saddest thing, Reed?

I won't never see where it is I'm going. I'm entering God's country otherwise known as nowhere with my eyes looking out the back of my head and that strikes me as an awful shame.

Dark out anyhow, Reed. At least you'll arrive at where you're going. Not everybody can say that in this world.

Myself personally I'm looking forward to it. I'm looking forward to it even while I'm looking behind. I just want to know one thing, Henry. My circulation's sub par. How cold does it get out there really?

Where? Tyee? Tell you what. I only drive the train, the engineer did muse and he measured his words with care. No one has ever let me steer the bus.

REED KITCHEN CHATTED IN THE CABOOSE free from standard issue railway gags in the logging town of Terrace. The detective they awaited climbed aboard. Your name is Reed Kitchen and I am pleased to meet you, the man said. He put his satchel down beside the green gunnysack. I've heard tell about you.

My reputation has preceded me, Kitchen said.

He felt captive here and cuffed. The detective was a chummy fellow with a respectable paunch for a man in his midforties who was losing his hair well before his time. He possessed a naturally friendly demeanour and his eyes were expressive and kind which provoked in Reed Kitchen's belly a parsimonious spirit. He had come into contact with railway detectives before when mischief had occurred on a jobsite—none of those men had taken cognizance of him. Now that one had expressed an interest he was inclined to fret about the cause.

I suppose you have climbed aboard this caboose to tell me that hereby as of five o'clock this afternoon talking has become an illegal recreation upon the railway like spitting swearing drinking possessing a firearm and unauthorized fornication. Talking is the only crime my friends and enemies tend to hold against me. So that must be it. But I do believe that you will find a prohibition against recreational speech to be a difficult regulation to enforce and my best advice today is that you don't bother. Don't even try. Let it go. Permit chat.

The railway detective looked from Reed Kitchen to the conductor and back to Kitchen and it was easy to see that maintaining his podgy smile required effort. Pardon me there, friend?

Did the conductor here put you up to this? Reed Kitchen inquired. Because before we get down to discussing any investigation that you might wish to commence concerning the merits or the demerits of talking or not talking on trains—or if you want to get fussy about these things walking on trains—I want to speak first and at some length about the ethical nature of a gag upon the mouth. And after we have had done with that discussion we ought to have a little chat between and betwixt ourselves about trainmen and mickeys and the life of the railroading man. We should have that talk here today.

The conductor was looking right at him from the opposite settee. I don't think our guest is interested in those discussions, Mr Kitchen. He was staring right at him and Kitchen took the inference that he meant more than he was willing to speak aloud.

This man says he has heard of me. He has heard of me in a land where I have never been. In a land where my name has never been mentioned before this day.

A brakeman had assumed the conductor's duties and the train eased its slow cumbersome snake of a body down the tracks.

Not from me he hasn't. The conductor seemed to invest his honour as a man and as a railroader in his chosen words.

Maybe you should talk, Reed Kitchen said to the detective. Maybe I have said too much today for one more time in my life.

The detective seemed uneasy now. I'm having trouble following the gist of this conversation.

Don't worry about it, the conductor said and he got to his feet. Mr Kitchen has the gift of gab. Sometimes it's necessary to follow the detours of his logic. Is that a fair statement, Mr Kitchen? Have I got you pegged right?

As fair as fair's fair, Kitchen agreed.

See what a mean? Make yourself at home, he told the detective. I'll be back in a bit.

He stepped past them and climbed into the sanctuary of his turret.

Reed Kitchen wanted to be up there too with the stars and the moon
and the light of the train reflecting off K'shian—the River of Mists,
the Skeena—and aglow upon the high mountains of nowhere in the
transparent heart of God's country where youthful human giants and
grievous men dwelled. What had become apparent to him was that
the railway detective had chat on his mind and he was the one duly
obliged to listen.

You've been with the railway a few years, the man said. All your
working life. They were seated on the same settee and Reed Kitchen
scrunched himself down at one end nervously and the detective
leaned sideways into him and slightly forward.

Longer than that point of fact, Kitchen told him.

How so?

You don't know about that part?

You have me at a loss, Mr Kitchen.

So you have gazed upon my record but you have not found it necessary to nose any further than that. That's a good sign. I don't know
if I can breathe any easier but at least I can breathe.

I want to assure you right now, Mr Kitchen—

Oh, Reed Kitchen said.

Pardon me?

I said oh. I'm worried. I have never been assured of anything by a
railway dick before. I'm a cautious man. To be assured about something
of which I know nothing is a worrisome thing. Especially when the
person who is doing the assuring has yet to tell me his own good name.

The train achieved full throttle. They spoke under the soft light of
kerosene lamps that swayed with the motion and repeated the waltz
with partners reflected in the glass. The air was faintly smoky and del-
icately oily and the sounds were of the caboose and train clickclacking on the rail joints and the quiet frizzle of wicks aflame.

I'm beginning to catch the drift of what our friend here calls the
detours of your logic, Mr Kitchen. I like you. I'm not surprised by that.
We're both railway men. When I learned you were headed out here I had
a peek at your record. That's my main interest. The place you're bound.

Nowhere, Kitchen said.

Pardon me?

The outer perimeter thereof. God's country some say. The creator of the universe likes his weather damp. He prefers the wet to cold so at least we will have that in common should ever we meet. God likes to walk around in the rain in the nude where people aren't I have been warned.

You don't need to feel uneasy about this conversation.

Never before have I been told by a railway detective that he likes me. Point of fact I have never been told anything by a railway detective before except maybe the time of day and I won't swear to that. I like you too. I like most people. I'd like you a whole lot more if I knew your name—that's all I'm trying so hard to say in this caboose.

Pardon my manners. Long day. Donald McBain. The man held out his hand and Reed Kitchen was happy to shake it. He pressed his hard calloused hand against the detective's mitt and the palm was soft but the grip was firm enough and he felt better. Friends used to call me Yellowhead McBain because I hail from the Tete Jaune Subdivision. Not that I use the nickname much anymore. Cops in other jurisdictions started calling me Yellow for short—or Yellowbaldhead if they really wanted to get my goat. They don't honour railway traditions. I encourage my friends now to call me just plain Don.

I don't know why I have these worries, Just Plain Don. I don't know why I have these grievances about my life.

I'm not sure I follow you, Reed.

It's like this, Don. You're a detective.

That's my job, Reed.

I'm sure you got your reasons why it's your job and they are none of my beeswax. What I don't understand is this. Is it more worrisome for me to be investigated by you for some matter I know nothing about or is it more worrisome for me to be talking to you today about a time in your life when you were called Yellowhead Don McBain? I don't know what to think right now but I do have these worrisome worries.

I'll come to the point, Reed.

That would be splendiferous.

Don McBain cracked up. That's a twentyfive cent word, Reed. I've never met a man who talks quite like you.

A buck and a half, Yellowhead Don. But I'll run you a discount. I got lots more words where that one comes from.

The caboose rocked violently on a fast curve. Both men put a hand out and treated the jarring ride with aplomb.

Where'd you learn words like that, Reed?

I been a railroader from the time I was a nipper at my daddy's knee. Before that even. He was a section foreman. North Ontario. I was born railroading. I was railroading in the womb. My daddy knew words.

That cinches it, Don McBain said.

Cinches what? Kitchen asked him. You're giving me a worrisome mood here, Don. His glance darted about the caboose and off reflections in the glass and back into the eyes of his inquisitor. The man had not asked him to be quiet and without repeated interruption Kitchen felt uneasy. Being free to speak stirred him up. Stories were moiling around inside him aroused by the notion that they had again found their key ingredient—a confederate listener.

You're the man I want to talk to. I had my secretary take a peek at your file and after I got off the phone I thought to myself that here is a man whose record speaks for itself. It's easy to see you have the railway in your blood.

You're scaring me half to death here, Don. You think the railway is in my blood? Let me tell you a story about me and the railway and what's in my blood. My momma was long gone before I knew her. Never got the chance to say hello. My father I guess talked her out of the house or if he didn't talk her out of the house she did not take to the life of a section foreman's wife living in a one room shed in some outpost in the middle of nowhere not to mention smackdab in the frozen heart of winter in the centre of nothing in north Ontario. That's how I grew up. A chip off the old iceblock. My daddy now he was my teacher. Of words and of many things. He would take it upon himself to hold my hand and walk me out to the track. We would wait for the freight on the morning of the day before the sun's up. Which would keep. First we see the bright eye beam. Then we hear the train roaring sliding on the track and that is our track—the track my daddy had laid down and hammered the spikes home for and tamped the ties.

We would stand on the track and this would keep. The train would come right at us. We'd feel the train up through our feet and legs and that was the earth's very own commotion. The blackness of the loco-motive is right in my face and only when I can't see nothing because all I am is shining in the light—only then does my daddy pull me off that track. Every time that train had to get a little bit closer than the last time before he'd pull me off that track.

Why did he do that, Reed? Don McBain asked quietly.

Because he was inclined. Do you know what my daddy would say to me, Yellowhead Don? I mean after he was finished screaming at the train and he would make me scream at the train. Do you know what he would say to me after the train had gone on down the track?

He was screaming at the train?

I am a man! he would holler in my face. I am a man! How do I know I am a man? I am a man because I work upon the railroad. Do beavers tamp ties? He would ask me that. Does a moose lay track? Do bears chip the ice from switches? Do wolves ride in the locomotive or in the caboose? No! He'd yell at me two inches from my face. They are the animals. I'd feel his spit upon my face. I am the man and I know I am the man because I have the predilection to work upon the railroad. We are not the mooses. That would be his lesson to me. We are not the bears. How do we know that? And I'd ask him, How do we know that, Papa? And his answer would always come back the same. Because we work upon the railroad. So ask me again, Don, if the rail-way is anywhere in my blood.

Reed Kitchen noticed that he had an audience for his story. Yellow-head Don McBain and the conductor and one brakeman lingered by.

Sounds to me like your daddy spent too much time alone in the bush, Don McBain said. That happens sometimes.

How close did that locomotive get to you? the young brakie wondered.

How close is the air in front of your nose? Reed Kitchen asked him. Let me put it another way. How close is the last breath on the lips of a man who's kicking off? How close is that breath? Let me put it another way—

That's okay, the brakie said. I get the picture.

Gentlemen? Don McBain said. Would you excuse us a moment? Thanks.

The quarters were tight in the caboose and the brakeman glanced at the conductor who shrugged and they inched toward the back end reluctant to be dislodged within their own premises. The conductor was the sovereign authority here and he chose not to pull rank.

I have a problem, Yellowhead Don whispered. It's one you can help me with.

I hope this is going to be a really small problem, Don.

Infinitesimal.

Because I'm very worried now that you are whispering to me in this caboose. In this caboose which I am beginning to believe you got on in the first place because you already knew I was on it myself.

It's a small favour, Reed. Honest. I know you got the railway in your blood. Your file, Reed, it's exemplary.

Then why do I have this grim feeling you're going to hold that against me?

A report came across my desk. When someone applies to the railway for a job that individual fills out a form. On that form is a question. It asks the applicant if he—or she—has a criminal record. I think it asks, Have you ever been convicted of a criminal offence? This is how it is, Reed. If the applicant answers yes to that question he or she won't get the job. We don't discriminate but there is competition in life and we move along to the next applicant.

You're making me so worried. I don't know what this has to do with me, Yellowhead Don. Reed Kitchen in his stark anxiety flexed his neck and rotated his shoulders.

It has nothing to do with you, Reed. Relax.

Relax! A railway dick is talking to me in a whispering voice about convictions of a crime. How do I relax?

Bear with me, Reed. Okay. So someone lied. Someone checked the No box when the honest answer was the Yes box. We can't throw somebody off the railway just because he has a criminal record. There are laws about that sort of thing. I happen to think that they are good laws and necessary laws. If you say to an excon, Nobody will ever hire you, what's he going to do but become a criminal in good standing? I believe in giving almost every man a break.

I'm glad to hear that, Don. Kitchen noticed a lamp smoking but he felt fixed in his place and did not move to adjust the wick.

Problem is, Reed, the railway has an ironclad rule. An unbendable unbreakable rule. That rule says that anybody who lies on their application form must be dismissed from the company as soon as that lie is revealed. So we don't kick somebody out because he has a record—which is against the law—we kick people out because they lied. We can do that. It's not a problem. It's legal.

That's how things work I guess, Reed Kitchen said.

That's how they work. So I have a problem, Reed. We check people out. Information has come across my desk. Someone has lied to get a job. My duty is to present this evidence to the B & B Master so he can dismiss the employee. Of course if I forget that's another matter.

The blackness beyond had enveloped an alternate sheen for Reed Kitchen—a liquidy dark reflecting incendiary flares of moonlight below the hostile brigades of cloud. No longer would the night be shot with stars. He felt himself crossing from the solace of this day through the darkness of night toward the unknown country ahead.

You don't look like the forgetful type to me, Don, Kitchen told him sadly. But you look like a man with a redeeming sense of compassion.

It gets me into trouble sometimes, Reed.

Why are you telling me this? I'm feeling very worrisome here, Don.

I want to share this perspective with you. This is your opportunity to do a fellow a favour. If this fellow—he's on B & B Gang 4—your gang—if this fellow is making an honest effort then it seems to me that this mission might slip my mind. But if this young man is a wise guy or if he's still a thief or if he's a lazy worker or maybe he's got a drinking problem then we might conclude that it is in the best interests of the railway to let him go. But how do I know that? How do I find out about him? How can I decide something of this nature? Any ideas, Reed?

Reed Kitchen thought about it. Don, what do you suppose would happen if I don't have a single idea in my head about this matter? What would happen here today if I can't think up a single way to help you out?

Yellowhead Don McBain rubbed the back of his right ear a moment. In that scenario I suppose I'll be obliged to do my duty and have the fellow dismissed. Do you see any other option, Reed?

Reed Kitchen saw no other option.

I can't take the chance. If he's trouble I can't risk letting him run loose on the railway and live in a camp where who knows what might occur. I'll detrain at Kwinitsa myself. Why bother the B & B Master with this minor affair? I'll let him go myself. Right away. Tonight.

You mean personally? Reed Kitchen asked him.

I mean personally.

And that will be the end of it? Kitchen wanted to know.

I'll try not to let anybody know that you could have saved his skin. But who can guarantee these things? Something might slip. You know the railroad. Word gets around.

You'll see to it that I get blamed. That's what you're saying. I'll be hated on my new gang before I get started. You're more cruel than you look, Yellowhead Don McBain. Kitchen was speaking quietly now and he studied his fingers which he wove together.

I'm searching for other options.

Why do I feel so stuck? Reed Kitchen asked him. Why is it up to me to spare this unknown criminal his life upon the railway? Why do I get the feeling—I don't know what it is, just this worrisome commotion—that this is only the beginning? You won't ask me for anything again will you, Yellowhead Don? That's not your plan? This is all there is to it, right Don?

McBain slumped back on the settee and smiled with wry amusement. Again he massaged the lobe of his right ear. You are a wise man, Mr Kitchen. An astute man if I may be permitted a twobit word. He sighed and clamped his own hands together. Let me put it this way. You know how your father used to hold you on the track in front of the locomotive until the engine felt like the cold air of north Ontario on your face?

Those times remain particular in my head.

You have my promise. I will never let a train get that close to your skin before I pull you away.

I have so much to say. You have no idea. There are things you should not know, Yellowhead Don.

The detective placed a comforting arm across Reed Kitchen's shoulder. Are we going to give that boy a break? Do we kick him out? Do we ruin his last chance to go straight? Do we take the time and trouble to check him out? Do we find out together—you and me in secret—if this chap deserves a break in life?

I have this grim feeling this isn't the end of it. That it's only the beginning. Why do I have this grim feeling, Don?

Yellowhead Don McBain smiled and took his arm off Reed Kitchen's shoulder and chose not to answer.

Your silence is so worrisome to me, Don. You have no idea. Nothing maddens me more than a man's unnecessary and loathsome and loud pitiful quiet.

REED KITCHEN SWUNG HIMSELF and his duffle off the rear of the caboose and hung suspended awhile as the train tramped slowly through the whistle stop known as Kwinitsa. Thank you for your kindly courtesies, he said to the conductor and he stepped off running onto the crushed stone grade.

The train gathered speed and he watched it recede and the sallow lights of the caboose winked upon the wilderness of his life as a distant dim lantern. The sadness of another departure incited an emotional discourse and Kitchen turned and surveyed the nocturnal view of this unknown destination and an ache of portent did reside nurtured and hushed upon his heart. Nowhere had again unfolded as a place where he had come and now he dwelled within that unknown country.

At an elevation higher than the rail on which he balanced the lights of mobile bunkhouses illumined smoke that wavered in a draught of evening breeze. These would not pertain to railway people.

He had neighbours—a construction crew most likely—an opportunity for chat. The pitchblack patch above the camp rising to the sky
he took to be mountain high and steep. Down the tracks in the opposite direction neither light nor shadow disturbed the pervasive dark.
At his back Reed Kitchen caught swatches of moonlight and the scud
of warring cloud reflected upon a river's night sheen and the river was
broader than his imagination had foretold. A bonus—the air in this
place was warm enough. The clouds appeared to be grievous and low
but for the moment dispatched no rain. So God in His country did
not especially enjoy His weather terminally wet.

He applied his attention to the spectral deportment of the gang
upon the siding immediately before him. Nothing newfangled here.
The bunkcars were converted wooden boxcars that in daylight would
be a dull railroad maroon. Light emitting from the high windows
exhibited the flicker and the ochre tinge of coaloil lamps and alu-
minum chimneys exhaled white smoke. No generator was heard and
somewhere a dormant locomotive groused. Reed Kitchen resolved
that something was out of sync in this unknown realm. The lack of
wood steps to the bunkcars. The speeder strapped to a flatcar. The
locomotive churning up ahead. The gang was in its mobile mode.

A cigarette glowed red.

I have come to the place where I am going, he announced in a firm
voice to the figure moving through the darkness of this night.

The figure stopped walking and did not reply. The red bud of the
smoke moved down to the man's side to further conceal his visage.

This is the unknown destination to where I've come.

The cigarette was raised again to the man's lips as an indication of
peaceful intention. The smoker said, You're the talker.

Kitchen felt immediately glum. A swell of despondency broke lat-
erally across his chest like a disruptive breeze rummaging across a
meadow and sadly he did reply, My reputation has preceded me.

Hhohghdverdoma, the man said.

That's a strange language I do not know, Kitchen told him, though
I do recognize that sort of talk. All chatter is the same I have found
no matter what the tongue. To my mind the only gobbledygook is on

the t.v.—never can I figure out those voices. They talk a lot but they never listen to me. He chortled and the sound was amplified by the darkness and bounced off the wood slats of the boxcars.

A great roaring like the vestigial yawn of a somnambulant god shuddered across the camp.

What's that? Reed Kitchen had never heard such distinctive bedlam. The ghastly yawn was followed by a barking as by hounds hellish and furious and set loose upon a trail with the scent of him redolent in their nostrils.

Sea lions, the smoker told him.

Lions? Lions who float upon the sea? What place is this?

They ride in with the tide on the icefloes.

Ice! Reed Kitchen said. Ice! How can that be? Ice is cold. It's chilly. I was promised a total lack of snow and ice.

They run down with the currents from Alaska headed south. Mexico. California.

I am a migrant also but I don't want to hear that story.

The man moved again through the darkness with long and loping strides. Faint light leaked from the bunkcars.

I'll come with you. Wait up. Is this Gang 4?

Get your ass in gear, the man suggested.

Wait up. Kitchen ran with his duffle bouncing on his shoulder. The man ahead of him climbed a ladder into a bunkcar and was promptly inside and the door shut behind him. I'll be right with you, Kitchen said and he violated his promise immediately and walked in the opposite direction. In the dark he hurried down to a discreet end of the train by the flatcars and dropped his duffle on the ground and opened his fly to piss against the steel wheels. He was peeing and to his left a red lamp waved where the freight had vanished from sight if not entirely from earshot for its rumble carried upon the river upstream and upon the floating ice where sea lions bawled. The red lantern swung in a broad arc. No, Kitchen objected. I just got here.

One by one the cars slammed together and the noise shook him and B & B Gang 4 shuddered and inched forward with screaks and groaning.

I just arrived. I haven't settled in. Hey? Now I got to leave? He was finishing his long piss against the side of the moving train. Moonlight through a convoy of cloud combined with a scent on the wind and he discerned the shapes on the flat going past him. Alongside the speeder lay outhouses knocked onto their sides and strapped down. He caught a whiff. This gang was on the move not simply to another spot in the yard but right on out of here. The gang had waited for the freight to clear Kwinitsa so that a train with lower priority could haul them away.

Reed Kitchen tidied up and grabbed his gunnysack and jogged after the moving train.

He made it to the door where the smoker had absconded. He clutched the grab rail on the run and used his momentum to swing himself onto the lower step and both feet were secured on the ladder and he wedged the gunnysack between himself and the door and used his free hand to trip the latch. The gunnysack tumbled into the bunkcar ahead of him and Kitchen climbed higher. He kicked the bag farther inside and entered where his dunnage had collapsed.

To his left a man napped on top of a bunk wearing workclothes for pyjamas. Four others to his right had commenced a hand and paused in their play to observe his arrival.

Gentlemen, Reed Kitchen announced and he knit his fingers together and turned his head to address those men awake and the one asleep. This morning I embarked upon a journey to an unknown destination and now I have arrived. This is the place to where I've come. Where this place is remains in doubt for as you can plainly see we're on the move so technically speaking we're not there yet. I have so much to say. About the wonders that I have observed and heard tell about. Let's talk. What we need here tonight is some high level chat. Myself personally I suggest a discourse on the aforementioned peculiar puzzle of predicaments that all of us have known so well. He shut the door behind him. Friends. Railroaders. Let's have a word. I have so much to tell you. You have no idea. I have so much to say.

The sleeper and the four men at their card game were united in a forbidding and solemn quiet. The most that Reed Kitchen managed to extract from anyone at that moment was a grunt and one muffled moan and a whispered expletive conveyed in some unknown foreign tongue.

Into this place where I have come and where I have never been my reputation has preceded me, Reed Kitchen said. Bear in mind that generally speaking people suffer from a tendency to exaggerate and this is true of railroaders although I will not mention particular names tonight. Where do I bunk? Here? Is this my place? Speak up. Somebody. Don't be shy. Come on you guys. Say something. Introduce yourselves. Talk. It's only human.

The train rumbled on into the darkness of that night.

2

REED KITCHEN SNAPPED the clip into place and sighted down the barrel at the man contorted on the bed and he asked him again what calibre. The man pulled the grey woollen covers to his chin and edged back against the wall. Thirty-ought-six, he said. His voice jammed in his larynx. He repeated the message. Thirty-ought-six.

Packs a wallop, Reed Kitchen said. Moonlight's halberd fell upon the sinew of his forearm and upon the gun.

Hey there pal, the man on the bed was whispering. He held the covers to his chin as though railway blankets might prove coarse enough to deflect bullets. Don't do this okay? I got a habit. I get myself into the wrong place at absolutely the wrong time and I really don't mean to die for that fault. We're sorry about the things we said all right but you can't go around shooting people on account of a shithole there pal. It's not justifiable.

Reed Kitchen did not respond to the man crimped and misshapen on the bed. A wimple of moonlight veiled his throat. He was dressed in his pants and shirt and eiderdown vest and he returned with the rifle to his own bunk and hauled on his socks and boots and laced them and pulled on his cap and adjusted the peak to shade his eyes in the lesser dark. He stepped through that tier of light again and opened the bunkcar door on the highway side and hoisted the rifle in one hand and leapt down. The man on the bed sank back and grabbed his crotch awhile and breathed before he raised himself astounded as a Lazarus aroused from the surely dead. He went to the door and watched the new man move through the shadowed segue at a crouch. His knees were bent and his back bowed with the rifle cradled in the crook of an elbow now and the scud of clouds gave chase to the moonlight before him and ducked in behind him like compatriot wraiths—comrades-at-arms on this night patrol.

The man watched him cross to the highway and go on down where it parted from view and divided from the tracks into the higher range and he urinated from the top step of his bunkcar into the darkness there until his bladder ran dry of its abundant fluid and fears.

FERENC VAN LOON STRETCHED HIS left foot to the top rung of the dining-car ladder and used the handholds to haul himself up. He snapped open the latch and stepped inside then lowered behind him a set of wood stairs with iron straps which he nudged into place with his boot heels. He shut the door.

Van Loon moved down to the far end of the table where he studied the yawning mouth of a jigsaw puzzle in its genesis. The four sides had been completed and the expansive middle remained blank. Masking tape held the beginnings of the puzzle secure to the table and the table was screwed to the floor. On the rough ride down from Kwinitsa a few breaks had formed and Ferenc Van Loon stripped the tape away with care and reconnected the sections that had gone awry and removed the string that tied the puzzle's box to a chair. The picture on the box guided the men toward recreating a meadow of wildflowers and mountain grasses. Among thousands of pieces Van Loon spread several hundred with a bias for the darker greens across that end of the table. He concentrated on adding a piece to the vast unsolved array.

Kai Jensen stepped through the door at the end of the car that connected directly to his quarters and stood opposite Ferenc Van Loon. He studied the puzzle as well. What're you working on? he asked upon a moment's reflection.

A bee's butt.

Kai Jensen grinned and scratched his scalp.

The men of B & B Gang 4 clamoured in together knocking mud off their boots and wiping the damp from their hair. Two Italians and a Portuguese and a Canadian and a Romanian refugee sat down with the Dane and the Dutchman to a breakfast of pancakes and artificial maple syrup that was Ruby Lake's morning specialty. Ruby stepped in through the pantry and picked two coffeepots off the stove and carried them over to the table.

Kai asked Van Loon to tell him about the new guy.

What's to tell? Now you see him. Now you don't.

He took off, Dino Pratolini said.

What're you saying? You scared him off?

The men denied culpability. Caleb Farrow told the story of being accosted in his sleep by the new man wanting ammunition and the gang laughed at the thought of him squinting into death's encrusted eye.

So what happened to him? Where's he at? Kai wanted to get at that.

I gave him ammo. He put his boots on and bugged off. I got up after him. Had a piss out the door you bet. Last time I seen him he's walking through the wet slop out back to the highway in the moonlight. I'm standing at the door watching him go down the highway with my rifle in his hands which he doesn't carry like a hunter. More like a soldier more like.

Farrow slid four pancakes onto his plate and in the same motion stretched for the butter.

So he didn't actually take his stuff? Kai persisted.

Why should he take his stuff? He took my rifle. He's gone hunting you bet.

In the middle of the night? Van Loon objected.

It's not night now, Caleb Farrow pointed out and he poured maple syrup and cut himself a wedge of pancake.

What did you guys say to him? Kai Jensen wanted to know. Come on.

Nothin, Frank Croce testified.

Ivor Radic agreed. The new guy did the talking.

Once or twice we told him to shut up that's all, Van Loon said.

Maybe six or seven times, Ivor Radic reconsidered.

Dino Pratolini vowed to his boss, We told him to shut up about twenty times. No more than that. It's not like we beat him up or nothin.

We said the next guy who talks digs Ruby's outhouse him, Frank Croce put in. Guess who talked first?

Van Loon laughed at the memory. Like taking candy from a baby.

The door on the highway side received a thump and the men craned their necks to see what neighbour might reside in this wet land and if that neighbour was man or beast. Ruby Lake went over but the door was stuck and she had to pull hard and it swung open fast and she fell back and the doorway was immediately barricaded by a slab of venison that dribbled blood and hung suspended in the air.

She did not speak. Her hand snatched at her throat.

The room had gone quiet. The men gazed upon the bleeding carcass that had knocked and now intruded at the door.

The red slab moved and Reed Kitchen's face poked out above it. Venison, he announced. Scrawny deer in these parts but at least there's deer. Are we going to eat mighty fine in this place they call Tyee or what?

The bridgemen murmured and one whistled and one whooped. Ferenc Van Loon gazed at the apparition and his bloody booty athwart the door.

The first man to break off his study was the foreman who turned and crouched over his breakfast. The men shifted their look away from the slab and waited for their boss to speak his mind. Kai sipped his coffee. Then he looked around at those watching him and he scowled. The man shot a doe, he said. What're you waiting for—Christmas? See it gets hung without dripping deerblood across the floor.

THE GREEN RIVER BRIDGE WAS seven miles west from Tyee and they travelled on the scraped orange speeder for a first look. Word had been passed along to the men of B & B Gang 4 that the new man would be trouble. He had a reputation. He was a chronic yakker who did not know when to shut up and he could not voluntarily shut up. Bind him. Gag him. Drop him aboard a freight train. Ship him Parcel Express across the continent and he'd be back talking a blue streak. The word was out that the new man would drive them mad and mad they would become in the confines of their camp in the depth of forest and winter's dark prevail. The men had worried about him and they had been teased by train crews passing the word along and they had exchanged strategies amongst themselves. Imaginative ways of assisting his disappearance had formed a part of their nightly entertainment. They worked together. They ate together. They slept in the same bunkcars and listened to one another snore and babble and they swung into town together whenever a day off was granted or seized. A new arrival sponsored an innate fear that the harmony of their camp might be upset and rumour and hearsay had alerted them to the danger. Now the new guy had wandered away in the predawn hours and bagged a deer. Venison over the next few weeks seemed adequate compensation for his legendary welloiled tongue.

Heads down out of the wind and crowded on the speeder the men were warm comfort to one another in the chilling damp air. The jigger towed a pushcart weighted with old timbers and plywood. The rain held off. Along the mountaintops and in the ravines the mists baffled the breeze and the sopping spectre of the woods reminded them that they dwelled in wet country now—peripheral rainforest country—and that the morning's respite would be shortlived.

Bald eagles observed their transit.

Ravens like shrill defrocked priests cawed.

At Tyee the railway and highway diverged. The tracks followed the Skeena River and the road disappeared to wend a convoluted path through the Coastal Mountains to the sea. Kai had driven down the previous night in his Buick and Ruby had followed in Van Loon's pickup to avoid the inevitably rough ride hitched to a freight train. Van Loon had preferred to play cards only to regret his luck and choice later. The speeder puttered down the track west from Tyee and the wildness and remoteness of this place invigorated these men and the morning air soothed them and the beauty of the river and mountains sustained their spirits and the spectre of a winter away from the deep freeze of the interior engaged by a worthy project warmed and welcomed them.

Kai Jensen slowed the speeder. The Indian cabins were built on piles above a soggy bog close to the Green River Bridge. Raised boardwalks connected the two main buildings and the five sheds and the outhouses and ascended to the tracks. No roads here. On the opposite side of the grade a small tug and a dory bobbed in the chop alongside a vacant log boom.

Smoke drifted from the chimney of the main house.

The speeder crept across the Green River Bridge. Kai stopped on the opposite side.

The aged trestle bridge was cracked and rotted and worn. The trick required of them was to replace the old bridge over the course of the winter while keeping the tracks clear. Rip out the old and insert a new wood structure with steel spans and delay no train for long.

Kai Jensen and Van Loon walked on the bridge and talked. The bridge was not especially high—thirty feet above the river at low tide. The banks rose quickly and much of the work would be above shorter drops. Tide reversed the flow of the stream. The Green was a meandering peaceable creek rarely more than three feet deep as it emerged from the mountains into the broad Skeena. A flooding tide increased the depth to ten feet and in lunar frenzy to fifteen. The width of the stream varied from six to thirty feet depending on the tide and that was a factor to influence their schedule. They'd have to do some digging and build a seawall. Kai Jensen and Ferenc Van Loon ruminated about these things as they strolled across the bridge.

A shower accompanied their walk and this rain was to be their daily affliction. Twothirds of the way across they stopped.

I've got a question, Van Loon said. He was listening to the rain rhythmic on his silver hardhat and listening to that sound as though it was a hymn.

Only one? Kai asked him. He wore his pixie grin.

Can we do this? Van Loon wondered. We've lost good people. We don't have an experienced crew anymore. The new guy—I don't know about him.

You got your doubts about him?

You don't I suppose.

Not anymore.

Van Loon took a look around. Kai was grinning and offering no clues. Then he pointed down. Reed Kitchen had descended through the reticular structure of the bridge and he was climbing amid the trammel of the timbers with the dexterity of a monkey. He walked on the braces and shimmied down the piles and swung from tie beams. In the maze of wood he moved with the agility of a cat and steadily worked his way down to the river.

They watched Reed Kitchen descend and test the waters with a hand and his reaction was immediate. It's cold, he alerted them all. It's chilly. I was promised subtropical climes. This water is freezing. It's a harbinger of winter.

I got a hunch he can work on bridges, Kai said. He's just got a few screws loose.

Loose? Missing, Van Loon said. He waited for Reed Kitchen to climb back and Kai Jensen checked on the men building the speeder stand. Van Loon watched the new man emerge from under the ties and regain the top of the bridge. Kitchen swung above the river and moved himself to the edge of the ties on the strength of his fingertips and he seesawed and gained momentum and manoeuvred a leg up and Van Loon could not believe what he was witnessing. He would never do that. He did not have the strength although he was strong and he lacked the dexterity although he was nimble and he'd never summon the guts although he was known to be foolhardy.

Nice climb, Van Loon told him.

How do you pronounce your name? Fence?

Ferenc. Fair-ence.

That's Dutch?

Hungarian.

You're Hungarian?

I'm Dutch.

The new guy continued to look at him as though he expected an explanation.

My mother's Hungarian, Van Loon revealed. I'm Dutch. My father's Dutch.

A man born of nations, Reed Kitchen determined. With me time's my matron. She's my disciplinary mom. My daddy? Truth be told I'm the son of a railway man. The offspring of a train. Myself personally I know I am a man because I work upon the railroad. How does it feel to be a man born of nations, Van Loon?

Ferenc Van Loon looked at him and said nothing and walked off.

If a man's got someplace to go, Reed Kitchen said behind him, it's not up to me to stand in his way. Point of fact I'll come with you. Maybe we'll have ourselves a nice long chittychat. Get acquainted and stuff like that. Ferenc? Me and you and these other fellows will build ourselves a bridge. What do you think about that in your heart of hearts?

THE MEN FINISHED CONSTRUCTION on the speeder stand and waited for the morning passenger out of Prince Rupert followed by a special freight. They sat around. Caleb Farrow tramped into the soused woods to do his business and called the others down to verify a discovery. He had located a dank and mysterious cave and two men at a time took turns sitting within the hollow rock where they considered with respect the lives of their forebears. The trains cleared and the black fortyton Wellman Crane waddled down slow and cantankerous from Kwinitsa shoving a flatcar of pilings. Kai gave the order and the men prepared to unload in time for the crane to clear the track again before the next freight from Prince Rupert arrived.

Where's the new guy at? Frank Croce asked.

Reed Kitchen was missing.

Ivor Radic had spotted him bound east. Frank Croce said west. Caleb Farrow said that someone had tramped by him while he shat in the woods. But he explained that the hiker could not have been the new guy because the stranger in the woods had talked to no man and neither to himself.

Maybe he fell in the river, Dino suggested.

Then look for bubbles. He's probably still talking, Farrow said.

There he is. Joe Ribeiro pointed him out.

Reed Kitchen emerged from an Indian cabin. He saw the men looking in his direction and he waved and chomped on a hefty slab of johnny cake.

Time, Kai Jensen said. Let's work.

Dino Pratolini and Reed Kitchen when he arrived and Kai Jensen toiled above the track on the flatcar. Dino hooked the pilings to the crane's cable and the other two balanced the load and steadied the timbers as they were lowered into the hands of Joe Ribeiro and Frank Croce. The men on the ground guided the timbers across to the stack and passed each timber into the hands of Ferenc Van Loon and Ivor Radic. Caleb Farrow unhooked the cable and worked it loose from the grip of the piles.

You know those Indians? Van Loon called out to Kitchen. I thought you said you never been around here before.

Never have I stepped a foot in this place, Reed Kitchen maintained. They call it God's country. Know why? I'll tell you why. If it's not raining it's pouring. This is a place not suitable for human habitation. God appreciates the walking around room free of human intrusion. I don't need to know Indians to talk to them, Van Loon. They are a quiet people much of the time. I like that. I can talk and they can listen and they don't bother to interrupt me when I have something to say. You guys can learn from Indians. They don't wander off someplace else just because I happen to be speaking my mind.

The men chuckled amongst themselves.

We have to make friends with them, Kitchen avowed.

Why's that?

They're the only people around with a boat. You can't live beside a river without a boat.

Van Loon gazed out upon the broad water. There's the river. Find a boat. The logic made a magical sense.

Hey, Joe, the talker called down. Aren't you yourself a Portugoose?

Portuguese, Joe Ribeiro corrected him.

You can't be a Portugeese because there's only one of you. You got to be a Portugoose. Trust me. I know the language. Let me tell you a

story about the Portugooses that I have known. Meander River. North
Alberta. Indian country. Nothing there but a Hudson's Bay Ripoff
Post. It's where Old Man Winter spends the summer. Nutfreezing cold
let me tell you. I was the foreman on an Extra Gang. Sixty workers and
everyone from Portugal. The world is on the move. We are the wan-
derers across its undesirable regions. A few of those Portugooses were
in the country legally and the others were not and I had to establish a
system. Indians and the kitchen staff were in on it too. Anytime the
Mounties raided the camp to round up illegal aliens we'd get tipped off
in time. My men beat it into the bush before they arrived. The Mounties charged in where we're laying track and the sergeant says to me,
Records show you got sixty men working under you. I'm looking
around and I'd say, Nothing under me but my boots and nothing under
them but railbed, sir. I used to have more men working alongside me
that's true, sir. But they quit, sir. Said I drove them too hard. Go figure.
All I got left is these eight hardcases. Those eight men left were legal.
We had a good time me and the Mounties and the Portugooses.

Reed Kitchen was the hero of his own tale but the bridgemen were
pleased with the story anyway.

You were a foreman? Kai Jensen asked him.

I'm not after your job. Don't pin that on me. All I want is warmer
weather. I said in plain language to the railway I wasn't going to
expose my nuts to the Arctic air again. I told them I might not be a
married man but that does not necessarily mean I won't get lucky
someday and if I do get lucky I want my testicles A-OK and on the
job. I want testicles that don't crack off in the breeze. Where I work is
hereby more important to me than what I do. I have only ever been a
section foreman and an Extra Gang foreman, Kai. What do I know
about bridges? I'm not after your job. Period. End of sentence.

All right, Kai said.

All right what?

All right I believe you.

Heads up, Van Loon warned and another eightyfooter swung down.

REED KITCHEN SHARPENED THE CHAINSAW running a file along each tooth. He gabbed and took sidelong glances at the job Caleb Farrow performed on the spikehammers. Caleb Farrow expanded the wood shafts by inserting screws and he demonstrated no affection for tools. Farrow was messing up and the finished hammers were not much improved and often in worse shape than before he had begun. A loose hammerhead can be a lethal weapon, Reed Kitchen said and soon he was fixing the tools that Caleb Farrow put down.

Farrow started working on the peevees oiling hinges to keep the rust out. He seemed capable of that task. He finished and took over sharpening the chainsaw and doing a botch of it and Reed Kitchen had to assume that task again and hope that Farrow did not turn his attention back to the spikehammers. Finally Caleb Farrow said, I'm going out for a smoke and a few minutes peace and quiet do you mind? Reed Kitchen looked at him. He didn't say another word. Caleb Farrow broke off their mutual stare and jumped down out of the toolcar.

Reed Kitchen admitted to himself that he could not remember what he had been talking about so perhaps his partner had a case.

Caleb Farrow returned and Reed Kitchen tried to patch things up between them. So far it looks to me like you didn't tell nobody about last night.

Last night, Farrow said. He was hitching his trousers with his right hand then letting the hand hang at his waist with the forearm upraised. The mitt of his hand looked limp or deformed but it was not.

The guys know I took your rifle, Kitchen said.

You bagged a deer so I guess borrowing my rifle without asking me is all right with them. He had begun to roll another smoke.

I didn't ask?

You asked for the ammo. I guess to save yourself the trouble of looking.

I asked for the ammo. Dino mentioned that. But nobody's told me the truth so I guess you kept that to yourself and I want to thank you. I don't know why you're doing me any special favours.

The truth, Caleb Farrow said.

About my sleepwalking. I want you to know that doesn't happen too often. That's what I want to say. I don't want you to worry about living in the same bunkcar with me. Point of fact it doesn't happen too often and I want to thank you for not mentioning it to the guys. Myself personally I got enough of a mountain to climb with them.

Caleb Farrow had struck a match and he held it now inches from his lips. His cigarette was nestled between the fingers of his other hand which he held at his waist. He said, Sleepwalking.

Reed Kitchen shrugged. It happens sometimes.

Farrow shook his match out before he was burned and struck another. This time he brought flame and cigarette together. Tell me. He took a long draw. When was it exactly you woke up? Before or after you shot that deer?

Reed Kitchen hesitated too long for Caleb Farrow.

You tracked down that deer in your sleep.

Thought I was trailing a wolf. Maybe I was. Probably the wolf led me to the deer but I can't say that for sure on account of my being asleep and dreaming about other things at the time. Reed Kitchen scrutinized his work on a saw tooth and ran a finger over the steel.

Hell's bells, Caleb Farrow intoned almost reverently. He was amazed and he was fearful. Right now, he said. At this moment. Are you taking a nap or may I presume that you're awake and among the living?

Reed Kitchen laughed at that. I can do you a favour too, he suggested.

Caleb Farrow picked out bits of tobacco from the tip of his tongue. What kind of favour? I can think of one right now off the top of my head. Don't go on a shooting spree while you're still fast asleep and I'm in the bunkcar with you.

You can keep to yourself what you know about me. I know what you're thinking. If I'm a jabbermouth what good is my word? Point of fact I might talk a lot but I don't spill the beans when I don't have a mind to.

You lost me, Caleb Farrow said. His pants were baggy and crumpled. His continuous hitching was a nervous habit not precipitated by a loose belt.

Reed Kitchen looked at him directly. You keep to yourself that I hunt deer in my sleep.

In exchange for what exactly?

I keep to myself all that nasty business about your criminal record.

Caleb Farrow continued looking at him awhile and Reed Kitchen resumed his work and he moved over beside him. Caleb Farrow flicked his partially smoked cigarette out the broad doors into the rain. Train, Reed Kitchen said. Later they heard one coming. Reed Kitchen moved to the doors and the locomotive whistled on through and Kitchen sang out, *Traaaaaiinnnn!* and the great beast of a freight shook their car and the tools clattered and the two men held on and the wind from the train swirled inside the toolcar like a dervish summoned from beyond the grave and the men watched the freight roar by. Caleb Farrow's brow was furled more compactly than usual and he would not take his eyes off Reed Kitchen.

It's not exactly a secret, he said at last. But that don't tell me how you found out so soon?

I know more than any man should. Reed Kitchen smiled. But that doesn't say I have to talk about it.

Like I said it's not exactly a secret.

Reed Kitchen was standing at the door and gazing across the Skeena River where sea lions bawled. I know what you mean. My sleepwalking is not exactly a secret either point of fact. But that doesn't mean the people I don't want to know about it have to know if you take my meaning. The people you want to know about your criminal background know because you told them. Some of the people you don't want to know also know but that's another story. The point is there are people you don't want to know who don't know and that's the same situation with me. We're alike that way. That's how I'd like to keep things between you and me. Alike. I want to keep the situation more or less the way it is.

Caleb Farrow studied the worn gouged floorboards of the old boxcar and Reed Kitchen contemplated a dreary sky. I don't remember you from Okalla, Farrow said. He looked up. Can't say I recall seeing you there. If you were there somebody would've cut out your tongue or snipped it back some.

You don't say. I have never been to this place you mention. It is an unknown destination where I hope I don't arrive. We have not met before, you and me. You must tell me the story about this place you call Okalla. I look forward to that yarn on a dark night. Just don't tell me any gross convict stories okay because I despise those. In the meantime, Caleb Farrow, are we in agreement? I hope the guys will never learn from you that I shoot animals in my sleep.

You're a strange beast, Kitchen. You are awful strange to me.

Do we have an agreement?

I'm not sure I believe you anymore. I'm not sure that you do hunt deer in your pyjamas. Why do you want to put me in this position? You dump your secret on me. Then you threaten me if I happen to tell it. What's with you?

You know my secret. I didn't tell it to you. But if you want to pretend I told you go ahead. If you think you're free to betray me go ahead. We'll see what happens.

Stranger by the second, Caleb Farrow said. You are one weird duck there pal. Quack quack.

We'll be friends, Caleb. I look forward to that. You'll listen to my tall tales and my short ones and I will listen to yours about this place called Okalla where no man wants to go and for that reason alone men get sent there. I look forward to those chats.

Caleb Farrow shook his head. He removed his peaked cap and scratched his scalp with his knuckles. I have to listen to you or else? Is that the picture? Kitchen, is that the picture you're painting here?

Reed Kitchen smiled and arose from his labour. When you think about it—when it comes right down to the nitty gritty—we all have to listen to each another. That's how it goes. We all do. As you say. Or else.

OIL LAMPS WERE CARRIED IN FROM the bunkcars to add to the pale luminosity and flashlights were lashed together and hung overhead. On the jigsaw puzzle the hue of a ridge had become discernible and the men were motivated by their breakthrough.

They drank coffee and munched on biscuits and Kai Jensen and his bottle of rye were dispatched back to his quarters in compliance with Ruby Lake's rules. He raised no objection and did his day's paperwork and later returned bolstered and repentant. The puzzle was their focus and the men searched for shapes amid the chaos of hue and foraged for the dark green welter of the ridge and the leafy green of the solitary elm that would dominate the meadow. The puzzle occupied their hands and bound their attention and their voices were busy all the while. Chat was continuous and Reed Kitchen embarked upon a story then requested one from a fellow worker. Stories were heaped one upon another as an incoherent chronicle of wit and history and lore stacked high.

Joe Ribeiro told about his children accumulating university degrees. I have a son a doctor and a son a lawyer and a son an artist. That would be very good except I have just one son and he is still in school. My daughter she has also enough education for three daughters but there is only one of her. Today she's a scientist but I don't know what she will be tomorrow. He had not seen his children in twentyeight years and neither had he seen his wife and monthly Joe Ribeiro did the honourable thing and dispatched the bulk of his paycheque home.

The men laughed and they were quiet awhile in the aftermath and attentive to the puzzle. Each man wondered if he could return to his old life again and resume where he had left off or if he was forever cast away in these woods and upon this track.

My turn, Ruby Lake announced. The puzzle reminded me. She told about the time the family collie had raced through the den after Christmas and knocked over the kids' jigsaw puzzle. She had sent the smallfry off to bed and picked up most of the pieces herself and in the morning she would enlist the children to stretch under the sofa for the pieces that remained. I forgot the maid came early the next day. I was having my morning coffee and heard the vacuum cleaner running. Me and the kids spent the entire afternoon picking jigsaw pieces out of a giant furball stuffed inside the vacuum bag.

Ruby Lake laughed merrily at the memory.

The men were quiet around the table.

What? Ruby Lake asked and Reed Kitchen smiled and patted her hand.

You have told us one story, Ruby, and you have revealed to us another. It's that other story we'd like to hear from you some night.

What other story?

The story of how you once had a maid and now you are a cook upon the railroad.

Oh, Ruby Lake said. That.

I had a servant once, Van Loon piped up and the others did protest. Swear to God. In the marines. I was stationed in the Dutch East Indies. Jungle patrol. We went out for a week at a time then had two weeks off in camp. In camp we'd sit on the beach or play football. Our native guides were the same as servants. They'd do what you asked. Those guys were unbelievable. They never wore boots. No shoes. They didn't feel pain. One guy I remember cut his big toe half off—that's what it looked like. He didn't stop walking. Didn't even notice. Just kept walking until the end of the day and he brought me water when I asked him. I called out for water just to look at his big toe halfflapping off. He never took medical attention until the end of the day.

The men nodded in appreciation of the guide's nature. Among them only Frank Croce was unimpressed. I work on a bridge and I got haemorrhoids, he said.

So that's your excuse, Kai said.

None of you would laugh if you had haemorrhoids.

They laughed anyway.

The whistle blew on Ruby's kettle and she poured the hot water into her teapot and carried it to the table to steep.

Something I could never figure out, Van Loon said. I hated it out in that jungle. I can't tell you how much. The heat in the day. The wet at night. Mosquitoes as big as crows. Snakes were like slugs here—everywhere. Twentyfooters about. You lived in the jungle long enough you had a stench. You couldn't wash it out. I hated the forced marches. Wading through swamps with leeches. My boots were soaked all the time. The food was lousy. At night you couldn't sleep right. All day you were hacking your way up some mountain just to come down the other side. When I was in the jungle all I could think about was—

Is this going to be a dirty story? Ruby Lake interrupted.

That's the point, Van Loon said. You didn't think about girls. Girls didn't exist. All you could think about was getting out of the jungle and making it back to camp so you could sit on the beach and play football.

Van Loon tried a piece on the jigsaw and failed.

I'd make it out of the bush alive. Sit on the beach. I'd get picked by a team and play football. Two days later I'd be so bored I'd sign up for another patrol. The second—the instant—I got back into the jungle I remembered how much I hated it and I'd dream of the beach again and swear to myself that I'd never volunteer for a mission the rest of my life. Then my patrol would end and I'd sit on the beach and get bored and sign up all over again.

I knew that about you, Reed Kitchen said. He examined a piece more closely to the light. You're a modern man that way.

What's that supposed to mean? Van Loon scoffed. He sounded offended.

I've seen your type before.

What type's that?

You can't live in the world and you can't live outside it neither.

That's a modern man?

Not exactly. Reed Kitchen lifted the puzzle piece aloft for everyone to inspect and the eyes of the men and Ruby Lake's eyes also followed the slow descent of his arm and he placed it where it was a perfect fit. Others scrambled to see if their own favourite pieces were a match for his. A modern man, Reed Kitchen said across the table, who has the wilderness wedged in the marrow of his soul—I have met such men before. They have a tendency to work upon the railroad.

Van Loon figured he was kidding and he wanted to receive the jest with ease and he wanted to hit him also. I'm going for a walk, Ferenc Van Loon said and he extricated himself from the bench seat. Ruby Lake alone said goodnight to him.

Did he say a walk? Caleb Farrow asked. In the history of this gang nobody has ever taken a walk for the sake of taking a walk. What's the matter with the man?

Now you tell a story, Reed Kitchen said.

I don't feel like it. Don't pressure me, Reed. I don't tell stories on demand.

Then I'll tell one, Reed Kitchen said.

Caleb Farrow uttered an expletive which aroused Ruby Lake's censure. He looked helplessly at her.

If you don't want to listen to one of Reed's stories then just tell one of your own, she said.

Reed Kitchen smiled and awaited the tale.

FERENC VAN LOON STOPPED AT HIS bunkcar for a jacket and sweater and walked the tracks west. He moved in the darkness and the steel rails guided him and the telegraph poles and the tracks reminded him of the world in which he dwelled.

He walked away from the lights of the bunkhouses and away from the lights emitted from the cabins of the section crew. A modern man. The wilderness wedged in the marrow of his soul or something equally halfassed. Reed Kitchen talked too much and talked nonsense besides.

Van Loon was upset by Reed Kitchen's remark and upset with himself for telling a story he deemed private. In the marines and in the merchant marine he had encountered men foreign to his existence. A quality of manhood and dignity and tradition inherent in the Malaysian guides had invoked a personal shame. Van Loon had returned to Holland after his tour of duty and learned that he had changed and that he could not conform. His life felt foreordained as though imprinted on his forehead from the moment of his birth. He would marry. He would work in the tool-and-dye factory. He would live with his bride in the home of his parents for ten years or more until his name surfaced on a public list for an apartment of his own. He had hated being a marine and he was learning that he dreaded civilian life more. His life seemed fixed and Van Loon received the engagement ring from the finger of his fiancée and hurled it into the centre of a pond in a small manicured park in Rotterdam.

The family was mortified by his behaviour and Van Loon talked to his father and at the conclusion of that exchange consented to ship aboard a steamer bound for Hong Kong. Van Loon's father was a senior steward in the merchant marine and he arranged the duty and charged his son with examining his life and determining his future on the voyage. His father had talked to him in a solemn tone about his choices in this world and the honour of the family name. Following a layover in Shanghai the ship's manifest was modified. Before he returned to Holland Ferenc Van Loon had circumnavigated the globe and in the course of that voyage he had made no choices and had reached no conclusion.

In Rotterdam Van Loon learned that his fiancée had taken the tossing of her engagement ring to be a meaningful gesture and she had married another man. In a nation of beautiful women she had been stunning and he believed that such beauty would not deign to consider him again. He told his father in the evening of his first day home what he had told no other nor himself. He would emigrate to Canada. He desired to live on the fringe of wilderness.

Factory and family and civic routine were the links he sought to avoid. He wanted to elude obligation. He wanted to flee the known to embrace a mystery. He refused to be encumbered and encompassed. The Dutch considered Canada to be their nation's opposite. The Netherlands were congested and compact. Canada void and huge. Holland was civilized and sober. Canada primitive and inebriated. The tame Dutch were a cultured and discriminating people. Canadians were the rambunctious liberators of Holland during the second world war. Van Loon's father had expected the dull monotony of the Pacific to master his son's reckless fervour and he had to concede that the great ocean had failed him. Ferenc would snap the family yoke and emigrate to Canada.

Van Loon walked down the tracks hatless in the drizzle. Cold water leaked in around his collar and he thrashed his sides to warm himself.

He longed for stars to dispel this continuous scud of cloud. At times a halfmoon emitted a glow. More often it was obliterated. Van Loon walked on. He believed that he had gone far enough but repeatedly added more minutes and greater distance to his trek and he walked on and time went by.

Walking to the bridge was out of the question. Yet with each step forward the bridge loomed as a possible destination.

Sometimes he ran stumbling in the dark.

Out of breath he doubled over and water dribbled off his scalp.

He walked on despite himself.

Often the night was pitch. The glow of the unseen moon shone on the rails and the shoreline emerged and retreated from view. At times he could not see his hands and he walked between the rails and tripped. He had a mind to remove his boots and walk barefoot and damage his toes and walk on bleeding and impaled and walk on anyway and Van Loon kept going and he did not know why.

He had waded through jungle this dark and had despised each step. He had volunteered then and he had volunteered now. Why had he signed on again and again? Why? He pressed on through the misery of this night as though the answer lay embedded in the dark and he walked on toward that unseen and unheard and unknown mark.

Across the Skeena lights from the hamlet of Port Essington twinkled like starlight awash on the horizon. A few Indians lived there among castaway white people and fishermen and bedraggled loggers. A few river scavengers lived there. They dwelled on the edge of the primitive realm remote and obscure. Van Loon wished and did not wish to number himself among their tribe.

He had rejected the beauty who had come into his life to follow an ideology of wistfulness. He had denied the world he had known to seek another which surely did not exist. Now he was condemned to live with small men and endure an absence of women and he was condemned to perform small tasks under weather he despised and he was condemned to go on living that life because he had no place to go and no place to which he could return.

Van Loon ran again. He traced the dim moonlit sheen of the rails and ran away from where he was and where he had thought he was going. He was escaping to nowhere and he fled through the seamless vacant night and the rain.

Van Loon was a builder of bridges and a maker of jigsaw puzzles and a cardplayer and a lover of worn women. He was a carouser and a man with no country save the company of friends and his friends were loners all. What a fool I am, Van Loon concluded in the silent sphere of his flight. I give up everything for nothing and consider that a bargain.

Van Loon stood still. He had heard a sound. Predators of this realm should not be out stalking at night and the nature of the sound and the depth of the darkness and the tempest of his own musing spooked him. He endeavoured to see through the mongering dark toward whatever ill might pitch his way and Van Loon was fearful of speaking as though the night and the river and the forest would judge him harshly for his fear.

Begrudged he moved more slowly now and believed he would achieve the bridge and he could not understand why that mattered. So seldom was he alone. In Rotterdam—a congested city—in an apartment eternally represented by at least three generations he had always relied on solitude. On the gang he was alone only in the outhouse and that did not preclude someone pacing outside and a conversation being struck. He was never alone here. Not on the bridge and not on weekends and not during idle time. So odd. Solitude in the city. Out in the wilderness such a thing was both venerated and feared.

Van Loon heard a sound again and stopped. His heart beat startled in his chest and he strove to be calm. In the expanse of wilderness Van Loon was beset by claustrophobia.

He spun. He waited.

He muscled his courage. Who's there? he called to the vacant dark.

An answer was returned to him out of the void. Reed Kitchen, the voice said. Where're you going, Van Loon?

The two men could not see one another and their voices were distant and disembodied in the dark. Van Loon felt grim with loathing. What are you doing out here? he called back.

Kitchen's voice when he spoke was closer now and strange how the man was moving yet he could not hear his steps. I don't want you to misunderstand me, Kitchen said. His voice carried the timbre of the night itself. Pervasive. Invisible. Provident.

What? I don't know what you're talking about. Why are you following me?

I'm not following you, Reed Kitchen said. Myself personally I am walking down the railway tracks. Any plain fool can see that.

A shape emerged as a darkness culled from another and the shape moved silently under cover of the rain. Van Loon distinguished Reed Kitchen and he was walking perfectly balanced upon a rail. Kitchen moved without hesitation and with speed and he was blindly confident of each step. He moved so quietly upon that rail. No crunch of stone and no soft thunk upon a tie. He had no need to determine his position. He moved with a ballerina's incalculable grace and in a trice caught up to Van Loon.

I suppose I got to listen to your gibberish all the way back.

Are we going back?

Where else would we go?

To the bridge, Kitchen said. Aren't we going to the bridge?

Why are we going to the bridge?

You're the one who's going there. You should know.

Van Loon could not make out Kitchen's eyes in this dark and his face was shrouded by the peaked cap. His breathing indicated that his fast walk upon the rails had required scant exertion.

I don't want you to think I was trying to get your goat, Van Loon. If you think that I apologize. Point of fact I thought we were having a pleasant conversation.

What do you want from me, Kitchen?

Now or later?

There's a difference?

Van Loon had turned and he was walking again. Reed Kitchen moved alongside him as though he strolled on air. Van Loon spun and knocked him off the rail.

Why'd you do that for?

Don't creep up behind a guy. It makes me nervous.

Train, Reed Kitchen said.

What?

Train. Kitchen moved towards him and Van Loon stepped back.

What does that mean? What do you want, Kitchen?

I'm your wilderness man, Van Loon. I'm your jungle guide with the sore feet. I wear boots but I'm like him. I remind you of him. That's why you brought him up. I know things like that. Van Loon—I'm your wilderness man. Do you know what you are to me?

I hate to think.

My shot, Kitchen said. I can't cope through this particular world. It's too much for me. I can travel on the train but myself personally I can't get off it. You could be my friend, Van Loon. You got that potential. I could teach you things and you could teach me things. I grew up in the wilderness. It's what I know. And laying track. What do you know? I'll tell you. How it is with people. You know you're a man because that's what you are. You never mistake yourself for a moose or a bear or a raccoon. I know I am a man because I work upon the railroad. What would I be without this track? It's up to you, Van Loon, to help me out here. That'll be your job. We'll make a trade. You show me the way through the modern world and I'll guide you into the wilderness and teach you how to get back out. I'll show you how to walk so silent you can step up behind a deer and tap it on the shoulder and when it turns its head to say hello blow it off. I can teach you that, Van Loon. All I need is your cooperation.

Van Loon loudly sighed. We need you on the bridge, Kitchen. So I'm ready to put up with you. But only so far. You have more than a few bolts missing—the whole assembly has come undone.

What you say may be true, Van Loon, but how come I know a train is near and you don't?

They waited in the darkness and rain. How far? Van Loon asked.

Three minutes to the Tyee whistle crossing.

No way. You can't hear that.

Two minutes fiftyfive seconds.

If it doesn't come, Van Loon stipulated, you walk back alone. I get to return in peace.

Two minutes forty seconds. You're a cruelish man, Van Loon. I know that about you. What happens if the train does arrive on time?

You tell me.

You face the train with me. Side by side. It should keep.

What's that supposed to mean?

Are we agreed on the bet?

Van Loon listened to the quiet of the darkness behind the rain and to the stillness behind the flowing water and the wind. Sure, he said.

Kneel, Reed Kitchen said. He tugged on his sleeve and Van Loon was surprised and he got down on his knees. Grip the track with both hands. Firmly! Now put your ear against the rail. Remember. You are not listening for a sound. You are using your eardrum to pick up the transport of nations and the motion of a continent.

Van Loon obeyed instructions and imitated the posture of his tutor and bent down to place his ear against the wet steel rail.

Gently gently, Reed Kitchen whispered.

I can't hear a thing with all your talk, Van Loon complained and his head jerked up. He heard the whistle of a freight crossing the highway at Tyee.

I win, Reed Kitchen said. Even if it is forty seconds fast.

Now what do we do?

Hold the rail. Hold it now. Think about this, Van Loon. The continent is connected to your hands. This track connects to New York and to Panama and to Colorado and to Halifax and to the Yucatan. You are connected to the railway and the railway is connected to the transport of nations and to the lives that are the lives of nations. Feel this train, Van Loon. Feel it. It's coming here for you. It's prowling up. It is our train point of fact. Ships from Rotterdam dock in New York and load their cargo onto flatcars and boxcars and hoppers and you are connected at this moment to all the sea lanes of the world and to all the commerce of history and to the voyages of antiquity and to the lives of the people here and everywhere who are served by the train and who rely upon the train for their income and for their sustenance and one way or another for the wellbeing of their days. Hold the rail, Van Loon. Hold it now. Feel this train in your blood and feel it thunder across the wilderness of your sorry soul, Van Loon.

You're an idiot—

You lost that bet now hold this rail, Van Loon.

Van Loon held and heard now faintly in the distance the freight's approach. Van Loon held the cold wet rail and waited for the locomotive's advance. He saw the light. Faint at first and intermittent the light swerved with the contours of the track and river. Then the light shone heading right at them.

Now we stand on this night, Reed Kitchen said.

Unhunh, Van Loon said.

Do as I do and don't make jokes. This is serious business.

Hhohghdverdoma.

I think I know what that means, Van Loon. If I were you I would not be saying such a thing at this point in time. Now. We stand side by side. Clutch my jacket at the shoulder. I clutch yours. Face the train. Keep one foot outside your rail and one inside. One jump to clear. Shift your weight to the outside foot and fly. Fly, Van Loon. When the time comes—fly. This will keep. It's a good dark night. The light is bright. Are you ready now? We face the train.

Reed Kitchen raised the level of his voice as the train approached.

When do we jump clear? Van Loon shouted.

You want to do this right? Kitchen asked him.

Van Loon was game but he did not respond.

We jump clear after it's too late. I'll hold you if you go too soon and you hold me. I'll push you when the time comes and you push me.

Van Loon was willing to place his life in the hands of this crank on the darkest night of this eternity in the outback of a foreign land with nothing to hold or sustain him here and Van Loon would do it and the train approached and the whole of its triple eye beam shone in his eyes and the light was a shock to his pupils after the grievous dark and all he could hear was the bellow of the diesel and the outcry of the steel wheels upon the rails and the joints clacking like gunfire and Reed Kitchen's voice sang, Traaaaiiiinnnn! Traaaaiiiinnnn! and he joined him in ranting, *Traaaaiiiinnnn!* and the train was suddenly abject and close and he flinched and thought that he was jumping except Reed Kitchen held him back and he slid through panic and

dread and death awaited and Van Loon was laughing now in the face
of the locomotive's pure oval light and rampage and the engine of the
world was upon him and he almost did not respond when Reed
Kitchen tugged him then shoved him over and he dove and the train
ripped the garment of this night down its seam and the light was gone
and he was sliding down the grade on his belly with the fright thump-
ing across his soul and screeching on the curve behind him and Van
Loon was scared and exalted and rapt as the caboose passed him by
and he remained pinned on his stomach ass high and petrified and he
could not budge except to tilt his neck sideways to see Reed Kitchen
upright on the tracks in the light of the peeking moon as though he
had never moved as though the train had stormed through him and
Kitchen said quietly and calmly, Are you alive or are you dead, Van
Loon? I would appreciate knowing this thing.

Van Loon did not know what to say. The question was a tough one.

Now you got me wondering and worried, Reed Kitchen said.

Van Loon managed to breathe first.

Now you got me scared.

Alive, Van Loon answered.

Myself personally I'm pleased about that. Come on out of that
darkness, Van Loon. I got some friends I want you to meet. These
friends of mine live down by the Green River Bridge.

Indians? Van Loon asked. He had a hard time turning himself right
way around. He contended with the slope of the grade and the wet-
ness of the long grasses and discovered that he had slid right off the
stone. His limbs had lost coordination and his good sense was
upturned and his muscles lacked tone and tension.

People are people, Van Loon, Reed Kitchen reminded him.

Why are we going to see them tonight? I don't mind. I just want to
know what you got planned. If you're going to throw me off a bridge
just for your kicks I'd like to know ahead of time. Van Loon had made
it to his knees and faced uphill.

Always keep a contingency plan in the works, Van Loon. I know
I do.

Van Loon crawled and for the last few steps he walked up the grade. Moonlight faded fast as though in flight from the desolate view. It's a simple question, Reed. His knees were shaky. Why're we going there?

For a little conversation, Van Loon. To have a chat or aren't you human? We're going down to the cabins to shoot the breeze. To gab. To gossip. To revive tall tales and to remark upon the wonders that we have seen. You've seen a few haven't you, Van Loon? I know you have. Just tonight you saw the white light of a freight train barrel down into the base scaffold of your soul. That's a story, Van Loon. A story worth experiencing is worth the telling. You got to let those stories get told. Can you walk?

Barely, Van Loon admitted.

Your strength will revive upon you. You've had a generous fright. We'll walk on slowly and we'll talk as we go. I'll start.

The two men carried on down the railway tracks and one man balanced on the rail and the other crunched his boots upon the stone and stubbed the steel toes against the ties and they walked on toward the Green River Bridge and one man talked and the other listened.

LIKE SPECTRES REED KITCHEN AND FERENC VAN LOON emerged from the darkness of the night and stepped down from the railway grade onto the boardwalk. Kitchen went on ahead and Van Loon followed behind and he was reticent and abashed. Kitchen rapped on the door and without waiting for a response opened it and stepped inside. Kitchen held the door for his partner and shut it behind them.

Coaloil lanterns illuminated the room and the dark figures there. Reed Kitchen said, It's me. I have come to pay a visit on this night. We thought you might enjoy midnight chat. This is my buddy Ferenc. He's a Dutchman. Dutchmen are from Holland. I don't know why they aren't called Hollandmen but these things occur when men are born of nations. Ferenc works with me on the bridge if you didn't guess that already.

Van Loon inhaled the scent of coffee and the acridity of oil lamps. In one corner a woman knitted and rocked and the wick of her small lantern flickered beside her. The lamp that hung from the ceiling above the long wood table cast the man who sat slumped over his coffee in a shadowy shroud. Reed Kitchen sat down opposite the man within the penumbra and Van Loon sat also.

This is Wilf, Kitchen said. He lives here.

Hi, Wilf, Van Loon said. I'm sorry to impose on you like this.

We're not imposing, Reed Kitchen said. Why would you say that? Wilf and his wife live alone out here. They have nobody to talk to if you can imagine that. They don't mind company once in a blue moon. They're not like you, Van Loon. They don't walk down a railway track in the middle of the night with no place to go.

Wilf must live out here for a reason, Van Loon said. It can't be because he prefers bright city lights.

A corner of Wilf's lip curled higher. His coffeecup blocked the view and he sipped. He put his mug down again. Have a coffee, he said. Pot's on the stove.

See? Kitchen said. He knew we were coming. Kitchen spun around on his seat and headed for the coffeepot.

I didn't know you was coming, Wilf said.

You just made coffee in case we showed up, Kitchen told him. That's neighbourly.

I made that coffee for myself, Wilf said. But you can have a cup.

Reed Kitchen's march across the floor shook the house slightly and the overhead lamp swayed and the shadows moved in a slow dance. He came back with two mugfuls and he and Van Loon drank their coffees black.

I guess you've lived out here a long time, Van Loon said.

Of course he has, Kitchen answered.

I been here a long time, the man said. He was short and squat with white hair and a moon face and dark eyes and he smiled more often than other Indians Van Loon had known.

What do you do out here for a living? The coffee was hot and eased the chill and damp of the long walk. Fish?

I fish some days, Wilf said.

He's a scavenger, Reed Kitchen said. The man's a certified beach-comber.

Is that right? Van Loon asked him.

Of course it's right, Reed Kitchen said.

I got a licence, Wilf said.

What do you beachcomb for out here?

Logs, Wilf said.

Van Loon recalled the empty boom on the Skeena across from the cabin. I didn't know you needed a licence for that, Van Loon said.

Sure you do, Reed Kitchen said. Anything that gets away from the logging companies belongs to Wilf if he can hook it. You and me, Van Loon, we'd get arrested if we took a log off the river without a licence. Unless old Wilf saw us first. In that case we'd just get shot.

Is that right? Van Loon asked.

Wilf shrugged and reiterated, I got a licence.

We're going to help him out, Reed Kitchen said.

How?

You will take apart that old bridge, Wilf said.

Yes we will, Kitchen said. What're we going to do with all those old timbers, Van Loon?

The railway takes those timbers back.

Make a distinction, Van Loon. The company wants those timbers. The railway has no real use for them.

I don't follow you.

Does the company drive the trains? Does the company build the bridges or lay track? Who loads boxcars—the company? Who smells what we smell? Who has creosote on the soles of their boots and oil on their clothes—the company? Who has callouses on their hands? The railway has no use for those old timbers, Van Loon. It's the company that wants to scavenge those old timbers to sell on the open market. Who're you going to help here, Van Loon? The company or old Wilf?

Kai won't go for it, Van Loon said.

That accident won't be his fault, Reed Kitchen said.

What accident? Van Loon sipped his coffee which had quickly cooled.

Stack those timbers too high and the whole thing will crash down with the wrong sort of push, Kitchen said. If that accident happens at high tide and Wilf is around to snag a few timbers—

I got a licence, Wilf pointed out.

That's right. Since we can't get a line on those timbers anyway because we don't have a licence Wilf gets them. What harm will that do? If you got something against Wilf earning a living, Van Loon, now's the time to speak up. Let's hear it.

It's okay with me, Van Loon said. I guess we'll have an accident.

I can feel it coming. I can feel it in my bones. Accidents happen. If Wilf has a talent for predicting when accidents happen then that's his own good luck.

Wilf looked across at Van Loon. I got a licence for good luck, he said.

Margaret, Reed Kitchen called out. Come on over here and have a cup of coffee with the boys. Now's the time for the telling of stories and you know what I appreciate most about you two. You're great listeners. Van Loon, want to hear a story about me and trains?

Another railroad story, Van Loon griped.

The best kind in my experience. Kitchen waited for Margaret to shuffle over and sit down beside Wilf and it took her awhile to fit her knees under the table.

Friends, my father was a section foreman. North Ontario. My mother lived with him there in nowhere land. She was having her troubles my daddy explained to me. She was pregnant and she was dissatisfied with this particular world. Don't ask me the details why because I don't know them. I wasn't born then. One night the late freight was coming through and she went out the door to watch it go by. Usually she did this to wonder where it was bound and where it had been and what places those were. What they were like. That's my best guess. Her husband who was the man who was my father had fallen asleep in his evening chair with one hand on his beer after the exhaustion of his day. My mother did not watch that train go by as normally she liked to do. This time she sat herself down upon that track. She watched the freight come at her and she was like a deer hypnotized by those bright lights. The train blasted through the whistle stop and either that noise or something else awakened the man who was my father. Some voice. Some call. He awakened in a sweat and discovered himself alone and he put on his coat and he was not sweating only he was shivering also for no known reason and he went outside too. He found only the pieces of his wife and the shreds of her garments—not her whole body whole. In the midst of his searching he found the child the train had severed from the womb. That child was alive and crying. That child was unhurt. It was born. I sure do love the railroad, Van Loon, I sure do honour trains, Wilf, because that train spared me my life. Margaret, I was that child. Some men are born between the legs of a woman and that's another scary and holy place—I was born between the steel rails of the tracks. I came into this world with a freight train ripping across my face and some say I've been talking about it ever since but I don't know much about the validity of that particular point of view. Myself personally I do believe that I was crying when I was born like my daddy told me I was and that I had no speech at that time. But I was crying so maybe I was bawling to get something out.

They sipped their coffees.

That's a story, Wilf said.

He's got a licence, Van Loon said and Wilf and Margaret smiled.

I like the sound of that, Reed Kitchen said. A licence to speak my mind. May it ever be so.

They talked amid the attentive shadows there in the dimming light.

3

REED KITCHEN BRACED both hands against the dash and presented his ultimatum. Brake or let me out right here boys.

Windshield wipers swatted the spatter of rain.

Outwardly composed and hysterical within Caleb Farrow sat in the middle of the bench seat and pitched his contradictory advice. No way. Either you accelerate there pal or we die.

Steeeeeerrrr.

Who's driving this crate anyhow? Ferenc Van Loon performed the three tasks demanded of him—braking and accelerating and steering through a snaking series of S-curves with deep gullies on both sides. He had not been prepared for a road where normal speeds and everyday driving techniques were hazardous.

You want to know who's driving? Kitchen squawked. I want to know whose peabrain built a highway like this one in the first place. I want the name of that man. His address. His phone number. The names of his children. I got a message I want to handdeliver to that particular human miscreant.

Government, Caleb Farrow deduced.

They drove on.

A rack of signs warned to take the next curve at five miles an hour and Reed Kitchen braced for the worst when Van Loon obeyed and slowed to crawlspeed. The turn amazed them and the idiocy bent them raucous. The pickup completed a virtual circle before the road pivoted in the general direction of the coast and Caleb Farrow did not hide his jitters now.

Either this is the road to hell or we're on a trek to Shangri La there pal.

Mists roved the valley below them.

Rain lashed the truck from above.

One good thing about this highway it keeps you quiet, Reed, Van Loon said. Relatively speaking.Though I could go for one of your tall tales right about now. Take my mind off the driving.

You kidding me? I want your mind on the driving. Keep your eyes on the road here in front of you.

Come on. Talk. Help settle my nerves. *Hhohghd—!*

A pothole large enough to sink a fox won an outcry.

Hang on a second, Caleb Farrow intervened and he lightly tapped his left ear with his palm as though suffering a faulty connection. Am I hearing things? You're asking Reed to talk? Has the road shook your marbles loose? We go out of our way to shut him up—that's what we do, Van Loon. Now you're asking this jabbermouth here to talk? No offence there, Reed.

None taken.

He's got some stories. You should hear them, Van Loon said and one in particular he wanted retold. Tell him the one you told me about the train.

That was a special time for the telling of that tale, Reed Kitchen said. He moistened his lips with his tongue. The time was right for the telling of that tale and you know what I'm talking about, Van Loon. We had circumstances leading up to that story that did pertain. It should keep. Not every story can be retold willynilly any old time of the day or month. Some stories are best retold at night.

Mist scrounged the wall of rock alongside them.

What're you guys going on about? Caleb Farrow asked.

Just tell the story, Reed.

Caleb first, Kitchen insisted and he folded his arms across his chest in a gesture of defiance. I haven't had a story out of him in some long while.

This beats all. Caleb Farrow slapped his forehead in a pantomime of dismay. Van Loon, not only are you asking the man to talk you are negotiating for the privilege. You are close to begging. What's the matter with you?

Caleb, Van Loon said.

What?

Shut up and tell a story.

Make it a good one, Reed Kitchen told him.

Caleb Farrow uttered a line of expletives.

I don't want to hear those gross convict stories either, Kitchen advised him. They don't count. You ask a convict for a story he tells you something truly nasty. I don't want to hear anything nasty on this day.

Gross convict stories, the man in the middle said as though Reed Kitchen had put a finger on the button of his inspiration.

How'd you find out he's a con? Ferenc Van Loon asked Kitchen.

The man knows everything there is that's pertinent to know, Caleb Farrow believed.

Reed Kitchen volunteered the source of his information. It's in his eyes.

Van Loon looked.

Get out of here. I'm telling a story. Caleb Farrow nodded at his listeners before he began with formality. In the springtime at Okalla Pen we had lambing season and we had calving season. I want you to know at the outset that I did not participate. I just saw a few things.

Is this a gross convict story? Reed Kitchen interrupted.

I've seen some things you will never drag out of me. This scene wasn't so bad. The men lined up. They took turns like they were off to the whorehouse. Only I found out later that in the barn they'd slip their dicks into the mouths of newborn calves and get their rocks off that way.

See what I mean? Ask a con for a story and he delivers something pitiful and nasty. That's an abomination that story and I don't want to hear it.

You already heard it, Reed.

It wasn't worth the effort. I do not consider that story proper payment for mine.

He's at it again, Caleb Farrow said.

At what?

Negotiating. Watch yourself with him, Van Loon.

Their skins stretched taut. Hearts yelped as the rock wall fell away and the pickup hobbyhorsed around a ledge where the side pavement was cracked and broken. Nobody dared look down to tempt a fall. Kitchen looked up and dug his fingernails into the dash.

They drove through cloud.

They drove on.

I will count this ride upon the highway proper circumstances for the telling of my tale because none of us is likely to live for the retelling.

Leaning forward to speak across the cab to both Farrow and Van Loon Reed Kitchen propped his right fist upon the dash to protect himself from sudden collision against the windshield. The wipers laid down a rhythm—a percussion he obeyed. The slant of rain as they neared the coast angled against them. The water was torrential. The hilly and winding road became manageable as they emerged from the mountains and Van Loon increased their speed. My father worked upon the railroad, Caleb, Kitchen began.

God help us. Another railroad story.

They are the best kind.

He told his story. The pickup gained momentum down a straight steep descent.

At the bottom of the hill Caleb Farrow told him, I'll let you know if I'm willing to believe all that or not. I'll reserve my judgment. I don't want the word going around that Caleb Farrow is a gullible man. I don't want to hear that sort of talk behind my back. Farrow was chuckling and having a good time.

They were in traffic soon with logging trucks and pulp mill pickups and construction Land Rovers and a few cars. Bald eagles alighted in the trees. The road under construction changed to mud and soon it was rocky and their heads bounced against the roof of the cab. They had arrived in Prince Rupert and Reed Kitchen remarked, This is the place to where we've come. A few minutes' reconnaissance led them to a strip of hotels and beer parlours a block away from the centre of town. We are on the edge of the sea, he said. There is no place more far than this. This is the end of the railway line to which I am connected. I have come to the last place where I can go. There is no place more faraway than this.

Reed, Caleb Farrow said.

What?

Make sense, man. You're babbling.

This is the place to where we've come, he repeated.

You do have a knack for the obvious.

All my life has brought me here, he said in a tone of lament.

What are you talking about when you utter bunk like that?

I thought it was obvious.

Ferenc Van Loon backed his GMC into a parking slot. Enough with the chitchat. Time to drink and shout and chase fine women. This is new turf. Let me tell you something, boys—I love new turf.

Caleb Farrow also smiled with wily mercy and Reed Kitchen pestered him. What're you grinning at?

Trouble, he declared. His smile dimpled into a sly grimace. I can smell it. I do love my trouble.

Reed Kitchen cranked open the door and stepped out into the downpour of downtown Prince Rupert and he could not say what he loved. Caleb Farrow bailed out after him. They sprinted through the cold slant of rain to the first doorway offering shelter and Van Loon landed close behind. They were standing at the entrance to a beer parlour and that seemed opportune. An omen. Ferenc Van Loon held open the door and the three men piled in.

Right you are, Caleb, Kitchen announced the moment he was through the inner set of doors. We drove ourselves down the road to Shangri La. Look at this place. It's heaven. It's brimming with chatter. It has been a painfully long time since I have heard so much boisterous conversation. I have come to the place where I've been going. I have come to the end of the line and lo—and lo and behold—look at this place. Look at it! It's paradise to me.

Caleb Farrow surveyed the hall congested with small wood tables laden with draft glasses and more than a hundred men and two dozen women smoked in their laughter and their voices fused with the ascending noise. He breathed rank scent. Heaven all right, he concurred and grinned again. I can find my share of trouble in a place like this you bet.

Van Loon shook water from his hair and shoulders and spruced himself up. He had already spied the woman of his dreams.

Now, Kitchen announced. Now today. Let us go into this fine public house.

FERENC VAN LOON UNDERSTOOD THE protocol of courtship. He had firsthand knowledge of the rules of romance as they pertained to beer parlours in this corner of the land. A man who pursued a woman would never find the field clear. Fallers and chokermen and fishermen and millworkers and catskinners and longshoremen also plotted strategies and made gruff moves. Animosity was easily aroused among these pretenders to a woman's affection and rarely would a rejected suitor gaze kindly upon another standing where he had slipped.

There are fighters and there are lovers in this world, Van Loon advised Caleb Farrow who was anxious to be initiated to his secrets. If you want to be a lover avoid the fighters. Be wary of them but don't let them notice you. If they pick you out of a crowd you can kiss your health goodbye.

What's your angle? Caleb Farrow asked. How do you walk out of a beer parlour with a woman on your arm other guys were crowding all night? I seen you do it when you and her never spoke two words together.

Secret communications, Van Loon decreed.

What's that supposed to mean?

Van Loon gave the matter some thought. You ever look a guy in the eye who's wearing a suit and you know—you just know—that he's a cop?

Natch, Caleb Farrow conceded.

And he looks at you and you know that he knows that you're a crook?

You bet.

Secret communications. It's the language of love, Caleb. The force of attraction. Can't be taught. It's something you have to learn for yourself.

You're a big help, Van Loon. You're some friend of mine.

I do my best.

In surveying his new terrain Van Loon chose to be prudent.

The focus of his attention travelled with an entourage. The woman came and went and returned again and different men enjoyed the indulgence of her company. I've never been in love with a hooker before, Van Loon admitted. Not since Hong Kong anyway where it was practically a daily occurrence—but that was different.

I admire you, Caleb Farrow said. You're one guy who doesn't have to pay for it. I don't want you to shatter my illusions there pal. Forget her.

Ferenc Van Loon brought his draft to his lips without drinking and his nostrils flared. Here's a promise. I won't pay for it. No fun in that. But she's the woman I'm after. She's the one for me.

Could be dicey, Farrow observed. Unless I'm blind it appears to me the lady comes equipped with her own small armoured division.

She rose just then and Farrow and Van Loon were attentive to her move. She was escorted to the washroom. Eyes across the beer parlour beheld a subtle and exquisite sashay although no patron felt free to pester her walk. She moved within five paces of his table and glanced at Van Loon—a cursory incandescent look and Van Loon swelled to the sadness explicit in her gaze and the hard brittle currency of her gesture.

For a mere fraction of an instant their eyes met and that communication proved provocative and rash.

Look, Farrow said and he gestured to the door. More action.

Two women tarried in the entrance to receive the appreciation of many. Van Loon considered the pair to be fine looking women and they were not here on business. Patrons stood at their tables and waved and whistled and hollered for them to come on over and in the annals of time no such overture had ever been accorded a sympathetic reception. The two women found a table for themselves and waited for suitors with sufficient courtesy and calm and courage and deftness to saunter on by and prove themselves amusing. Van Loon rejected the invitation. Most days he'd feel the need to entertain their gentle disposition for lively company. He could not be moved by their presence now. As the woman of his favour turned at the entrance to the ladies' room—a test—Van Loon passed muster. He had demonstrated that he had eyes only for her. His regard had not been swayed by the new arrivals. He felt himself aroused to the challenge conveyed by her look.

I'm going after the other one, Van Loon told his friend.

Two pretty ducks sitting on your pond over here, Van Loon. Take your pick. Do what you do so well. I'd be a happy man to pick up what's left over you bet.

Attitude, Caleb, Van Loon cautioned him. You're like the yahoos who whistle at women coming through the door. If I wasn't here you'd probably join in. You'd whistle your head off.

Maybe I would and maybe I wouldn't.

If somebody whistled at you would you come running?

Answer me this. Why go after the pro who gets to walk to the can with her own security guard when there's two amateurs sitting over here begging for your stuff even if they don't know it yet? Just tell me why that is, Van Loon. I want to understand these things.

The glass Van Loon had raised to his lips remained poised and he did not sip. I can't let her down, he said. This woman and me—we have exchanged our opinions of each other. I can't disappoint her.

Caleb Farrow breathed out a heavy gust of air as though this mischief was forever beyond his ken. He pocketed his smokes and chugalugged his draft. Fine. Chase whatever fluff you got going. I'm taking my chances with these two. Just tell me what to say.

Van Loon laughed. What?

Tell me what to say.

The whole conversation or just your opening line?

Get me started, Van Loon.

Van Loon sipped finally from his glass and put it down. His eyes remained steadfast on the door to the ladies' room. Unhunh, he said.

What do you mean unhunh? Come on. We're buddies. Help me out here.

I need you for something else.

What else? No offence but you know what comes before friendship.

She emerged. She wore a narrow black vest and a white sweater and black leather pants. She was petite and her curves were gentle and obvious also. For Van Loon the stoniness to her bearing and the plaint of her gaze sustained her beauty and enchanted him more than the lustre of her small breasts and waist. She had mystery. She had story. She possessed a wildness beneath the sheen of her look and beneath her look she kept company with some painful commotion. She gave him that quick glance again. For a fraction of an instant their eyes met again and Van Loon detected what he had earlier surmised—that she had found cause to be disappointed in him. I need you to buy a portion of this woman's time, Van Loon said.

She's out of my price range you bet.

Once you've paid for the pleasure of her company I'll take over.

Excuse me? I must have wax in my ears. Farrow boinked a side of his head.

Things could not be right between us if I bought her. You make the purchase. Then I'm free to horn in on your time.

Caleb Farrow mulled over the situation. He was looking at the table where the woman was seated and he recognized the men about her. He did not know them but identified their nature through the secret communications Van Loon had discussed. Mean cousins. One bad lot and these were not men to slander. Which did intrigue him. He did love his trouble. I suppose I can do this for a buddy, he said. I presume you're raising the currency?

Nope. Van Loon kept his eyes on the back of the woman's head. Her hair was lustrous and brown and cut short. I can't buy her. It wouldn't be right.

So I'm supposed to pay the price—

—and give her up.

Gee, Van Loon. I know you think I'm not too bright but gee. This doesn't sound like such a sweet deal.

You buy her. You give her up. Van Loon took another swig of his beer and finally removed his glance from the woman and looked at Farrow. I'll see to it you score ten times over with the ladies.

Emerging from his slouch Caleb Farrow straightened himself in his chair. I'm getting an interested feeling here, Van Loon.

All winter long, Caleb. He looked back at the woman. Just do me this one favour this one time.

Done. But explain it to me. How is this any different? If I'm paying for her and I'm your friend how is it any different from you paying for her yourself?

I just need to talk to her. Find out what makes her tick. Find out what's behind the story here.

Caleb Farrow shook his head in disgust and admiration. A waste of good dough, he decreed. But I won't look a gift horse in the mouth even if it is wide open. I'm willing to collect on your stupidity, Van Loon. All winter long like you said. Ten times over. I'm going to hold you to that. So. Who do you think's the cashier? Where's he at?

Ferenc Van Loon pointed the gent out to him. Then he said, Where's Kitchen? How long does it take to get us three rooms?

Probably he found somebody to talk to.

I'll make some calls—find out if we're booked in someplace. When I come back make your move.

Buy me a beer first, Caleb Farrow said. That and a promise is all I'll see out of this deal for my hardearned cash you bet.

Ferenc Van Loon raised one finger to the passing waiter and stood to leave. He put on his jacket. He dropped a single on the table. The woman turned as though she had been watching him through the back of her head. Van Loon left the beer parlour for a telephone in the hotel lobby and he could feel her eyes measuring the length of his stride. He sensed her watching his long lope. The woman was wondering why he had given up so quickly when he had not looked the type. It goes to show you, Van Loon could hear her thinking.

Hold your horses, he told the voice that was her voice that he imagined inside his head. Hang on for a minute longer that's all.

Hold my what? her voice was saying to him. She was laughing in his mind with her head thrown back and her long neck exposed to his lingering kiss.

Horses, Van Loon said. He was bending to touch her throat with his tongue and she giggled and when she quit giggling under him she sighed. Yeah, he whispered. Horses.

And she was saying, Whoa. Whoa, pony.

DRIVEN BY WINDS WHIPPING OFF the great natural harbour of Prince Rupert rain slashed one side of Reed Kitchen's face and streamed under his collar and soaked his chest and back. He walked slanted to the gusts determined to reach his destination—a place he had rarely imagined. Reed Kitchen needed to mark the spot. He needed to stand on the site with all due reverence and trembling as a prophet might behold the voice of his God upon His own altar. Reed Kitchen wanted to stand in proper awe at the cessation of his world and revere there the holy and empirical *end of the line*.

The rain had sting.

The wind had bite.

Kitchen did not know what to expect and the moment was upon him. He had arrived at the stagnant blocks butted up against a cliff below the paved road ascending to town. Here. The end of the world to him. He did not know if time stood fixed and the planets ceased their spin. He believed that it must be true. In this place time dissipated and God emerged and verified the rumours. Here the migratory patterns of civilizations from the east of China through Asia and Africa and Europe concluded and here no further step was set to be trod without crossing the Pacific and recommencing again. Here in this place where history ceased the shoddy closure of a rail link that traced its origins to antiquity was a muddy patch. Pools of water expanded at his feet. Moss grew upon the ties and grass between. The intensity of rain effaced the outer world. So it was true what people said. God liked it damp.

The world's end.

Time's curtain.

Beyond the edge of the world lay the void of sea. Reed Kitchen was schooled in irony and it seemed the greatest irony to him that at the outer rim of nowhere he had located God's country and at the edge of God's country the only place to go was back to the beginning because he had found the end.

We have nowhere to go, he wanted to say if someone would listen. He wanted to scream, *Trrraaaaiiinnn!* as though he could summon his own good God out of the pelting darkness of the squall and have his own rabid God roar through this point at the end of the line at this junction in time to verify what lay beyond. This tabernacle constituted holy ground to him and that reality was confirmed. At this juncture other worlds conjoined. In this grotto at the rail's end to all the world's trains and their accumulative links Reed Kitchen discovered that he could not speak. He could not shame the silence with his tongue. What convinced him and proved most credible to him— Reed Kitchen realized he had nothing to say.

He panicked. He fled that place.

Reed Kitchen ran back along the slippery rail and fifty yards down ducked into the train station to mop up. In the washroom he dried his hair under the blower and warmed his face and his heart raced. He dabbed his brow with paper towel and combed his hair with his fingers and returned to the waitingroom where two bearded men—an older and a younger—inquired about passage east. You have to return from here, Reed Kitchen heard himself say and he wanted to stop. He wanted to be quiet. There is no forward way. There are no tracks south and no roads and you must sail upon the sea or fly above it. If you wish to travel by land you must return east by the way that you have come. Two young women travelling with the men emerged from the other washroom and Reed Kitchen saw them recoil and fear him and blanch. They bunched up together to hide one behind the other. This is the place to where I've come and it scares me beyond my wits to arrive, he said and he railed to himself, *Enough of this! Get out! Go!* For Reed Kitchen feared his own words and his own self and the place to which he had descended.

Reed Kitchen walked partway back the way he had come and the

rain let up and he swerved toward the sea. The long sheds attracted
him and he walked to the side that confronted the harbour where he
observed a sombre and rusting vessel. A flood of light fell through the
yawning doors of a warehouse. He entered through those doors surprised to find women in white uniforms and they stood in long rows
and carved the day's catch from the sea. They laboured at makeshift
tables lit by bare bulbs and they talked and sliced the bellies of fish and
severed the heads and tails and talked and skinned the fish and Reed
Kitchen delighted in their conversation and they talked and he stepped
forward into the light and the women went mute. He drifted outside
again. The place stank. He observed the gangway rising high into the
hulk of the *Isu Maru*. Reed Kitchen looked at the men and two women
on deck. This is the place to where I've come, he said aloud and he
climbed the gangway to the ship's middeck. He walked around the deck
of the ship and no man challenged him. The crew were of different
races and most were Asians. Although the ship was Japanese he
assumed these men were not. The presence of women surprised him.
He had not imagined women travelling the seas of the world and Reed
Kitchen descended into the bowels of the boat. He moved through the
engineering works and stepped into cabins. He visited a messhall and
peered into the vast holds from above. What is this stuff? he asked one
Asian sailor who stared back at him without comprehension. Sand was
piled high in the centre holds of the boat. Reddish brown. Like rust.
Roughhewn logs partially filled the gaping caverns in the stern and
bow. On the dock more wood awaited loading. Below again he found a
place where men slept in bunks. Reed Kitchen curled up on an unused
bed and closed his eyes as though a nap was warranted. He wanted to
talk—to himself if to no other—to understand this place and discern it
with his mind. He could stow away. He could secrete himself away
aboard this ship and who would notice? He could perform duties and no
one would object. He could skip his watch and no one would be con-
scious of an absence. He could land in some foreign place as Van Loon
had done and see the nations of the world and no one would deny him
entry. Surely it was not necessary to remain attached to the railway.
What law had been written in stone? Blood alone bound him to the

tracks. I could stow away, Reed Kitchen thought to himself and he must have been thinking aloud because another voice answered. .

Not a great idea.

Reed Kitchen opened his eyes.

I thought I told you to meet me on deck.

It's raining, Kitchen said.

It's always raining, Don McBain said.

The railway detective rotated a shoulder and wiped rainwater from his cheeks on the back of his hand. He flicked the hand and water sprayed across the floor. He coughed as men did who came in from the cold and damp and he rubbed his nose on a handkerchief.

Kitchen sat up and his feet dangled off the edge of the bunk and he looked with worry into the eyes of the railway detective. You have found me in this place, Yellowhead, he said. His tone conveyed a hint of awe.

Don McBain smiled. You still have that strange way of talking. Yes I found you, Reed. In this place. You've forgotten something though. I don't appreciate being called Yellowhead anymore.

Not everybody has a choice in the names people call them by.

Don McBain was grinning and the grin evolved into a low chuckle. He rotated his hat in his hands. Actually this is a good place for a meet. It's better than the deck.

Are we having a meet? Reed Kitchen asked him.

In police work we call this a meet.

That's a good thing to know, Reed Kitchen told him. I have something to report, Don.

What's that, Reed?

You don't need me anymore.

Don McBain sat down on the opposite bunk. He took out his smokes and tapped the bottom of the package. Two cigarettes poked out their necks. He offered the pack across the aisle and Reed Kitchen helped himself. Don McBain was wearing a black slicker down to his ankles. He unbuttoned the front to get at his lighter. Under the slicker he was wearing a suit and his tie was maroon and zoo animals frolicked up its length—giraffes and zebras and elephants and hippopotamuses. Why's that, Reed?

There's a man you wanted me to investigate. An exconvict. I won't say his name out loud in case somebody is listening. I have checked up on that man, Don, and I am pleased to report to you that he's a fine fellow. He's an upstanding young man and an asset to the railway. I am pleased to say that I myself personally call him a friend.

Don McBain listened and lit his smoke and he passed the unlit lighter across to Reed Kitchen who cupped it in his palm. He wanted to hear a response before he flicked the lighter.

How're things on Gang 4? McBain asked him. Good crew?

Good crew, Don.

That's great. What were you mumbling about stowing away?

Kitchen tapped the unlit cigarette against the side of the bunk. I must have been talking in my sleep, Don. I was taking a nap out of the pouring rain.

Don McBain nodded. Something's come up, he said.

Reed Kitchen was staring at him. I knew it would, he said. I had this feeling that this was only the beginning.

We need someone who will talk to us.

I'll talk to you, Don. I just don't know if you want to listen.

I'd hate to see Caleb Farrow lose his job. Wouldn't you? A man like that can't have many options.

Almost none. Kitchen lit his cigarette and his hand trembled slightly. His face glowed a tawny yellow in the light of the flame and red in the glow of the cigarette. He looked around at the white steel of the cabin and felt imprisoned. I want to put my feet back on dry ground, he said. I want to get off this ship now.

Settle down, Reed.

You scare me, Don. You always do. You have that effect. You know why that is? Reed Kitchen drew a deep drag off the smoke.

Why's that, Reed?

Because you keep coming to me out of this world. I don't know nothing about this world. Why don't you let me go back to my own good world once and for all.

The thing is, Reed, we need somebody who comes from your way of life. We need somebody about whom it can be said that there is no doubt. Your credentials, Reed, they're impeccable. As far back as anybody wants to research you're a man working on the railroad. Nobody can dispute that fact. Nobody could think for two seconds that you're a cop. Or working for the cops. Nobody would ever think that, Reed. It's important for you to believe me.

Kitchen smoked as he breathed and stared at McBain. I believe that, Don. It just scares me why I should need to.

The detective crossed the aisle between bunks. He sat down beside Reed Kitchen and placed a hand on his near shoulder. He smiled. He took his smile away. There's some serious business going down, Reed. Serious muck. You know what makes me so mad?

What's that?

The bastards are using company property for their crimes. Railroad property. That really pisses me off, Reed. That's why we have to get involved. We can't let them get away with it.

Maybe we can. Maybe we can't. Myself personally I don't know nothing about this and I got to tell you, Don, that's fine with me.

Is it, Reed? Is it? Let me say this just once, Reed, then we'll forget that it was ever spoken. Okay? Don't get yourself all excited or riled but we can do more than remove Caleb Farrow from the payroll.

Reed Kitchen looked into his eyes to gauge his meaning. What else would we do to him? he asked quietly.

Not to him, Reed, McBain whispered. I'll spell it out. If you can't help on this one the railway might decide that you're expendable. The railway has its ways.

You can't do that.

McBain patted Kitchen's kneecap and assured him, Yes we can. Trust me. It won't be a problem.

I have a union.

Damn the union, Reed. Pardon my language but damn the union. Now let's not talk about this again.

This is an awful day, Reed Kitchen moaned.

Don McBain commiserated with him and shook his head. Rained cats and dogs for a month. You'll get used to it.

I'm not talking about the weather, Don. Although I agree with you it's bad enough.

Reed, Don McBain said quietly, we need your help. We have few resources up here. We have to make do with what we've got and now we're up against some serious muck. We need your help. No one will suspect you. If somebody checks you out what'll they learn? You're a bridgeman working for the railway. What's suspicious about that?

That's what I want to be—a bridgeman working for the railway.

Essentially that's what you are. All I'm asking for is a little of your time on your days off. Meet a few people. Hang around with a certain crowd. I'll take care of the introductions. All I'm asking for is that when you're not talking you're listening. Just listen, Reed. Then tell us what you hear.

Us? Kitchen asked him. He butted his cigarette on the steel floor and crushed it under a boot.

Me, Don McBain said.

Who's us?

I meant me.

Who's us, Don?

I am working in concert with other police forces.

The RCMP?

Yes.

Who else?

This isn't the issue, Reed.

Who else, Don?

The Coast Guard. It's a joint effort, Reed. We need your help.

You have your resources and you still want me? You don't need me. You have your resources.

Our resources are spread pretty thin. Besides— The Mounties—the Guard—you know how it is, Reed.

No I don't.

Those other forces don't expect the railroad police— They don't expect me to acquit myself with distinction. I need an edge. I want to hold my own. I can do what they can't do. I can run someone beyond suspicion. Someone like you, Reed.

So get somebody like me. Just don't get me.

Nobody knows you. You don't have friends in the area who can screw it up for you. Nobody in his right mind would think you're a cop. Because you're not. It's perfect.

It's like before, Kitchen said sadly. This isn't all there is to it. You only make it sound that way. This is only the beginning and that's something I know in my bones.

Don McBain stood up again. He buttoned his slicker. He dropped his own cigarette to the floor where it fizzled in the puddle that had formed at his feet. The floor was slippery with rainwater shed from their clothes. He turned his hat in his hands.

That's what I like about you, Reed. You have a keen sense of things. You know what's up. You're one of those people who can see what's coming around the mountain. You're important to us for that reason. That's why we need you. We need that sense. Come on. I'll take you to dinner. We'll talk about other things and drink a glass of wine and have a good time.

Reed Kitchen followed him up to the deck and he stood in the rain looking at the lights of Prince Rupert above the blackness of the railway yard. He could hear the diesels wheezing in their sleep although he could not see them beyond the rooftop of the warehouse. That's fine, he said. Take me to dinner. But when it comes time to talk about things I'll be the one who does the talking. That's the price you will have to pay.

Don McBain laughed out loud and took him by the elbow. It'll be my pleasure, he said. That's God's own truth, Reed.

The phrase struck Reed Kitchen as curious and they descended the gangway. He called out to the detective, What do you know about it? God's own truth. What do you know about that?

Yellowhead Don McBain had lost track of whatever his dupe was saying. He was unable to provide a satisfactory response.

BOTH MEN WERE EXCITED AND WEARY and halfpast sober as they drove down to the floating colony annexed to the Port Edward canneries. Ferenc Van Loon and Caleb Farrow had eaten and napped and done their laundry. They had showered and shaved and scented themselves.

They drove off Kaien Island and found the turn to the secondary road in the dark and in the rain followed a map traced on a napkin to the dilapidated shacks docked against the shore.

If Reed was here I know what he'd say, Caleb Farrow said.

Van Loon said it for him. This is the place to where we've come.

I know what I'd say to that.

So do I.

Something of that nature.

Below the height of the gravel lot the cedar and sheetmetal bunkhouses rocked in waves under the onslaught of nasty weather. Smoke rising from tin chimneys blew down onto the boardwalks below the slash of rain and the sallow light the windows emitted quickly diffused. Van Loon shut off the engine and kept the head-lights on and the windshield wipers flapped and the men stared out into the darkness as though some knowledge aforethought might be gleaned from the blackness or the highbeams or the shack lamps ablaze as distant fires.

Sure do love my trouble, Caleb Farrow said.

We'll find out how much.

Never have located the bottom to that desire.

Tonight'll be a test.

You bet.

They sat in the cab awhile.

This infernal rain, Van Loon grumbled. It's going to piss on us for-ever. Who can live and work in a climate like this one?

Not me, Caleb Farrow said. It's got me beat.

It's ridiculous. You're wet all the time. You're cold all the time. You're soaked through to the skin most of the time. You can't walk six inches without getting drenched in this rain.

Not to mention the sixty or the eighty or the ninety or the one hundred feet we got to cross to get down to those floats.

I don't know why we bother to wash up or do our laundry when both jobs get done walking around outside.

You're getting yourself into a mood there pal. That's okay. What-ever it takes. So turn the engine back on and give us some heat.

We got to go on down there, Caleb.

I've been told. Turn the engine back on, Van Loon. There's something else you got to do.

What's that?

First turn the engine back on.

Van Loon started her up and gunned the engine and Caleb Farrow rubbed his hands in front of the side vent. What else? Van Loon asked him.

Don't go calling me names or referring to my dark past but there are a few things any crook knows and number one on the list is you always point your getaway vehicle in the direction you'll be getting away. Turn this thing around. Make sure your rear tires aren't buried in some mudhole. As much time as we're taking arriving you never know how fast we might want to be moving along later.

That made sense to Ferenc Van Loon and he turned the truck around so that it faced away from the sea and he drove forward and back a few times to test his traction. Then he shut the motor off again and turned off the lights and they sat in the dark and listened to the noise of rain slashing the roof and glass and under that sound the murmuring distant complaint of the generator that powered the lights of the floating colony.

Let's get going, Van Loon said after awhile.

Have a smoke first.

You'll only get cold again. It's cold and damp in here.

Then let's get going, Caleb Farrow said.

Let's go, Van Loon agreed.

They sat in the truck awhile.

Let's go, Van Loon said and he placed his palm on the door handle.

I'm waiting on you, Caleb Farrow told him.

You got the shortest way to go, Van Loon mentioned.

That's why I'm waiting on you to come around. I'm not going to wait on you outside in the rain.

Won't make no difference. You'll be as wet as you can get in six seconds.

I hate this weather, Caleb Farrow said.

It's not fit for humans.

Not these humans.

I'm going, Van Loon promised.

I'm waiting on you.

I'm gone, he said and he opened the door and he was running through the darkness. Caleb Farrow climbed out of the truck and put his head down against the hard cold snap of water and stumbled after his partner. A small lamp guided them to the head of the stairs where the way downward followed through the dark and they held onto the cold slippery wood railing and slid and slipped and tripped descending to the boardwalk. At the bottom they jumped across a small lit gap and stood under an eavestrough. Rain sluiced off the spout like a waterfall from the higher mountains.

Know what I heard Reed say one time? Caleb Farrow asked his friend.

What'd he say?

He said you get wetter if you run through the rain than if you walk. More drops hit you if you run even though you're out in the rain for less a time. Do you believe that's true?

Are you asking me if I walked here would I be drier than I am right now?

Don't seem possible does it? Reed says it's true.

How does he know? Did he count the drops?

The thought made them laugh and eased their jitters. Their laughter soothed their sodden discomfort.

Come on, Van Loon directed. We can't get any wetter walking or running. Better find out where it is we have to go.

I'm right behind you, Caleb Farrow said.

That's what I'm afraid of, Van Loon let him know.

What's that smell? Caleb Farrow asked.

Something else I'm afraid of.

We've got a problem, Caleb Farrow surmised.

They were walking under the overhangs of the homes constructed on the rafts lashed together. They could see into some homes and other windows were darkened. They could see men and women and children sitting about tables or watching television on black-and-white sets that lacked sufficient juice.

What problem is that? Van Loon asked.

If we're into the kind of trouble where we get chased and if we spend too much time around here before that chase begins who's doing the chasing can just about follow his nose. The word will be out around town you bet. Find two men who stink like fish. Like herring. Like coho.

I wouldn't worry about that, Van Loon said. They had come to a corner and he was stopped by the curtain of rain. Around the corner lights spilled toward the sea and that seemed to be the way he wanted to go. When it comes to stinking like fish we'll blend right in, he said.

We're going back out in the rain aren't we?

You can't get any wetter than you are right now.

That's not the issue and you know it. The issue is this. When do we begin the drying out process?

Look at it this way, Van Loon said. The sooner we step out into this rain the sooner we'll find a place to get dry.

I'm going to take that as a promise.

Let's go.

I'm right behind you.

That's what bothers me the most.

Ferenc Van Loon took one step forward and two steps back.

What's wrong? Caleb Farrow asked him.

This can't be the way, Van Loon surmised.

Why's that?

It's too damn miserable. Let's see if there's another way around or a back entrance somewheres. Something like that. I want to know where we're going before I go there.

Makes sense to me, Caleb Farrow said.

Under the eavestrough they were sheltered from the most furious blasts of wind and Van Loon lit a smoke and passed the pack across to Farrow. Caleb Farrow lit his smoke off Van Loon's.

Van Loon smoked and he said, Shit, for no particular reason and he tried to wrap his neck in the collar of his denim jacket.

You know what this reminds me of? Caleb Farrow asked him. The flood. Which is a good thing because I do believe we might be standing on Noah's Ark right about now. Smells like it anyhow.

Let's go, Van Loon said once more.

I'm right behind you.

You know what?

What?

Nobody else is here.

What do you mean?

Everybody else—Kai and the gang—they didn't show. They didn't come to Rupert. We're here alone.

Maybe that's a good thing.

They let us think they were coming then took off for Terrace. They never told us they were going to Terrace.

Maybe they didn't want you causing them trouble in Terrace.

Me? You.

Kitchen.

Yeah. Kitchen. That's it. They didn't want Reed talking to them. They let us take him to Rupert while they went to Terrace.

That's a dirty trick.

I didn't know they had it in 'em.

They walked back the way they had come and turned at the edge of the pier and walked along the rafts parallel to shore. They were out of the wind this way and only when they crossed between rafts did they get wet. The rafts rocked slightly under their steps and were jarred by the waves they heard sloshing underfoot. Van Loon stopped and Farrow said, Hell.

That's where we're going, Van Loon said.

Has to be, Caleb Farrow concurred.

Let's go.

Do we have to?

Yellow light up ahead lit the way. Outside a doorway two rafts down a towering man stood guard. The man did not look at them as they moved through the dark smoking their cigarettes and Van Loon was in the lead.

Hi, Van Loon said.

The man observed him without expression. He was wearing a broadbrimmed sou'wester and a slicker that covered him down to his boots. The man's girth was as impressive as his height. He said, I don't know you.

First time here, Van Loon told him. He straightened himself up despite the wind. Addie sent us.

Caleb Farrow said, Let me guess. Folks call you Tiny.

The man clutched Farrow's jacket and shirt at the chest and lifted him up so that he was falling out of his clothes and slammed him against the side of the cedar shack. He held him there pinned against the wall above the boardwalk. The man held him there and Farrow slid down inside his clothes so that his chin rested on top of the man's fist. The man said, Slug. You don't call me Tiny.

Understood, Farrow said.

The man released him and Caleb Farrow slid down the wall until he found his footing.

Who are you? the man asked Van Loon.

Ferenc Van Loon.

Kraut?

Dutch, Van Loon told him. He flicked his cigarette into a gap between the rafts created by the waves. The rain had already snuffed it.

The Dutchman, Tiny said. Under his black sou'wester they could not make out his face. Where're your wooden shoes at?

Van Loon shrugged.

I suppose you want to stick your finger up my dike. Van Loon stared at the black patch of face he could not see. The man chuckled and the sound was a rhythmic grunt. Dutchmen don't wear wooden shoes indoors. Take yours off.

Van Loon continued staring at the unseen visage.

Or get lost, Tiny added.

Van Loon bent down and took off his boots. He skimmed off his socks and stuffed them into his jacket pockets. He held his boots in one hand to shelter them against his stomach.

We'll keep these outside, Tiny said as he took the lowcut black boots from Van Loon. He moved down a few paces and carefully positioned them under a stream of water funnelled off the roof. The boots quickly flooded and overflowed. Tiny went back to the door where he had been standing guard and opened the door and he shouted inside with a boom of a voice, We got first timers! A cheer arose from the patrons at their tables. Everyone faced the door. First we got The Dutchman. His wooden shoes got left outside.

Van Loon entered the room barefooted before the mirth of many. Caleb Farrow tried to squirm past Tiny but the big man dropped an arm down and that arm possessed the authority of a steel gate.

Next we got The Slug who crawls in here on his belly.

The two men looked at one another and Farrow checked with Van Loon. Then he got down on his knees. Then he got down on his belly and he slid into the room like a slug on a leaf while the place was raucous with laughter and calls. Farrow stood up inside and the players applauded and turned back to their games. The woman Van Loon had met earlier brushed past him. She opened the screen door and said to Tiny, Take those boots on down to my cabin and dry them on the space heater. Bring them back here—dry, Tiny—in one hour.

The large man said nothing. He stooped to retrieve the swamped boots and walked off.

I see you have some pull around here, Van Loon whispered to the woman without looking at her.

She walked around in front of him and folded her arms across herself and she said, You're in. Congratulations. That leaves you with three more problems to solve. Play at the big table. Win at the big table. Then get out of here with your skin intact.

And yours, Van Loon said.

I would think that one over if I was you.

Wait for it, Van Loon said and while he continued not to look at her he smiled. All good things will come to pass.

The woman looked from Van Loon to Farrow and back at Van Loon and she said, Follow me. She took them out of that room and into the next and found them seats at a blackjack table. This will have to do for now, she told them. Gentlemen, this here's The Dutchman and The Slug, she announced to the other players. They're sitting in. Good luck to you guys. I'll bring your chips over. Two hundred to start?

Van Loon nodded still not looking at her and she waited for him to look at her but he did not and he would not and she shrugged and moved away. She came back and said to The Slug, He's gorgeous. He's got a great tush. He's stubborn enough. Does the guy have a clue?

The Slug looked over at The Dutchman. He sat down and brought up his right hand as a thing deformed and unnatural and tapped the loose fingers on the table to demand a card. We got to trust him, he said looking at the woman who had told them that her name was Addie Day and whose name mentioned at the door had been their ticket into this abode. He's our only hope.

The woman smirked and went off to collect the chips.

When she came back she passed each man a towel and their chips and she took the order for two beers and told them that next time they had to get their own beer—that she was not a waitress or anything like that—and she went off again.

Hit me, The Slug said.

The Dutchman lightly tapped the table.

Life, Farrow said, has just begun. He won the first hand on nineteen points and smoked two cigarettes down to nothing before he won again. I've been alive for twentyeight years and I don't know what's worse—my life or my luck.

Card, Slug? the dealer asked him. He hadn't put down a bet. The dealer was a tall thin man with a goatee and a narrow face and a pinched brow. Farrow touched the table with the fingers of one hand and slid a chip across with his other and the cards were a blur across the table and this game seemed too fast for him and this kind of life too cruel and he lifted the corner of his card and knew that quickly that his luck had changed. He counted cards by curling his toes and he perpetually lost track but this time his toes were on a roll. They seemed to be in sync. He won that hand and folded a few times and he pushed the ante higher and won again.

Lady Luck's sleeping in my bed tonight, he said. Me and her and

Goldilocks. A few laughed and Van Loon left the table to scout around.

He strolled through the three gaming rooms and passed the poker table where he wanted to play and circled back to cross near again. Van Loon returned to the blackjack counter and sat down and Tiny's voice bellowed from the doorway, We got a first timer!

Those in visual range of the door turned to witness the initiation and humiliation Tiny would inflict this time and Van Loon and Farrow looked too and they kept on looking when they saw who stood inside the door now with his peaked green cap stuffed in his mouth.

This is The Jabbermouth, Tiny announced. I had to shut him up long enough to get him inside.

Safely ensconced the new arrival pulled his cap from between his teeth and addressed the rooms. Gentlemen! Ladies! People of the gambling den! Let's play a few friendly hands and hey—while we're at it—tell of the wonder we have seen. Let's talk about the joys and the perils each of us has known and the aforementioned peculiar puzzle of predicaments that dogs us through our days.

Both The Dutchman and The Slug were staring at The Jabbermouth and The Slug was whispering loudly in The Dutchman's ear, How did he get in here? How did he know where we were? How did he find this place, Van Loon? There's something about this guy. I'm telling you. It's uncanny. I never told him we were coming here. I didn't know how to get here myself until we arrived.

Wasn't me, Van Loon said. He was equally impressed. I haven't seen him since he left the beer parlour.

Me neither, Caleb Farrow concurred. How does he do it?

He could screw things up for us, Van Loon said.

That's not the half of it.

Addie Day met The Jabbermouth with a towel and after he had mopped his head and neck and chest dry she escorted him to the same blackjack table where the bridgemen were playing. Gentlemen, it's a night! The Jabbermouth enthused as he sat down. Raining cats and dogs and if I may expand upon that particular theme I would say that it's pouring nanny goats and hyenas and wolverines too. It's wicked out there. Hi, he said to Caleb Farrow and extended his hand. I'm the one they're calling The Jabbermouth in here. What's your handle in a place like this tonight?

Caleb Farrow looked at him and at his hand and he shook the wet palm. I'm The Slug, he said. This here's The Dutchman.

Good to meet you boys. How're the cards falling? The house raking it in or can an honest working man be spared half a chance?

Van Loon and Caleb Farrow looked at each other and back at Reed Kitchen and back at each other. Their companion was not willing to indicate that they were acquainted. Van Loon and Farrow shrugged and faced their cards.

This is a night for ducks, Reed Kitchen said. This is a night for seals. This is a night for shadows and spooks. This is a night for the ace of spades and the king of clubs don't you think so?

Ferenc Van Loon reached around behind Caleb Farrow and leaned over behind him and tapped Reed Kitchen on the shoulder. I think I know you, Van Loon said so quietly that no one else could hear.

Kitchen was equally circumspect. I know I know you, he said in a low voice.

So what gives?

You have your identity in here and I have mine, Kitchen said. I don't know how and I don't know why you got in here any more than I know how I did but I would appreciate it one hundred per cent if for your sake and my sake too you don't happen to know me by my real name in this place here tonight and that would be fine all around. It's not a good thing to know me here tonight. Point of fact I will not ask what you are doing here when from what I heard you got a reputation for chasing women—

That may be the case here too, Reed—

That's not my name in this room. You may call me Jabber for short.

We'd appreciate it also if you don't happen to know us either.

Two more people who don't want to know me in public. Say no more. I understand. We are like ships passing in the darkness of this night. I don't know who you are or what you are or why you are—

I'll explain another time—

Splendiferous.

What?

It's a word. Part of the English language. I don't know what a direct translation in Dutch would be.

Kitchen. Caleb Farrow swivelled on his chair and interrupted their conference. You're one weird loony guy you know that?

Reed Kitchen sat up. I told him. I'll tell you.

What?

Call me Jabber.

Is anybody playing cards at this table or are you girls here to chat? the dealer demanded to know.

Two things, Reed Kitchen told him. First and foremost to chat is human. Second of all we do not play at blackjack. Blackjack is serious business.

Do you or don't you want a card? the man asked.

First I want a new deck, Jabber said.

He reached across and stripped the remaining portion of the dealer's deck from his hand which he hurled across the room and the cards fluttered out of the air like giant flakes of confetti.

Then I want a drink. Then I want my chips. Then I want a card. Do you got that? Deck. Drink. Chips. Card.

The dealer looked at the mess of cards strewn across the room and back at Reed Kitchen. He commiserated with him. You sorry sonofabitch. Excuse me a second. I gotta get Tiny's attention.

Certainly, Kitchen said. I'll be here. While I'm waiting I'll have a few words with The Sip.

The dealer continued staring at him without moving. In the end he chose to leave Tiny outside and to retrieve a fresh pack of cards from under the counter. He stripped off the wrap and dealt cards to the row of seven men.

Who's The Sip? Caleb Farrow asked Kitchen. He didn't get an answer so he asked Van Loon who simply nodded. He's the guy we're here for? Farrow whispered and Van Loon nodded again. No shit. He turned back to Reed Kitchen. You know The Sip? He's some dude I heard. How do you know The Sip, Jabber?

Reed Kitchen changed the subject. Let's talk about something else.
Like what?
Like how did you come by the name The Slug?
That's a long story, Jabber.
I got all night.
I bet you do, Caleb Farrow said. I bet you got all night.
I'm listening.
It all started when I was a little boy, Farrow said and the men up
and down the table and the dealer chuckled amongst themselves and
the man drinking heavily at the far end guffawed. Only the mien of
Reed Kitchen remained implacable as he waited for Caleb Farrow to
continue.

ON A SECOND FORAY THROUGH THE gaming rooms Ferenc Van Loon
scanned the action at the other blackjack counter. A craps table was
also in operation there and under the swinging bare lights circles of
men played draw poker. Van Loon slowed down passing the table
where he wanted to sit and he rolled a smoke above a gambler and
wet the paper and tapped the man's shoulder for a light. The man
they called The Sip glanced at him from the table's opposite side and
returned to a study of his cards and the woman known as Addie Day
crouched behind The Sip on an elevated bench and put her knees up
and she also observed Van Loon with curiosity and intent. Addie Day
lowered her head then raised her eyes and squinted through the
smoke. Two players were close to busting. Their spirits and their cof-
fers had taken a drubbing.

The Sip was a large man in his fifties with broad sloped shoulders
and a rotund waist and high dark stringy hair above an impressive
weathered forehead. Van Loon guessed that he was strong. He had
worked in his time. In recent years that mass of muscle had softened
but Van Loon believed the pulpiness concealed a convincing strength
as under that quietude and cardplaying acumen prospered real venom.
Van Loon caught his glance and their eyes met for a second—long
enough—and he walked off.

In this room Van Loon sensed his spirit rekindle. Among these damp and darkened figures who swayed upon the gentle roll of the raft his inner excitement acquired a resonant thrum. This was why he had thrown away his lover's ring—to be here. This was why he had pursued wild women. This was why he had emigrated and why he had lived on the cusp of wilderness and why he had chosen the jungle over the soccer pitch every time. This was why he had roved through the brothels of Hong Kong and Shanghai and shipped out across the oceans of the world—to be present when the time came and to be free when the time came to enlist in a moment such as this and to splice his elation at a time such as this onto a gathering sense of doom.

Reed Kitchen had cited Van Loon as a man who could guide him through the muck of the civilized world and Van Loon had not understood what he had intended by that or what was expected of him. There in that room Van Loon captured an inkling of his friend's power of discernment. Kitchen had confused the civilized world with his own experience. He had referred to what was corrupt and debased and violated—for that was what he knew the outer world to be. Kitchen had recognized that Van Loon could lead him through human nettle like a spider awalk upon a web of its own devising. Reed Kitchen could ramble through the wilderness of the forest and tap a deer on the shoulder and shoot off its snout. Or so he claimed. In here Ferenc Van Loon could swipe a woman from under her patron's nose. Or so he believed. In salacious dark quarters Reed Kitchen would have trouble foraging for himself and yet his uncanny sense had attributed those necessary talents to Ferenc Van Loon. Here and in this house Van Loon reigned. As stalker. As lord. As infidel. Reed Kitchen might move through wilderness with mystery and silence. Van Loon floated through a shadowy hinterland with equal facility.

Blackjack was not a game he enjoyed and Ferenc Van Loon did not play aggressively. He aspired to hold his own to keep his stake intact. He did not count his toes like Farrow endeavoured to do with varying success. He took chances from time to time to beat the dealer and maintain a realistic view of solvency.

Addie Day returned to their table. She said to Van Loon, So that's your angle.

What is?

It could work given time, she said. Eventually. For the moment it's not—as you shall see. She revealed what she meant by that and asked The Jabbermouth to join The Sip at his table.

Me? Myself? Yes. That would be an honour, Reed Kitchen said. He slid off the blackjack stool. To play a sporting game with the proprietor of this realm—that's a tribute for a lowly working man like me. A privilege. Myself personally I feel overwhelmed by this blessing bestowed upon me here tonight.

Caleb Farrow was listening to this talk and Ferenc Van Loon told him, Never mind.

But—

Keep your mouth shut.

See you later, guys. Best of luck to you with your game. I'm going to play me a few hands of real poker with the proprietor of this realm.

Good luck, Jabber.

Thanks. Luck or no luck it's an honour bestowed upon me here tonight.

Van Loon watched Reed Kitchen walk off with Addie Day to sit in the chair he coveted for himself. Male hearts and the male minds of this estate moved with her across the room.

Let me get this straight. Right now Reed Kitchen's sitting at our table playing our game against the man we came here to whup. Caleb Farrow summarized the situation for him in case he was having trouble absorbing the details himself. How do you figure that one out?

You said it yourself. He's uncanny.

No doubt about it. The man hunts deer in his sleep. The man might be a friend of ours but you got to watch him now and then.

Hunts deer in his sleep?

He might be asleep now it's hard to tell for sure.

The rafts were protected from the brunt of storm waves by the lee of the island and they rocked gently in the wash. A few men felt queasy. The call went out from tables in two separate rooms for poker

players. Van Loon and Farrow declined those invitations. Men from
The Sip's table overheard the requests and one decided to cut his losses
and try his luck where the stakes suited his impoverished condition.
Electric bulbs sporadically dimmed and brightened again and Addie
Day returned and invited Van Loon to sit at the high stakes table.

The corners of Van Loon's lips curled slightly.

Don't be so damned smug, Addie told him. This is only step one.

That's all it takes. One step at a time. I told you this would come to
pass. Keep ready.

Excuse me if I don't hold my breath, Addie Day said.

You're too cynical.

I have reason to be. Who do you think you are? Mr Ray of Sunshine in My Life?

I'm working on it.

So what am I supposed to do? Caleb Farrow asked.

Come watch.

Your boots are back, Addie Day said. More or less dry. Like everything else around here.

You mean more or less wet.

Now who's being cynical? She folded her arms and leaned forward
slightly and smiled and her tongue poked out to touch her top lip and
he was delighted and enthralled by her.

Van Loon put his socks on again and his boots which Tiny had
placed inside the door. The three of them moved through the smoke
and the dimming and brightening lights and they heard the generator
quicken and roar and bawl in the throes of its labour. The inner soles
of his boots squished. The Sip gestured to the vacant chair and Van
Loon sat down and Farrow took a seat on the elevated bench beside
Addie Day.

Van Loon put his chips on the table and The Sip's chest jerked
once in a measured laugh and he said, That won't cut the mustard
here. Caleb Farrow stood again and emptied a pocket and Van Loon
was surprised that his friend had done so well. Van Loon's pile of chips
was tidy and modest now and apparently sufficient to begin the game.
Five card draw, The Sip told him. One eyed Jacks wild. That's it.

That's all. The game never changes no matter who deals. What's your name again?

The Dutchman, Van Loon said.

They call me The Sip, The Sip said and he distributed cards around the table.

Does that mean something? Van Loon smiled as he asked the question.

The man looked at him. A logger who had a fat face and a thick beard and resembled an overstuffed cherub answered on his behalf. He's a Cypriot. A Cypriot from Cyprus. If you don't know where that is I'll tell you.

I know where that is, Van Loon said.

It's in the Mediterranean, the logger told him anyway.

Born of a Turk and a Greek—one of the few, The Sip said. I'm what you call a rape baby. The man's big chest shook again. My daddy took what he wanted. That was who he was. He never asked permission.

Now that's a story, Reed Kitchen said. That's a story.

You like to hear about rape there, Jabber?

No sir. I don't have that in mind. Myself personally I am not partial to disgusting stories. What I like to hear about is history. A little history once in a while lets us know where we are and where it is we've been. History points the way. Now if you don't mind please, Mr Sip, I would like one card and one card only. Since you're going to the trouble anyway you might as well make it a good one. Thank you very much.

Reed Kitchen was the skinniest man in the bunch and Van Loon was the next thinnest. The others at the table were loggers with massive appetites and forearms and thick beards. In this company Ferenc Van Loon felt alien and Caleb Farrow as tall as a dwarf. The cards went well for Ferenc Van Loon. Then they went badly and Reed Kitchen said, Just because it don't snow around here so much doesn't mean it's not cold. I was fooled, Mr Sip. I got to tell you. I got tricked into coming to this climate. I was lulled into an untrue belief that this land here was a subtropical clime. If you want to know the truth I

don't know who to blame for that base shenanigan but I do believe
certain persons lied to me in the hope that I would believe that
untruth and leave the place where I was and come to this place where
I had never been and where I have now arrived. Some people wanted
to get rid of me. I don't know why.

The Sip interrupted him. Better you play at another table.

I'm getting hot. I'm on a lucky streak. Why do I have to do that,
Sip?

You're driving me crazy, Jabber. Go sit at another table and we'll
talk about our business some other time.

Reed Kitchen looked chagrined and frustrated as he gathered up
his chips and stuffed his pockets and nodded to every player at the
table and went over to the very next table where they had room for
him. He sat down among them and announced, Gentlemen, this
game is too damned quiet. How can you concentrate with so much
silence? Nobody can play cards in a proper manner without enjoying
a smidgen of conversation. Open up your mouths. Speak. Say something. He crossed the second and third digits of his right hand and
held them aloft and claimed, Me and The Sip we're like this. So you
better do what I say.

My buddy here is looking for a seat, Van Loon told The Sip.

He gave you his chips. I saw him. You got to pay to play.

Both Van Loon and Farrow went to their wallets and passed money
across to Addie Day who slid off her bench and went over to collect
more chips. The Sip shrugged and Farrow took the seat that Reed
Kitchen had vacated. Addie Day returned and stood behind Van
Loon and after that his bets became increasingly rash and he began to
lose on a regular basis.

The time came when he was close to be being busted and Caleb
Farrow was dealing and Van Loon said, You don't mind if Addie quits
standing behind me do you, Sip?

What are you telling me, Dutchie?

It makes me nervous that's all. She's in my light.

The Sip crooked his neck and Addie went to sit on the elevated
bench behind him again and The Slug dealt the cards and The

Dutchman moved what remained of his chips into the pot.

I'd like to raise the ante here, Dutchie. But it don't seem to me like you can cover it.

Maybe we can come to an arrangement, Van Loon said.

Arrangements make me uncomfortable. They get messy when one party doesn't pay off. I have to send my people around and I don't approve of their behaviour. I regret the need. Arrangements are inconvenient for all concerned.

Van Loon and The Sip were looking at each other and other players were looking at them and a mood seemed to infiltrate the room and other men stopped between hands to watch from a distance or they stretched their legs and wandered over to watch from close up.

You know, Van Loon said, I got in a game with a friend one time who couldn't make the stake so I made an accommodation. We bet who would dig an outhouse hole the next morning. I lost. I dug it.

What's your point?

Money is not the only currency in the world.

I'll be damned if I know what I value second.

Tell you what, Van Loon said. You don't have to raise me cash.

What else is there, Dutchie?

Raise me free time with Addie. I'll be more than happy with that. An hour. That way you have nothing much to lose yourself.

The Sip was looking at him now with harsh attention and men were watching The Sip and they did wonder how he would respond.

Why would I do that, Dutchie? The Sip spoke in a quiet voice. If I raise you you're out. You're gone. You get to walk away from this table with empty pockets and it don't matter what you're holding in your hand. The only thing you might be holding in your hand if I raise you is your dick.

He did that laugh of his again.

Maybe's there's something I can put on the table that would interest you enough to call the bet, Van Loon told him.

You mean like your dick? The Sip was still laughing and others joined in.

Van Loon continued to stare at him until The Sip quieted down.

The man said finally, I can't think what that would be.

Somebody give me a pen and paper, Van Loon said. Someone did and The Dutchman wrote and he folded the note carefully in quarters and passed the slip of paper across the table to The Sip.

I don't take IOUs.

Just read the note.

The Sip accepted the paper and began unwrapping it and others leaned in close to him to read it themselves and he held it against his chest and looked at them and they got the message and backed off. The Sip took a peek at the note and folded it up again and smiled as though only a part of his mouth consented to grin and he said, You're on.

You want a card? Farrow asked him.

Two, The Sip said.

Farrow struggled with his seemingly deformed hand and two cards slid across the table into The Sip's giant paws.

You? Farrow asked Van Loon.

Two.

Van Loon glanced at Addie Day who blinked in the smoke and he smiled and he picked up his two cards and placed them in his hand and looked up at The Sip who was smiling also.

I'll take one, a third player said.

No you won't, The Sip decreed. This hand's between me and Dutchie.

There was no argument.

I'm going to raise the ante here again, The Sip said.

We had a deal, Van Loon objected.

I'm going to raise your time with Addie to all night long. You can raise your bet accordingly. Is that a problem?

Van Loon looked through the smoke at The Sip and across at Addie Day and she blinked and sucked on her cigarette and he nodded his consent. Then he said, I call.

The Sip placed his cards on the table. Two pair. Sevens and sixes.

Van Loon showed two Kings and a one-eyed Jack. The game never changes, he said. Three Kings.

You win some you lose some, The Sip said and he was smiling still. He turned sideways to Addie Day and told her, Looks like you're working tonight, girl.

She stood and held out her hand with the palm up. The Sip did not take her meaning and she gestured with her chin and he passed her the folded note. If she was going to work all night for nothing she wanted to know what the payoff might have been. She didn't look at the note in the room to the regret of many. She stuffed it into the pocket of her blouse and followed Van Loon to the counter to cash his remaining chips. She told him and she told Caleb Farrow where her room was located and she walked through the main door into the darkness and the rain. Caleb Farrow left after her and Van Loon waited for his chips to be cashed and he departed the gaming room and Reed Kitchen bade several people farewell and he lined up as well for his money.

This has been a night, Reed Kitchen said. A night for ducks and geese and wolverines, he told anyone who might listen.

IN THE RAIN FERENC VAN LOON followed the clatter and muffled weep of the generator to the shed where the machine was housed and he shoved open the rotted door. The shed stank of diesel fumes and mould. He ran his hand along the inside of the doorframe and located the light switch at hip level. Van Loon flicked it on and in the light plucked a splinter from his thumb. The machine was painted bright orange and looked relatively new and the floor was mosscovered. With proper attention the machine would purr and cease bucking on its blocks like an impetuous stallion in captivity. Rainwater or condensation had mixed with the fuel and Van Loon had come to extinguish the beast's misery.

He helped himself to an oily rag off the shelf and knelt down and traced the copper fuel line. Van Loon used his fingers to loosen a nut and pulled the fuel line free and stuffed the loose end with a corner of the rag. He did not believe in making an unnecessary mess and he plugged the line and thought how this was so typically Dutch that in a moment of urgency and risk he took the time to be tidy. The generator coughed with greater exigency and the overhead light flickered once and twice and a third time. Van Loon opened the door and returned to the rain and shook his head and hair and took two steps and the lights went out across the floating colony.

Behind him the generator spat and died.

People within their homes groaned and ranted as he made his way with the wind and hard rain at his back and found his footing in the darkness and stepped off the rafts and held onto the bannister climbing the stairs to the parking lot. Below him as he turned within the omnipotent blackness an odd candle was lit and one handy flashlight had been summoned into the breach. Before he detected the shadow he sensed a presence converge upon him in the pitch black night. Van Loon jumped. His heart quickened and the top of his head felt severed. The shadow spoke and Van Loon understood that he should have expected one person to function in the blackout and one had.

This is a mendacious place, the wraith said.

Reed. Don't creep up on a guy. I just about pissed my pants.

This is a mendacious place and I don't know why you're here.

Taking care of business. What's that word mean anyhow?

Wicked. This is a wicked place, Van Loon.

What're you doing here, Reed? Wait. Don't answer. Forget I asked. You came down here to mooch a little conversation.

I want to know what that gambling man is going to do, Reed Kitchen said.

About what?

What's he going to think—what's he going to do—when you turn him down like that not accepting his winnings? I'm interested in the answer to that question.

What're you talking about?

You won that woman fair and square—you did, Van Loon—but you are not down below enjoying your winnings in the darkness of this night.

I'm not a man who has to win his women in card games, Reed.

That's what you did though. And that's not all you did.

What else?

You cut off the lights down there and I don't know why you did that. It does worry me some.

Van Loon wiped water from his mouth and face and he said to Reed Kitchen, You shouldn't sneak around after people.

This is a mendacious place filled with wrongful iniquity, Kitchen said.

What's iniquity?

Bad stuff.

What do you know about iniquity, Reed?

I'll tell you what I know about iniquity, Reed Kitchen said. Do you want me to tell you what I know about iniquity?

Can I stop you?

I do not believe for one minute that my mother walked out of her section foreman's house and sat down in front of that train that gave me my life. Myself personally I do not believe my daddy was sleeping like he told me. I sorely believe that my daddy held her in front of that train and he did not let her go until the time was too late for her—pregnant with child—to get on out of the way. When I was spared by that train and born out of the caboose of that train he was a frightened man. He took it as an omen and he was a man who believed in omens and he took it as a sign from God and he did consider me to be the witness of his crime and of his folly and he did consider me to be protected by God on high and perhaps by the ghost of his own dead wife and perhaps by the railroad itself and perhaps by locomotives and he raised me up as best as he was able. Scared shitless to do otherwise. Trouble is he raised me in his own particular fashion and he made standing before trains a game—an exercise—our sport. Some kids play hockey with their dads—I played chicken with trains. I want to tell you something, Van Loon. There's something you should know.

What's that? He kept his back to the rain and his ears tuned to the sounds on an upward draught from the floating colony.

My daddy did not push me away at the last possible split second like I told you when those trains came riproaring athunder like the voice of God down our throats.

Didn't huh?

No. He didn't. He held me, Van Loon. He kept his fist on my shirt
and held me as long as he could and longer than the time before and
the time before that. Only when he jumped clear was I free to jump
clear myself. Do you see what I'm getting at? I had to be quick afoot. I
do not believe my mother was a willing participant in her time of
dying, Van Loon, so ask me again what I know about iniquity and
mendacity. I dare you to do that.

Van Loon was quiet. He listened and breathed and wanted a smoke
and he could not risk igniting a match.

There's something else that bothers me, Van Loon.

You're full of problems tonight.

I want to know what you're going to do when you figure out that
Caleb Farrow is not here which means to me that he must be down
himself collecting your winnings.

Van Loon chortled. You think Farrow's screwing my girl?

I'm surprised that you find such a dire situation comical. Your very
best friend is down there screwing the woman that already you are
calling your girl. I don't miss much, Van Loon, but I think I missed
something here. Since when is she your girl? Seems to me like you
don't even know her yet.

Pretending not to know her was for The Sip's benefit, Reed. He
thinks I already screwed her for cash. He doesn't know I actually bor-
rowed her time to talk to her.

A conversation with a woman is a wonderful thing, Van Loon.
What I wonder is does Caleb Farrow know that? I bet you he's down
there screwing her now and I doubt he's saying a word while he's at it
to tell you the truth.

Don't worry about it, Reed. If Farrow's screwing her I'll kill him.

I don't want to hear this kind of talk. What good does it do? What
good does it do the one who ends up dead? Or the one who ends up
dead in prison because he did it?

I'll wait for Farrow and ask him, Van Loon said.

That seems like a reasonable alternative to murder. Talk it out. If
you want someone to moderate your discussion I'm available.

They heard them before they saw them through the rain.

Oh no! Reed Kitchen exclaimed. Don't tell me this!

Why's the truck not running? What's the matter with you, Van Loon? Caleb Farrow demanded.

I was talking to Reed, Ferenc Van Loon explained.

Oh no! Reed Kitchen announced again.

Take it easy, Reed.

You have stolen a woman!

Hey, Addie Day said. I'm along of my own accord.

Oh no! Reed Kitchen called out.

Get in the truck, Caleb Farrow commanded. He leapt onto the bed of the pickup and his fingers worked the combination lock in the dark and he lifted the lid of the supply box and dumped the bag that he had carried up the stairs inside. Addie Day passed him her second suitcase and he placed that inside as well and locked the cover.

Oh no! Reed Kitchen cried out again.

Van Loon grabbed him by the front of his denim jacket. She wants to come along, Reed. She's doing this of her own accord like she said.

You don't understand the consequences here, Van Loon.

You can say that again, Addie Day said and she opened the side door to the truck.

We understand a lot more than you know, Reed. Now get inside.

You don't understand. Don't you get it? Now that you have her there's no room for me.

Hhohghdverdoma. Reed! Get inside! There's room.

I'm a criminal now! I can feel it in my bones. This is an abduction.

Who is this yahoo? Addie Day inquired.

I'm known as The Jabbermouth in some places. But I would be pleased if you would call me Reed because that's my name. Kitchen clambered into the truck first and then Farrow and then Addie Day jumped in next and squeezed onto Farrow's lap.

The lights of the floating colony popped back on and the murmur of the generator was heard again and Caleb Farrow spoke in an urgent voice, Go! Go! Go!

Ferenc Van Loon had his key in the ignition and his foot on the

gas before he got his door closed. The truck fired and the rear wheels
kicked gravel as the pickup spun out of the parking lot onto the paved
road.

This is rather exciting, Reed Kitchen mentioned.

It's trouble, Caleb Farrow agreed. Trouble's a thrill.

I call it freedom, Addie Day said. Freedooomm! she sang.

Van Loon laughed. I call it love.

Whatever you want to call it, Reed Kitchen said and he insisted on
the final word, myself personally I don't like it one bit.

The truck sped through the blistering black rain. The windshield
wipers threshed time.

Step on it, Caleb Farrow said. You never know what they figured
out by now.

I don't want to get a ticket, Van Loon said.

It's not the police I'm worried about, Caleb Farrow said. Which
makes for a nice change.

Where are we going? Reed Kitchen asked.

Tyee, Van Loon told him.

We can't go to Tyee. My stuff is in Prince Rupert.

They had reached the junction of Highway 16. West to Tyee. Or
east back to Prince Rupert.

My laundry, Kitchen argued. My stuff!

We got to get out of town, Caleb Farrow decreed.

What are you doing here, Reed? How did you get out here?

What do you mean how did I get out here?

How did you get out here?

A friend dropped me off.

You don't know anybody here.

I do now.

If we take you back to Prince Rupert—

I'll catch the train to Tyee tomorrow. No sweat.

Risky, Farrow said.

What else is new? Van Loon asked and he turned onto the highway
heading back to Prince Rupert to drop Reed Kitchen at his hotel.

Typical, the woman called Addie Day determined. Typical typical.

We'll make it, Van Loon assured her. Their faces were suddenly lit by the headlights of an oncoming vehicle.

Sure we will, she said. She did not sound convinced.

We might, Farrow said. Just don't ask me to lay odds.

This should keep, Reed Kitchen informed them all.

What'd he say? Addie asked.

In unison the three men in the cab repeated, This should keep.

II

The
Earth
In Its
Devotion

4

REED KITCHEN ROUSED HIMSELF from bed and in his nakedness stood and lifted Caleb Farrow's rifle free from mounts above the other man's pillow. He was alone in the bunkcar and soundly asleep and he loaded the thirty-ought-six with ammunition pilfered from the drawer under Farrow's bunk and he was asleep as he stared down the sights at the tail of an oilstain winding like an intestine gutted and strewn upon the floor. He did not shoot. Kitchen remained asleep and he dressed in his workclothes and raingear and laced his boots and put on his cap and climbed down the ladder on the highway side of the bunkcar. He sloshed through the bog to the road. He crossed the macadam and ran down the ditch and entered the woods where he picked up a stream and followed deer tracks along the bank and later wolf and deer tracks intermingled. Beyond a bend in the partly frozen meandering stream he encountered a red Mack truck—an eighteen wheeler roaming through the woods picking its way among the trees and ascending and descending gullies and hillocks—which he shot through the snout and the windshield splintered and pink fluid from the radiator splashed forth as from an artery severed and the truck collapsed like an elephant slain in midcharge. The trailer pitchpoled and crashed through the underbrush and the blast of the rifle and the crack of the trees awakened Reed Kitchen from his walking slumber. He had been dreaming and he had also been strolling through the woods with a rifle in his hands shooting imaginary vehicles and Reed Kitchen was troubled to find himself again the proprietor of such an unsatisfactory estate.

He walked on.

Reed Kitchen used the stream and the ravine it cut out of the mountains as his cardinal geographical line. The tracks of a lone wolf zigzagged ahead of him in the light snow that persisted at this elevation as the rains set in again. He traced the steps of the wolf. He crept under branches and hunkered down on all fours to squeeze himself below fallen trees painted green and emerald and dark by moss. Kitchen needed to trace exactly the path of the wolf. He did not know why. He saw where the wolf had urinated a short while ago and Reed Kitchen sniffed the wolf's mark. He crouched on all fours and inhaled the olfactory information odoriferous on the yellow carnation blooming on the pristine snow. Wolf, Reed Kitchen said. A word he spoke quietly and with reverence.

Loose and ambling Reed Kitchen walked on. He scrabbled up a rock ridge where water cascaded alongside him.

He felt weak and dizzy from the agitation of waking up suddenly and after he had walked far enough he lay down in the snow and wept. He hated walking in his sleep—he hated that—and he hated waking up to find himself in some other realm in an unsavoury condition—this time with a rifle in his grip. He consoled himself with the knowledge that he had shot only a truck and luckily for him it had not been a Mack but an imaginary vehicle. Kitchen wept. The narrow case of his body shook and Reed Kitchen hid his eyes in the crook of an elbow and his ribcage quavered and tears and the rain wetted his cheeks.

He hated walking in his slumber. He felt great loathing toward that particular affliction.

He lay on his side and his body curled and low strangulated moans rose from his chest and throat. Reed Kitchen had to hold himself together or break apart. He rocked himself clutching his chest and stifled the pains of his body and moaned. He regretted his unsound dreams and he regretted walking in the pasture of those dreams and he abhorred awakening in the clamour of those dreams to discover himself wherever he had happened to wend.

To inhabit his dreams as a sleepwalking man had never seemed right to him.

Kitchen urged himself to get up and blow off the day's fret. He pushed himself onto his hands and knees and saw that his body had warmed the snow. He was lathered with mud and feathered by twigs now and old and decayed leaves. He pushed himself up and sat upon a rock and faced the rain. A convergence of mists obliterated the view from this height. He showered himself off and the mud and debris paraded down his yellow slicker and he looked less like a stump and more like a human with each passing minute. What a mess I am, he said and he did not want to talk about it anymore. He did not want to start up talking and get to a point where he could not stop and waste good words when no one was listening. I have so much to say, he lamented and he endeavoured to make those words the last he would utter on this hunt.

He forded the stream where it was most shallow and rocky and sensed that the lone wolf was following him now—pursuing him now—or just hanging around to hear a gentle dose of human language. So he spoke to that unseen wolf. I know I am a man because I work upon the railway, he explained to the creature and he hoped that the wilder beast would understand. Do bears tamp ties? Do beavers chip the ice from switches? Never. And if they do do they get paid for that labour? Rarely. I am a man and most of the time I work upon the railway. Today's Sunday, he added. I happen to be resting. Which means that if I see you, wolf, to ease my mind I will shoot you. In the outside world we call this recreation. We call it sport.

Kitchen walked in a generally westward and generally downward direction. Skeena mists hung to the cliffside and revealed the shore where they parted or swooped low or drifted high. The river and the slope of the mountain were Reed Kitchen's essential topographical guides. The cloudcover which appeared perpetual was too thick to guess where the sun might be. He tramped through evergreens and bushes clothed in a suit of rain and he was equally wet when it drizzled and when it did not. He walked on not looking to hunt and in pursuit again of his life's most crucial quest—someone with whom to share a pleasant conversation. Farrow and Van Loon had installed Addie Day down at the Indian cabins by the Green River Bridge and he presumed he'd find them there and he chose to believe also that he did not require an invitation to visit.

Reed Kitchen crossed the highway well above Tyee and scurried amongst the spindly spruce again. The land carved an uphill trace and he emerged at the height of a rimrock above the tracks. He doubled back and caught sight of a sodden grey shape moving through the underbrush. He did not know if he was dreaming or imagining or seeing something that was actually there. To be safe Reed Kitchen pointed his rifle into the air and fired. The mist—shot—whorled. He listened to the echo bounce a few times and decay at a great distance. Kitchen walked the long way around the mountain to get down to the tracks and he ambled on to the Indian cabins with his ears alert for trains and his flesh wary of wolves and his head steeped in the tremulous veil of mists that roved the mountainsides along the Skeena River and touched down upon stone like a hand that soothed the moist brow of a wanton and unregenerate earth.

SWALES WERE FLOODED AND THE tall grasses had collapsed under the weight of water and the air was pungent and perfumed by the rank odours of mud and moss and fungi. Reed Kitchen crossed the slick boardwalk in the rain to the main cabin. Rain sluiced off the roof and collected in pools under the house constructed above short pilings rotting for years now and reinforced often and the bolsters now also decomposed. Reed Kitchen did not knock but opened the two doors and entered the house and propped the rifle against the front wall by the coatrack and took off his peaked green cap and used it to slap excess water from his slicker onto the floor.

The beachcomber's wife Margaret was seated in her usual rocker by the window. Unaccustomed to the trespass of strangers on such a grand scale she was not knitting today. She wore a bright wool winter serape to shield herself from the damp and she rocked gently so that the sound of her motion answered the squeaks of a mouse talkative in the wall behind her. Her face lay impassive and observant. Her husband leaned forward over his steaming cup at the table across from Caleb Farrow who had his back to Reed Kitchen and the door. Wilf's face was weathered and pockmarked and his hands purpled from his life's labour on fishboats and logging tugs. In the furthest corner of the room Addie Day sat slumped in a sloped gutted armchair with the ankle of one leg crossed above the knee of the other like a man and Ferenc Van Loon sat in a wooden tablechair angled back on its hind legs with his feet propped on one end of the table and he smoked and dropped his ashes into the palm of his free hand. His boots lay on the floor beside him—one was upright and the other felled—and he wore the heavy woollen grey socks that were the comfort of bridgemen.

Look who's here, Van Loon announced.

You know that rain Noah bragged about? Kitchen mentioned. The one where he built that ark and took all those animals aboard two by two? That wasn't nothing but a sunshower compared to this. Forty days and forty nights my ass. What we have here today is a rain the likes of which Noah never experienced.

Wet out is it? Van Loon asked.

I hate to be the one to break it to you but our friend Wilf has a leaky roof, Caleb Farrow said without turning around to greet him. If you're looking for dryness you've come to the wrong place.

There is no dryness in a flood. I don't go looking for dryness in rainy weather because I don't expect to find it. Not around here. That's my philosophy. When it's hot out I don't expect a cool breeze. When it's cold out I don't expect warmth. I'm a realist, Caleb. If I'm thirsty in a desert do I do a dance for rain? He peeled off his raincoat and kicked off his rubberboots and unhitched his suspenders from his shoulders and pushed down his rainpants. No I don't, he said.

I'm with you, Addie Day piped up from her busted chair. That's what I've been saying in different words to these yahoos. She reached into her breast pocket for smokes. Where there's trouble I don't expect to find peace.

Addie, Van Loon said over his shoulder at her.

She's right, Reed Kitchen said.

What do you know about it? Caleb Farrow asked him. You're not part of this discussion.

I am now, Kitchen said. He sat down on the pew by the door that Wilf had salvaged from a place of worship in a defunct mining town. Fill me in.

No one was quick to jump to the task and Van Loon said, You been hunting? He nodded at Farrow's rifle standing at ease by the door-jamb.

I came through the woods over the mountains. Carried the rifle in case there was something to shoot worth shooting. There wasn't. Except maybe a wolf I tracked but I never caught sight of it for sure.

No wolf, Wilf said.

Looked like a wolf. Moved like a wolf. Left tracks that looked like wolf tracks to me. Pissed like a wolf.

Dog, Wilf said. Wild.

Any man who has the good sense to walk in here with a rifle in his hands has a head on his shoulders. You're a friend of mine, Reedie, Addie Day said. How come the rest of you turkeys don't have a clue?

Addie, Van Loon said without looking behind him where she sat.

Caleb Farrow noticed the rifle and he said, That's my gun. You don't bother asking my permission anymore?

I might have asked, Reed Kitchen said and he looked right at him.

Caleb Farrow returned his stare and a question and an answer were apparent in his eyes.

What we need around here is more weapons, Addie Day said.

Nobody replied to her and Reed Kitchen said, She's trying to tell us something.

Help me out here, Reed. It's an effort to drive sense into their thick skulls.

That's a tough job I know. I might have to fetch a spikehammer for that job.

They laughed lightly and Margaret asked Reed if he'd like a cup of coffee and he accepted her offer and asked if she would mind if he poured the cup himself. She nodded and he went over to the wood-burning stove and helped himself to a mug of joe that was black and strong and bitter from continuous reheating. He sat back down on the church pew and placed the cup beside him and Addie Day said, Speaking of Noah. I always said, He's proof there is no God.

Addie, Van Loon said and he took his feet off the table and turned his body halfway around to face her. What does that got to do with anything? What are you talking about now?

I'm having a conversation with Reed do you mind?

Van Loon explained to Kitchen, We're trying to get her to talk about her situation.

They want the fairy tale, Addie Day contended. They're not prepared to face reality.

What's this about Noah? Reed Kitchen probed.

What kind of a god mucks around destroying the world he created in the first place? It's a lose-lose situation. Either he's second rate for creating a world he has to destroy or he's not any kind of a god worth talking about because he's so cruel he drowns a planet. If that wasn't bad enough his friends and their pets get off scotfree on their yacht while everybody else drops dead. The Noah thing proves to me there's no God.

Now that we got that problem solved maybe we can move on to something more particular, Caleb Farrow said.

No, Reed Kitchen said.

Addie, you don't understand, Van Loon told her. You can't raise a subject like that under Reed's nose and expect it to go away.

It's a free country. He can talk. But I know what I know.

You don't know much about Noah, Reed Kitchen told her.

And you do? He's a friend of yours? Addie Day laughed and lit the smoke held in her fingers.

In a way, Reed Kitchen said. He stood up to tell this tale. He believed it to be the reverent thing to do. He paced. Some stories, he said, come down through time from one mouth talking into another ear and so on through generations. Stories survive like that for centuries. There are stories going around from time immemorial before they were written about in the Good Book but the Good Book put down the Reader's Digest condensed version—the Good Book never attempted to inscribe the details.

Now you're telling me you've got the full length version of the Bible in your head? You do ramble in and out of my favour, Reedie.

You asked for it, Van Loon told her.

This is a story that's been going around maybe five thousand years. The story gets told differently each time but its essence remains the same. You can't change the essence of a story even when you try. You can ruin a good story but you can't kill it. You can shoot the story-teller but the story can live on without him.

Shoot the storyteller, Caleb Farrow reflected. Now that's a start.

You're a more important person than anybody would think, Addie Day said. Know what you are, Reed? You're a font of knowledge.

Most of the time that's true, Reed Kitchen said although he knew she was teasing him and did not believe he was a font. But stories get retold and I have never been shy about the retelling.

No kidding.

You be quiet, Van Loon. Don't pester me so much and listen up. You might learn something.

Get it over with, Van Loon said. Today.

God flooded the earth because men and women had become like the wilder beasts. They had tails and some men and women had more than one head and they had extra sets of arms and they grew horns and things like that. Men weren't free to be men and they were becoming more like the animals every day and so the world was flooded to save the species. God wanted to save the human species and also what in his opinion he considered to be the fittest of the animals because nature had run amok and was running amoker. So sending that flood was a good thing point of fact. It was not a bad thing done. The flood was an act of love and an act of common sense.

Anybody who couldn't swim for a month drowned, Addie Day said.

People were crazy in their heads and the evil they did was abomination. Halfmen and halfwomen fornicated with the wilder beasts and reproduced greater monsters still. The demons made flesh were drowned so that the new generation had an opportunity again to transform themselves into human beings worthy of the name. Next time it won't be the flood we are forewarned. We are told that next time will be the refining fire. You wait and see.

How do you explain this rain? Caleb Farrow put in. It's raining worse than Noah's time. You said so yourself.

Reed Kitchen sat down and took the question to heart. I think it means that maybe we have not drowned all the monsters yet.

That I can believe, Addie Day said. Anyhow your story proves that God if there ever was a God was a major dud.

People are the duds. God gave them back a chance by drowning the abberations in the redeeming flood.

Can we get on with this? Van Loon asked.

On with what?

We were trying to figure out Addie's situation before you barged in here and changed the subject.

Same subject, Addie Day told him. Monsters.

Right, Van Loon said.

I kid you not.

Fill me in, Reed Kitchen asked again. He got up from the pew and sat down beside Caleb Farrow and straddled the bench. He said to Wilf, Your dog?

Used to be, Wilf said.

Good dog?

Once.

It's a terrible thing when a good dog acquires a taste for venison. Forgets its a dog.

You think it's rabid?

I think it's a mad dog.

It's a terrible world we live in when our pets become the wilder beasts.

Addie Day disentangled her legs arising. The men watched her. She stepped to the stove and refilled her mug and stared at the rain bejewelled on the window and at the smudge of darkgreen forest beyond wild and impenetrable here and sopping and the steam of the coffee and the smoke of her cigarette moiled below her chin. The men had their eyes upon her now and upon her displaced loveliness and their hearts did ferment and flare and the sadness of her aloneness awash upon this shore moved them to an affectionate and yearning and sheltering spirit. She had been carried here less by the intervention of these men than by floodtide and happenstance and current and by an unnamed duress and by her own puzzling logic too. She had been carried here like a sea lion upon an icefloe yielding to the tide and she appeared damp and beleaguered and chilled. She resembled a fugitive whose own mysterious presence seemed unremarkable and natural and somehow the land to which she had fled was made foreign and forbidding by her pose. A change in their lives was apparent and Addie Day was not that change herself and she endured by the window and put her mug down and poked her fingertips into the tight front pockets of her jeans the elbows splayed. She seemed like the norm—the constant—while all that was customary and familiar in their lives had been transformed and they were unable to look at this place through their own eyes and saw this place through her eyes now and what they beheld was wet and desolate and removed from the world of people and artifact and memory.

She pivoted and her gaze was upon them now and they saw themselves through her eyes as wayward and fettered and impaired and she gazed at them asquint through the smoke of her cigarette that dangled from a corner of her lips.

These boys want to know about my past, Addie Day said.

We want to know what hold The Sip has on you, Van Loon corrected her. And will he let go of it.

He has no hold, Addie Day stated. The fingertips came out of her jeans and one hand chose the cigarette and the other the mug and she returned to her shipwrecked chair and sat alone and crossed an ankle above a knee again and blew out her smoke and sipped and she reached down and put her cup upon the floor. Nobody has a hold on me, she told them. Not even you guys.

Not even The Sip? Van Loon asked her.

Especially not him.

You're as free as a bird.

I didn't say that. I wouldn't say that.

That's what we're trying to get at. What would you say?

Van Loon, you have no idea—you have no clue what you've done. I don't think this place is safe enough. It's not secret enough. It's too damn public if you ask me. You promised me the wilderness and what do I get? Practically Grand Central Station.

I'd like to go there someday, Reed Kitchen said. Grand Central Station. I'd like to sit and watch the trains arrive and depart.

I might be safer there than I am here, she grumbled.

Van Loon has been around the world, Caleb Farrow pointed out to her. I've done time in the joint. Wilf knows this country and Reed knows everybody and everything that's pertinent to know. He knows The Sip. It's not like you don't have people looking out for you who don't know a thing or two.

You have to trust us anyhow, Van Loon said. You don't have a choice.

Addie Day sat for awhile and stood for awhile and sat back on the arm of her chair this time.

You should tell us your story, Reed Kitchen said. You should tell us the one you don't want to tell because you don't think we'll believe it. I've got news for you. I will believe it. I always do. Even if it's a lie.

Addie Day walked past them and opened the two front doors and tossed her smoke out into the rain and Reed Kitchen said, Train.

They listened and Addie Day held open the doors and they heard the unrelenting rhythm of the rain and Caleb Farrow said, Never doubt him, and in a few minutes the train was heard—eastbound— obeying the Slow Order and bellyaching across the Green River Bridge and Addie Day watched the train until the caboose emerged into view and she closed the door to shield herself from the trespass of unwarranted eyes.

I know you think The Sip is my pimp, Addie Day said after the train had gone.

That's what we think, Caleb Farrow said.

He's not. I don't have a pimp. I had one in Vancouver once. That was the last time. I'm my own boss. I was on a summer tour. Did a rotation through the north country. Edmonton. Prince George. Rupert. Back home to Vancouver. A bunch of us girls. Cops allowed hookers so long as we didn't stay long and I don't want to brag or nothing but in this part of the world I was something special. I wasn't just another pin cushion waiting to get pricked. So I quit the big city and came back here. Intended to freelance. There's no lack of single men here. There is no lack of cash. There is a lack of women—professional or otherwise. I called the shots. Somebody don't like it he can take his paycheque someplace else. I had more business than a girl could handle by her lonesome. So I raised my prices and I decided what we do. Take it or leave it. Some things this girl would do for nobody. Other things I would not do if I did not feel like it at the time. I was calling the shots so I called them. Take it or leave it.

So how does The Sip fit into this? Van Loon asked her.

You think it's easy for a woman to call the shots? With some guys it's not a problem. You make a deal with them and they have honour and they keep their side of the bargain. Other guys get ideas. They get a flag up their flagpole they figure they're the king of their own country. You guys aren't exactly the best examples and that's another problem we have because you guys aren't exactly weightlifters if you know what I mean—

What do you mean? Caleb Farrow asked her.

She means you're short, Reed Kitchen told him.

You're a skinny runt yourself, Farrow shot back at him.

You're good looking, Addie Day said to Van Loon, but some of these loggers up here eat your weight for breakfast.

So you needed protection, Van Loon surmised.

I needed companions who had reputations, she said. I wasn't going to be nobody's money machine. The Sip liked my company. Maybe you can guess why but if you can't I'll spell it out for you. He prefers his lovers to have hair on their chest. He likes them burly. He likes loggers and fishermen and longshoremen. I don't have to tell you what that means in this part of the world.

What does that mean in this part of the world? Reed Kitchen wanted to know.

Addie Day sighed and looked at him and decided, I don't think I could explain it to you even if I could be bothered.

So he liked you hanging around, Van Loon deduced.

I made him look good. People made assumptions and we let them. We needed those assumptions in our lives. The Sip looked like a man who kept company with a sexy woman and who lived off the avails. I looked like a woman who had a friend nobody ever crossed.

So you didn't hand over a share of your earnings?

Never split a penny with him. Sometimes I got a cut out of johns I brought down to the colony for craps or stud or blackjack. So you could argue I was pimping for The Sip.

Is that why he won't be pleased to see you go? Because you reel in suckers to his game? Caleb Farrow asked.

He won't notice the loss much, Addie Day admitted.

Then why? Van Loon asked.

She sipped her coffee and chose not to answer.

Caleb Farrow slumped forward and supported his chin on his fists one piled above the other and shut his eyes. He had endured an inquisition in his time and now appreciated how authority could be worn away with patience and resilience and by the mute evocation of all things vital. He thought he might get himself arrested again to see if had learned anything and to discern if he could exhaust his accusers instead of being worn down by the vigour of their enmity and right-eousness and by the choler of their evidence.

Van Loon nodded at Reed Kitchen as though to ask him to use his powers to oblige Addie Day to talk again.

When you went around the north country did you take the train? Reed Kitchen asked her.

Train. Boat. Bus.

Boat?

She smiled. Down the inside passage. That was the best part. Even when it rained hard. Some rare times the skies would clear and I have travelled down in sunlight and those were amazing days. We live in the rain so long up here when the skies clear the world appears sharper than it is. We get used to this drabness until we see the whole world shine. It's like stepping into heaven. I have a fantasy about living along the passage.

Where is that exactly? Reed asked her. I'm not from around here.

Prince Rupert to Vancouver Island. It's an old Indian sea route protected by islands.

The railroad does not go there.

That's the beauty of it, Addie said. No trains. No roads. No people. If I could live along there that would be heaven.

Live your fantasy here, Van Loon said.

Meaning what?

The Skeena's like the passage. Mist. Rain. The river's as wide here as the passage ever is.

There's a railway line beyond the door, Addie Day pointed out to him. Trains go by.

Minor detail. You're here. That's better than only dreaming about it. And you have friends to take care of you.

You're my friends, Addie Day said, until one of you screws me.

I won't, Reed Kitchen said. Everybody including Wilf and Margaret looked at him and he said, I'm not like The Sip. I just happen to know that I don't stand a chance.

Van Loon promised to set me up with the ladies in Prince Rupert, Caleb Farrow said. I plan to have my hands full. So to speak.

Addie Day pushed herself out of her chair and she came at Van Loon from behind and wrapped her arms around his neck and pressed the side of her face next to his and leaned herself against the back of his shoulders. She kissed his temple and she kissed his cheekbone under Van Loon's right eye. What about you, pardner? You love 'em and leave 'em, hhmmmh?

Van Loon crossed his arms and placed his hands on her elbows and endeavoured to turn to face her but she held him too tightly and rocked him slightly forward. You have my attention, he promised her.

A quiet migrated from the focus of their embrace outward as a ripple swells. Reed Kitchen was uncomfortable with this silence and crossed and uncrossed his legs and recrossed them again and stood up and sat down to deal with his distress. The betting was on Reed Kitchen but Caleb Farrow talked next. So what's the big deal about The Sip? he asked her once again.

Addie Day straightened herself up and placed her hands upon Van Loon's shoulders and she inhabited the quiet that had entered the room as a taciturn mood and she massaged the muscles of Van Loon's neck before she moved away.

You don't owe us anything, Van Loon said. But this can be your place. The kind of place you've dreamed about. We need to know exactly what we're up against here. Why are you so afraid of The Sip? If he doesn't have a hold on you why are you afraid of him? If you don't have a business agreement what kind of an arrangement do you have? Help us out here, Addie. We're only working on your side. We won't go ask The Sip for his point of view.

She stood in the room with the sound of the rain resuming on the rooftop and twiddled her fingers and brushed back her hair. She cupped an elbow and brought a hand to her mouth and pressed her mouth hard until tears welled in her eyes and she said, He gave me knowledge.

They waited.

Prince Rupert's a wide open port. There are controls but if you are quiet about it and smart enough you can step around those controls. That's why The Sip is here.

They waited.

The Sip brings in people. Filipinos mostly. Sometimes Chinese. Indians. Mostly Filipinos. People who want to get into Canada or the States but they can't get it done legally so they knock on the back-door. Not many people know this but Prince Rupert has become the backdoor to North America on the west coast. That's something I know. The Sip gave me knowledge so I will fear him. The more knowledge he gave me the more I have to fear him.

He's all talk, Caleb Farrow said. We can handle The Sip.

She turned sharply then as if to lash out. She stopped herself and turned away again. She studied the ceiling and the floor.

Talk? There was this girl one time. A Filipino. Very pretty. She was causing trouble. She had come with her father only her father had died on the voyage and The Sip disposed of the body by dropping it on an icefloe for the tide to take out to sea. The daughter was causing trouble saying she wanted to go to the police and get the body back and she wanted to go home to the Philippines to her mother and she was saying their dream of sending for the rest of the family someday was over now anyhow. She spoke some English. The Sip listened to her and then he and his punks boarded his fishboat and I was out watching with the Filipino girl so he signalled us to come along too. He said he would see if he could find the corpse but really The Sip wanted to make me a witness. He wanted me to see this so I would know about him. He wants me to have knowledge so I will fear him so that I can't ever think about having a life of my own for long. Not even here. Not even in this place. This nowhere place that doesn't even have a name.

She returned to her broken chair and sat down but she did not cross her legs this time and brought them under her like cushions and sat curled. I said to The Sip when we got out in the channel—because I had a premonition—I said to him, You're not going to find the body. And he said, We'll just shake her up a little. She's got a big yap. That's what I believed I guess because that's what I wanted to believe. We bumped up against this icefloe and The Sip took a swig of his beer and he made a point of telling the girl that this looked like the ice he had put the body on and he told her to get out on the ice and look for her dead father. She was hesitating but she was willing to get out of the boat onto the ice and The Sip asked her if she wanted a beer. She shook her head no. Then he said, Sure you do. She was frightened. She was worried. She was looking at me like she wanted to ask what this meant. I couldn't tell her because I didn't know. She felt safer with me there and at that time I still felt glad to be there because I was scared for her myself and I thought she was safer with me along. They put out these hooks that moored the fishboat to the icefloe and that made me and the girl think they weren't just going to leave her—that maybe she could get off the boat and look for her father's body.

The Sip said to her, You want a beer real bad don't you? This time she said, No thank you. The kid was polite. The Sip said, Sure you do, and I remember that look he had on and that's when I got so scared I just about stopped breathing. But I still didn't know what was happening. The way the other punks were sniggering made me scared. One of them was a guy named Wart and I'm always scared when he's around. You don't know what to expect with him. Then The Sip said, You want a beer real bad don't you? You're a drunken little whore aren't you? And the girl didn't know whether she should say no or whether she should say yes and get this over with. She didn't say anything at all. The Sip said, I'm a generous man. He put his thumb over his beer bottle and shook it and he asked her again, You want a beer? She shook her head no this time and he said again, Sure you do. I remember I said his name and I said stop it and I remember he gave me a look like I swear to God made my blood run as cold as that ice. The Sip just nodded to his punks and Wart and the other one grabbed the girl and now she was screaming a bit and he sprayed the girl with his beer and I jumped on The Sip but it did no good. He pulled her dress up and exposed her crotch and he stuck the bottle inside her—it disappeared right inside her—and she was crying and moaning on the deck.

I tried to help her but they pulled me off her. She tried to get the bottle out of her but they wouldn't let her and they told her to get on the ice. So she did. She wanted off that boat. She wanted to take her chances on the ice. Taking her chances with the tide and the sea probably seemed like an escape to her.

Addie foraged for her cigarettes and then threw the package on the floor. She had been talking without reference to those who were listening and now she seemed to discover them in the room with her. Aware of them again she spoke more slowly—her words like the twist of knives. She got out on the ice. Then the men got out on the ice with her. Which made me think and maybe it made the girl think that they had had their fun and now that they had punished her they would look for the body.

Addie was looking at Van Loon until she could not look at him any longer and she lowered her gaze to the floor.

Reed Kitchen asked, What happened?

You know what happened.

No I don't.

She was crying when she looked up and she did not attempt to stop the stream down her cheeks to her chin and to the corners of her mouth. Addie Day said, They broke the bottle.

A quiet was sustained in that room under the rhythm of the rain.

What? Reed Kitchen said within the dimension of that quiet.

Wart smashed the bottle inside her, Addie Day said and the quiet persisted in that house for a long time until a train's whistle blew.

Van Loon said, Listen up. We don't tell anybody about Addie. Not even the rest of the gang. We pretend that this is where she lives— that she has always lived here. Nobody else will ever know that we pulled her out of Prince Rupert.

The men nodded and Addie Day nodded also.

We'll have to give you a new name.

Eleanor, Addie said in less than an eyeblink. She smiled at their surprise and wiped her tears with the palm of her hand. My mother's name, she said. I forgive her now so call me Eleanor.

Reed, Van Loon said, you have a big mouth. You don't ever talk about this understand?

I got lots more to talk about than this.

Caleb?

Wild horses won't drag it out of me, he said. We'll keep you safe, Eleanor, he promised her.

Addie Day smiled through her tears and nodded her head.

They were quiet.

Reed Kitchen asked, What happened to her? In the end? They left her out there?

Addie nodded. The last time I saw her she was pushing herself off the icefloe into the sea. The last I saw she was on her back and she found a slope and slid down into the water which was cold—it was winter—and I never saw her after that.

They breathed and the men hung their heads and shook them gently.

I don't know what to say, Addie, Reed Kitchen said.

Call me Eleanor.

Another eastbound freight slowed down crossing the Green River Bridge.

Eleanor. I don't know what to say.

5

FOR LONG WEEKS THE MEN dug down into the muck and rock and slop
and sandbagged the side of the river at low tide and watched as the
water rose above their levee shouldering their wall apart again and
lowering it again and the gang's progress was incremental before it
became substantial. Finally the levee was born and the wall withstood
the river until the crest was breached by tide. As the tide fell they
went down into the slew again and dug out the riverbottom and
waded in the clay and pitched thick mud into the river and at the end
of the shift they opened one end of the levee to let the riverwater
back in to let it back out again when the tide once more retreated.
The sky was dark and the rain never stopped. The whole time they
worked below the bridge it rained. The rain did not quit for five minutes nor for a pause nor a breath. They knew not a moment's respite
from the deluge above or the tidal inundation alongside them. They
dug. They used their picks on stone. They used crowbars and when
crowbars lacked sufficient heft they used clawbars to prise rock loose.
The sluice of water off the peaks of their hardhats snuffed their damp
smokes. They cursed the weather and they cursed the wind and they
cursed the rain and they cursed the river and they cursed the bridge
and they cursed the railroad and they cursed each other and they
cursed their lives and they cursed their Maker and they cursed all
apparent powers of this realm. They dug to expose the riverbank to

allow them to lower the superstructure of the new bridge. Still it rained. Still it never stopped raining.

Ice rose with the tide and they felt the cool breath of the icefloe on their wet faces and necks. Their knuckles ached from the chilly damp. What's the name of this river again? Caleb Farrow asked no one in particular.

Which river? Ivor Radic asked him back.

This river. You think I mean some river on the moon?

There's that river, Ivor Radic said.

What river?

That river. He pointed.

Not the Skeena, Caleb Farrow protested as the Skeena coursed past them against itself. The river flowed against its own current with ice upon it offered up by the tide. This river. The one we're working on, dodobird.

It's called the Green River, Kai Jensen said.

But it's not green, Caleb Farrow said.

It's green all around it, Reed Kitchen said.

The river's not green, Farrow said. He put up his shovel and took out his smokes. The water's not green. This is a hellhole of a place. With a name like that somebody might look at a map and see that name—Green River—and he might think to himself that this is a fine place to be. A place worth visiting. It's misleading. A name like that is not honest. I think we should give it a new name.

It's a shitty name, Frank Croce agreed.

We can't name the river, Kai Jensen said, but nobody said we can't name the bridge. We could give the bridge a name.

Old Fart, Van Loon suggested.

The Arsehole Bridge, Caleb Farrow said.

Reed Kitchen said, Bridges have the same name as the rivers they cross. This is the Green River Bridge. We can too rename the river. Who says we can't? Who would know? Myself personally I would call this a hard bridge. So that means the river is called the Hard River.

Van Loon said, If you got to name the bridge after the river and the river is called the Hard River then you can't call it the Hard Bridge.

You got to call the bridge the Hard River Bridge.

Except it's not the river that's hard—it's the bridge—and you can't blame the river for the bridge except for making it necessary and you can't blame the river for the rain—so call it the Hard Rain River.

That means you got to call the bridge the Hard Rain River Bridge, Van Loon told him.

Better a name like that than the Green River Bridge, Caleb Farrow said. At least somebody looking at a map would say to himself that that's not a place he'd ever want to find himself in.

They were putting up their shovels now and taking a break.

They were quiet awhile contemplating the bridge and the river and the muck and their smokes and Reed Kitchen said, You can call it the Hard Rain River Bridge if you want but it seems to me with a name like that you can call it the Hard Bridge for short if you want to. I don't hear nobody saying you can't do that.

All right then. We'll call it the Hard Bridge, Kai Jensen said and he wanted to make that official too because he had announced it.

Except it's not appropriate really, Reed Kitchen said and he shot down his own argument. In this instance when you think about it you don't want to name the bridge after the river because we would never be here if it wasn't for the bridge so really it's better to name the river after the bridge because we never would've found the river if we hadn't been told to go look for the bridge—so really the river should be called the Hard Rain Bridge River.

Too hard to say, Frank Croce said.

Joe Ribeiro agreed. Don't roll off the tongue exactly.

Ice butted up against the superstructure and timbers complained and the men looked and Caleb Farrow said, I think we should call it the Cold River. Then for sure nobody would want to come here to look at it. Then we call the bridge the Cold River Bridge.

I'll pay you to swim across it, Van Loon said.

How much? Caleb Farrow asked him.

Five bucks.

For five bucks you can kiss my ass.

Ten bucks then.

To swim across the river?

Ten bucks.

It'll be cold, Reed Kitchen warned him.

Ten bucks won't do it, Caleb Farrow said.

I'll put in five, Frank Croce said.

I got five, Joe Ribeiro said.

We'll all chip in five, Kai Jensen announced.

Except Van Loon. He puts in ten, Farrow said.

Hhohghdverdoma. Van Loon laughed.

Thirtyfive bucks there pal, Caleb Farrow said. If Dino was here instead of bullcooking I'd make forty.

So we'll charge him five bucks to hear the story.

Forty it is.

It'll be cold, Reed Kitchen said and each man looked seriously at the water now. The tide was about halfway up the levee swelling the river to fifteen feet wide. Ice drifted up the river and the surface along the opposite bank was frozen.

I'll do it, Caleb Farrow said.

For forty bucks? Reed Kitchen asked him. Don't seem worth it to me.

I'll do it because I'm a sonofabitch, Caleb Farrow said.

You don't have nothing to prove, Kai Jensen said. Forget about it.

I'm going. I'm gonna swim this river.

Caleb Farrow scrabbled up to the top of the levee where he pulled off a muddy boot and balanced on one leg like an awkward crane and peeled his sock away from his foot and deposited the sock in the boot. Then he removed the other boot and sock and took off his rainjacket and slid the suspenders off his shoulders and stepped out of his rain-pants.

He won't do it, Frank Croce said.

You wanna bet? Ferenc Van Loon asked him.

Frank wasn't sure.

You wanna bet, Frank?

Don't bet him, Reed Kitchen advised Van Loon. If you bet him Caleb won't swim just so you can lose that bet.

After that nobody said anything and they looked up at Caleb Farrow above them and suddenly he stepped down on the sandbags on the other side of the levee and they heard the splash and the men scrabbled up to the top of the levee and made it at the same time that Caleb Farrow bobbed to the surface letting out a yelp and then he was silent and the men were laughing even as they saw his face change and saw the grim fright and fear enter him and he swam for the far shore and what was a moment for them was a time suspended for Caleb Farrow and a time that continued to extend as he pulled himself onto the ice and pulled himself onto the rock and mud on the other side.

Now the men were hooting. They were applauding. Kai Jensen declared, You swam it, Caleb. Now you can name it. You want to call this the Cold River and the Cold River Bridge then that's what it'll be. You should know.

Caleb Farrow lay in shock and shivered and grinned on the other side. He could not yet speak. His body remained violated by the assault of cold upon his skin and bones and blood.

Cold? Reed Kitchen protested from the rim of the levee. Cold? If this river was called the Cold River I would never have come here in the first place because I was seduced by the promise of subtropical climes. I will show you what's cold and what's not.

Reed. What are you doing? Van Loon asked him.

He was taking off his clothes.

I've lost my five bucks. You're not getting another five out of me, Frank Croce warned him.

You guys will die of pneumonia, the foreman told them.

Don't do it, Reed, Caleb Farrow said from the opposite bank and those were the first words he had been able to utter since his swim.

Reed Kitchen was enchanted. He was entranced. He had seen Caleb Farrow descend into the water and now he had to do the same. Reed Kitchen stripped nude except for his hardhat and the men whistled and as the rain and the breeze caught his skin he had a premonition of heat and of fire and of blood aboil and he jumped down into the stream and the first shock was the depth for he could not touch

bottom and the second immediate shock was the indubitable sensa-
tion of cold and he fought through an immediate seizure and he could
not believe how his strength had vanished and how his muscles would
not respond and swimming he experienced himself go light and soft
and time slowed and motion slowed and his heart—his heart, he
knew—might quit this race for the faraway shore.

Reed Kitchen felt his heart stagger inside him and he stopped
swimming and sunk quickly as though he was weighted and when he
came up he was thrashing blinded by the water now and made deaf by
panic and his stroke became vigorous. He was aware of the shouting
but only ignorant momentum propelled him forward and when he
touched a hard surface it was not the frozen and welcome hand of ice
that greeted him but the wet slivered touch of a piling and Reed
Kitchen realized then that he had swum under the bridge.

He hung on.

He breathed.

He pulled himself up and hung himself on the scaffolding while his
accomplices cheered.

We should call this the Hardhat River, Kai Jensen called out,
because you lost yours.

Weakened Reed Kitchen hung on the bridge to keep himself from
falling back and his teeth chattered like jackhammers and shivers
quaked the whole of his body and he had to gasp for breath through
his mouth to stay alive and his lungs ached and yet he had to speak.
He had to talk. He had so much to say.

It's only right that I name the river, he croaked. This is my river to
name. I am the one who should give names to things. You know I'm
the one who does the talking. You remember, Kai. When we first
came here. I was the one who went down through the bridge and
tested the water first. You remember that.

And the men were looking at him and they were quiet now and
unsure of his sanity and equally uncertain of his passion.

Naked on the girders Reed Kitchen said, This is my home—at least
for now—because home is where the heart is. I will name this place
Heart River. But the actual river I will call the Hardhearted River

because when I was a drowning man my friends did not move to save me and therefore I christen this bridge the Hardhearted River Bridge.

The name was agreed upon in silence. The men stood staring at him and none dared budge.

FARROW AND KITCHEN BELIEVED they had placed themselves in the palms of mortal danger. Needing to warm themselves anon the two soaked and shivered men sat upon the pushcart as others rolled it down to the Indian cabins and dropped them off and hauled the cart back to remove it from the tracks. Reed Kitchen strode into the main cabin in his nakedness and worry and crossed the room to sit upon the floor next to the woodburning stove and in his sopping attire Caleb Farrow entered the home most shyly.

What happened to you guys? Margaret asked. She was standing at the counter turning the handle of her quern in a rhythm she did not interrupt.

I went for a swim, Caleb Farrow told her.

After a visit to the outhouse Addie Day entered by the back door and she heard Farrow speak and asked him, You fell in the river?

No. I went for a swim.

So d-d-did I, Reed Kitchen announced. We both took a d-d-dip in the Hardhearted River under that H-h-hardhearted R-river B-b-bridge.

Addie Day looked over at Reed Kitchen sitting in a squat on the floor and saw that he was nude and shivering and that his teeth chattered in a violent way and she turned back to Caleb Farrow and told him to stand out of his clothes. Now, she said.

B-b-better do what she says, Reed Kitchen told him. Save yourself. I can s-s-see that M-m-margaret has a good idea. B-b-blankets.

Farrow peeled off his shirt.

Hurry. You'll catch your death, Addie told him.

He looked down and then looked up. Ladies are present, he reminded her. He was gently blushing and smiling.

Addie Day studied him. There's one lady present by my count and I'm sure Margaret won't be upset by your bare skin.

I've seen worse things alive than a naked man, Margaret said.

Well I see two ladies present, Caleb Farrow told her.

Addie Day looked at him again. Then she went around the table and whapped him on the back of the head. Strip, she said.

Caleb Farrow was stalled by embarrassment and racked by chills and a harrowing cold shook him and made his fingers inert. He had to hug himself and dance by the fire while the worst of the shakes plundered his bones and he managed to unfasten his pants and slide them down. He was dressed only in his underpants when Addie Day grabbed the briefs from behind and yanked them down and in his surprise and mortification Caleb Farrow performed a quersprung jump right out of his shorts and Margaret tittered and kept on in a helpless giggle as Farrow covered his genitals with his hands.

The blankets Margaret draped around them were prickly and cold and the two men shivered in the heat of the stove back to back. Margaret opened the grate and stoked the flame and tossed on more logs.

I think I'm gonna die, Caleb Farrow lamented.

Addie Day sat down and in a moment bounded to her feet again. There's soup. That'll warm you up. She stepped across to the stove and removed a flaming timber from one side below the oven and placed it on the other. Fragrant smoke from the timber wafted through the air and the men breathed the smoke as though consuming heat. She added kindling to the second stovefire and more wood.

You can't d-d-d-die on me, Reed Kitchen warned him through his chattering teeth.

Why not?

Bec-c-c-cause where you go I go. You should have f-f-figured that out by now.

You mean if I die you die?

You got it.

Then will you shut up?

If there is a h-heaven it is a place where people can t-t-talk freely.

Heaven to me is peace and quiet, Caleb Farrow said.

That's hell. You sh-should figure it out or you m-m-might get lost. Myself p-personally when I g-get to heaven I want to s-s-sit on the right hand of God and have a nice long ch-ch-chat.

There's a few things I'd like to discuss with the Old Geezer myself.

Like what? Addie Day asked him. What would you say to God, Caleb? She was stirring the soup in the large battered pot on the stove.

I'd ask him why he had to invent the red convertible Corvette.

Addie Day smiled. She shook more pepper into the broth. Did you steal one?

Not me but that car tempted a life of crime. I was hanging out in Winterpeg when I was a kid with boys older than me. They got it into their heads to break into a department store. Make off with the fur coats. So many furs in that Christmas window they figured they'd need an extra body to help carry the loot away so they recruited me. I was dreaming of a red Corvette. I figured with a few fur coats I'd make a downpayment.

How'd that plan go? Kitchen asked.

Alarm bells were ringing like Christmas bells. Those boys lit out in every direction. On account of I couldn't see a thing—I was loaded up with fur coats above my head—I was moving a whole lot slower than the rest of them. Tripped over a hydrant there pal. Fell flat on my face. I didn't have to pick myself up because sixteen of Winterpeg's finest were piling out of eight squad cars and they were only too happy to do that for me you bet.

You poor sap, Addie Day commiserated with him.

I've said all my life that things would be different if God never allowed the red Corvette. He let it be built to demonstrate that I am a man of weak moral fibre.

What happened to your accomplices? Addie Day wanted to know.

They got away clean.

You didn't snitch?

Should've but I didn't. Those boys are policemen themselves today you bet. They're mailmen and lawyers and accountants and fathers themselves you bet with kids of their own running loose on the streets. I went to reform school where I got reformed. I went in there knowing I had to mend my ways and I came out of that place an educated B and E artist.

You didn't snitch. That tells me you are a man of high moral character, Addie said.

I eat my Wheaties.

Addie Day carried over two bowls of steaming barley broth and the shock of the soup revived their innards and Caleb Farrow believed that he might live awhile and Reed Kitchen determined that he could speak again with his familiar loquacious ire. I am in a dark vexatious mood, he said. My own companions would've let me drown today.

You weren't drowning, Reed.

Yes I was.

You were kidding around it looked like.

If that bridge didn't rise up out of that river to block me off I would've floated on out to sea no thanks to you.

The tide would carry you back inland.

You can drown in a bathtub, Caleb. You know we were not in anybody's tub today.

Caleb Farrow shrugged.

Go ahead, Reed, Addie encouraged him. You tell us a story now.

It's nice to be invited, Reed Kitchen said.

Farrow sat quietly and slurped hot broth.

I'm in a dark mood and it does bring to mind the time my daddy brought me out to the railway tracks to watch the bright eye beam of the locomotive bearing down upon us.

I've heard this story before, Farrow interjected.

Be quiet, Caleb, Addie Day said and he sat quietly in the warmth of her rebuke.

Not this version you haven't because it is not a version that I have told. When I saw you in that river I thought to myself that here is a man who has jumped in the water because he is under pressure. I wondered what that stress could be. Then it occurred to me what that stress could be. When I jumped in I was thinking about that other time in my life when the bright eye beam of a train bore down upon my daddy and me and my daddy was prepared this time for he had filled himself with fortitude.

I don't understand, Reed, Addie said. What are you talking about?

Caleb will say it in simple language. I'm in too vexatious a mood.

His daddy tried to kill him on a regular basis. His daddy would take him out to face oncoming trains and hold him there and jump clear at the last second hoping Reed would not.

Nice guy, Addie Day said.

I had to be quicker than him, Reed Kitchen explained. Because he jumped clear first and that left me with less time than he had left himself. So I had to be the quickest of the two. Only this time I could tell that he was aiming to hold me longer than before so that even the time he gave himself was limited and maybe he would leave himself none at all. As though he wanted to see if I would go under the train again and be shat out the other end by the caboose again as I had done at the time of my birthing and I had to wrestle him there on those tracks and I had to pull out my tricks and I knew that this would keep.

Reed Kitchen paused to place the bowl to his lips and drink the warmth of the broth inside him.

Tricks? Addie asked.

Slippery tricks. Wrestling tricks. I had to fight him on those tracks and this train was coming down hard at us and when the time had already passed for jumping I had to free myself and leap clear in one motion and my daddy—he was not part of that motion.

They were quiet in the room and waiting. Margaret returned to milling fishbones at her quern and she was the one who asked him what happened after that.

The train stopped. That's what happened. I walked on up to the locomotive and the engineer asked down at me, What'd I hit? I told him it was a small deer. I told him I'd take care of it—that there was no problem here. So he moved on. That train chugged on out of there and went on down the mainline and I waited for the deeper dusk to fall. I waited. When the shadows were dark enough to hide what I did not wish to see I moved myself around to those places where my daddy was and I put the pieces of him in a wheelbarrow and wheelbarrowed him away from the traintracks and the places where men might walk and that's where I dug his grave. I buried him in that place.

You white people have strange ways, Margaret said.

They were quiet awhile listening to the renewed force of rain on the roof and slanting against the windows and Caleb Farrow said, There's something I should tell you, Reed.

Yes there is, Reed Kitchen said.

What?

You're the one who wanted to say something.

You tell me. You're the one who knows everything.

Now is the time for me to be quiet and for you to talk.

Forget it, Caleb Farrow said. I changed my mind.

Is that all you have to say?

That's it.

What are you guys rattling on about now? Addie Day inquired.

Nothing, Caleb Farrow said.

Almost nothing at all, Reed Kitchen said. I just want to know why he went for a swim. I want to know why and he's too ashamed to tell me.

THE RAIN HIT HARDEST ACROSS THE great basin of Prince Rupert's harbour and Reed Kitchen found scant protection under the eaves of the long sheds. A Japanese freighter with a Filipino crew taking on copper sulphate blocked the direct wind that swirled in frenzied forays down the length of the dock. Kitchen hid his neck in the collar of his slicker and hunched his shoulders to brace himself against the cold and the wet and he waited in the shadows created by the ship's lights and the sluice of rain that flooded the eaves and concealed him as behind a waterfall.

He watched the man approach blackly luminous in the floodlit rain. He saw him approach before he was himself seen and he spoke his name.

Yellowhead Don, Reed Kitchen said. Over here.

The man hesitated and looked behind him to the deck of the ship. He stepped through the veil of the waterfall and extended his hand. Reed. Good to see you.

Reed Kitchen consented to shake the hand as frigid as his own.

The two men were attentive to the wet and wind and darkness and huddled their hands in the depths of their pockets.

I will be talking to The Sip tonight, Reed Kitchen told him.

Good. That's good. What's your agenda?

I will tell him what I can do for him.

Excellent. What can you do for him, Reed?

He needs to know a railroading man.

I told you. That's what our people heard. I admit it—he's a slippery fish when it comes to catching him in the act. He can transfer people from a mother ship at sea and carry them to any number of ports at night or in the rain. He can elude us even when we know he's coming. But ashore. That's where his problems magnify. That's his weak link. How does he dispose of his human cargo? One time he chartered a bus. He won't be so daring again. Another occasion we believe he shipped his people by truck. But trucks are subject to inspections on highways and he can't be comfortable with the risk. Sometimes he has shipped people south by boat. The Coast Guard pursued him once and lost him along the inside passage. A close call. Our people let us know the day the word went out. He wants to use the railroad. He let the word out and it happened to come through to us. Which made me think of you.

He will ask me what I can do for him.

Yes he will.

I'll tell him that empty boxcars often sit on a siding at Port Edward.

That's good. He sees them often.

He will let me know the approximate time. I'll relay the numbers of two boxcars.

Yes.

He will tell me when he wants the cars transported. In Port Edward the cars won't be checked. I'll explain that to him. They'll be picked up by a regular slow freight and delivered east. I'll explain to him that I will fix it for those cars to be delivered east as empty. This is the end of the line. We ship many cars east from here empty.

We do. Yes.

He learns from me the numbers of the cars—I learn from him the

day for the pickup. When I learn the day for the pickup you will know
to watch that train.

You're a good man, Reed. You've thought about this.

You should be worried.

About what?

I have thought about this. I am no longer an anxious man in your
company. Do you know that Caleb Farrow went for a swim?

What do you mean—went for a swim?

In the Hardhearted River. I wonder why he did that. I joined him
in that pool.

I'm not following you here, Reed. Your logic is getting away from
me.

Only desperate men go swimming in the Hardhearted River.

You've lost me, Reed.

I don't know why you don't go down to The Sip's gambling den
and bust him and put him in jail immediately. Why don't you go do
that?

Not my jurisdiction. Don McBain sniffed his leaking nostril. But
there's no point. The Mounties would only find him playing cards. He
is not the owner of that place. No one is. It's a raft afloat on the water
that doesn't come under the administration of any municipality. That
doesn't make it legal but it also doesn't make him the legal proprietor
of those games. All we can do is arrest him for gambling and in this
part of the world that's a lesser crime than jaywalking. He'll get a thir-
tydollar fine and time served and that's only if he's got a lousy lawyer.
If we arrested every man around here for playing a little cards our
industries would shut down for lack of labour.

If you arrested every man around here who gambles you'd have to
arrest yourselves.

No doubt.

Promise me one thing.

Name it.

This is what I do. I name things. You must catch The Sip.

Consider it done.

He must go to jail.

Fifty years will be too kind.

That jail must be located in a faraway place.

A federal pen. They're all faraway.

Promise me something else.

You have a list tonight.

Reed Kitchen was looking at the railway policeman but he was not able to see him in this outer dark. He saw only the shape that he knew to be Yellowhead Don McBain.

Shoot, McBain said in response to his stern quiet.

You will inform the Mounties. I know you want to be the hero. I know that's your problem in life. You want to be the hero. You want to be a real policeman and not just a railway dick. But you cannot take a chance. You can't screw this up. You need all the help you can get. If you screw this up—if The Sip escapes—my life will be in danger. If my life is in danger the life of my friends will be in danger also. It is for my friends that I want The Sip in jail. I am not doing this for you, Yellowhead. I am doing this for my friends.

We'll take care of our end, Reed.

If you don't—if you put my life in danger and the lives of my friends in danger—then I do believe you will find that your life has become more perilous also.

Whoa. Are you threatening me here?

I would do no such thing. I have a belief that when a story is told it has a life and an understanding of its own. A story travels to many places and no one can predict exactly where and no one can prevent the news that it brings.

You don't say. This is a moot point, Reed. We won't screw up. You get me the date and we'll have him dead to rights.

I will need an address for The Sip to communicate with me. I do not wish to give him my B & B address. I will give him an address with the Roadmaster's department. When the Roadmaster receives a letter for me you will know it is from The Sip. The Roadmaster can carry it across the hall to you. Call me on the radio in Tyee. Give me the numbers of the boxcars. When you radio through to my foreman pretend that you are calling for some other reason. Tell him I have a dying relative. Then I will travel to a telephone to call that relative but I will call The Sip instead. I will tell him the numbers and he will tell me the time when he wants the boxcars shipped.

You have thought about this.

I have thought about this. Reed Kitchen frowned in the invisible dark. This is a cold wettish land, he told the detective. It may not be snowing here tonight but I'll tell you something—a man can freeze his bones stiff in a damp cold like this. A man can freeze his bones stiff standing around out here.

That's true, Reed. It's a verity.

Verity. The verities. With two bits and words like that I can buy a cup of coffee.

You can have the word, Reed. You can have it free.

I'm a rich man with a word like that. I'm what Caleb Farrow would call a citizen. Do you know Caleb Farrow, Yellowhead? Do you know he went swimming in the Hardhearted River on his own accord? Why would he do that do you think?

6

FERENC VAN LOON TOUCHED the place where the coaloil lamp's pale
light shone with human kindness upon the woman's outer thigh. He
lowered his head to her. She watched him and Addie Day lifted herself upon her tiptoes to kiss his mouth and she closed her eyes for this
union. As his hand moved to the inside of her thigh she smiled.

Smart guy.

I'd have to go back to Holland to find a girl as fine as you.

Sweet talking man.

You're beautiful, Addie.

Call me Eleanor.

Not here.

Especially here. Call me Eleanor here.

Your mother's name.

My daughter's too. All I have for my trouble is the name I gave her.

They kissed again until the pressure of her hand upon his shoulder
moved Van Loon toward the pallet in the corner of this outflung
cabin. Addie Day removed her T-shirt and with it covered her
breasts as she stepped toward him and this time she was laughing
welcomed into his arms and this time she licked his lips and touched
his tongue with her own and snuggled her tongue against the lids of
his eyes and her laughter this time was freighted with the huskiness
of her voice and her customary despondent nature. Addie Day strad-

dled him and used her weight to knock him onto the bed and she rose above him. With grave tenderness Addie Day slipped loose the first of his buttons.

When I was about ten or eleven, Van Loon confided in her, the girl who lived downstairs from my family—she lived on the first and second floors, we lived on the third and fourth. I've forgotten her name. Anyway. She was older than me. Thirteen. Fourteen. I was playing some game. I remember I was on the floor. She came in and about a minute later she asked to have sex with me. It was a request. I wasn't interested. I was too young. I think I invited her to play chinese checkers. When I got older I regretted that. I can't tell you how much I regretted that. I wanted her so bad when I was a teenager. She was all I thought about then. She moved on to older boys and I never stood a chance. She punished me for turning her down. She never forgave me. She used her beauty to punish me on a daily basis.

Now you don't say no to girls. Addie Day was smiling slightly and her eyes had become vague and she was enjoying the touch of him under her hands and between her knees.

I don't say no to girls. When I saw you. That day. In the beer parlour. In Rupert. I knew if I did not make a move on you I would regret it worse than I regret that time long ago.

You're sweettalking me because I'm the finest piece of white flesh to come your way since you turned up in this country.

That too.

She bent to him and kissed his nipples and rolled her tongue upon him and pinned him down and she did not let him up until she wanted to let him up.

When she stood off him she removed her panties and he unbuckled himself and shook off his boots and slipped out of his pants where he lay on the bed. She did a pirouette in the small room. She went to the window and drew a heart in the condensation on the glass and stabbed it with an arrow. The cabin was one room and small. There was no heating stove. They warmed the cabin with the chill of their flesh. She turned the lamp lower. In Rupert. In the beer parlour. That day. I was asking you to set me free.

I know.

She moved back to him for the warmth and hard comfort of his body and she whispered to him, Let's make this time—she scratched his chest—vicious.

Van Loon tossed her under him and she yelped and he placed her ankles upon his shoulders and she collapsed into the cavity of the mattress and the bedsprings jounced and he entered her where she was most willing and anxious and she looked at him and he explored the heartache of her desire and this time no solace soothed her eyes and this time no peace resided there and this time no comfort lingered to be gained or forfeit or won or defeated and he said, Wait, and she said, Hurry, and he said, Wait, and she said, Quick. And they rocked together and their bodies kicked one upon the other and the two gripped one another until their greater and lesser hurts prevailed before they did subside.

In the deeper night Addie Day disentangled herself from the limbs of her man and rose from the bed to snuff the lamp and she stood serene and still in that august darkness. The rain fell gently upon the roof. She had not seen the moon in weeks. Nary a star in months. The night was so black here and so complete and so mercilessly mercenary assailing her soul. She broached the dark with her hands and felt about for a raincoat and after the raincoat covered her she opened the door. Addie Day walked slowly in the darkness across the footbridge to the main cabin. There was no light save the twinkle that was the outport of Port Essington miles off on the other side of the river. A signal in the braver dark. Her fingers found the doorknob in the blackness. She opened the door quietly and entered into that huge stillness where Margaret and Wilf burbled in their sleep and where her true love did lie waiting. Addie Day removed her raincoat and placed it on a chair and naked lay down beside him.

I've got goosebumps. I'm chilly.

He placed his blanket over her and warmed her by his side. They lay in the temperate darkness while their eyes adjusted to the noble gloom.

I've had sex with animals, Caleb Farrow whispered to her.

Everyday it rained and every night was blacker than the night before. No vision here. No clarity. No light. Addie Day said, Me too.

Her voice was yet so near—as vital as her breath—as necessary as the air and equally unknown. He could not see her and sensed only the gentle rise and fall of her chest.

I mean with real animals, Caleb Farrow said. Fourlegged beasts.

Maybe this was the difference with Caleb she thought. Where other men drew allusions to their conquests he broached the grim matters of his defeats. You're lucky, she said. Mine were twolegged.

Caleb Farrow smiled within himself and within the respite of this room. I suppose I'm lucky at that, he said.

Is the whole gang in Rupert?

Be back Sunday. One long drunk.

Good of you to stay.

We don't dare show our face. Not me or Van Loon.

I hope nobody lets anything slip. It was good of you to stay, Caleb.

It's nice to be here. It's nice that you're here.

Tomorrow Van Loon wants to go scavenging with Margaret and Wilf.

I was thinking about it.

Decline. I'll decline. We'll have that time alone.

All right, Caleb Farrow said.

I'm sorry your best friend's Van Loon.

He still is, Farrow said.

They breathed that darkness awhile and tittered together as the flagrant sounds emitted by Wilf in his sleep gained courage.

Were you impotent with animals too? Addie Day asked him.

I told you I don't like that word.

Could you get it up for animals? she asked him.

It's animals that made me this way. It's animals that made me impotent. I believe it is because I have defiled and debased myself. That's why I want to be a citizen again. It would be nice to make love to my own species once again.

You'll be a citizen again, Caleb, Addie Day promised him.

She lowered her hand and placed it upon his sex. He was soft and small and worry arose through his skin. We're like two peas in a pod you and me, Addie Day told him.

You bet, Caleb Farrow said.

ADDIE DAY HUDDLED ON THE SHORE under a wool serape watching Wilf's tug move through the chop eastbound on a flood tide. The *Margaret M* was a stout and salty ship with high bow and bulwarks and a deep spring to the sheer and a rattly old diesel and Ferenc Van Loon waved back at Addie from the stern. Her lover was gone to work upon the wild river and she turned her back to him and to the boat to be with her one true love.

Crossing the tracks Addie Day took pause. This was the solemn circumstance of her life. She lived in exile upon an uninhabitable shore and in a place as primitive as Green River she confounded her life with situation. Two men meant trouble. Especially when those two men happened to be pals. This was asking for strife. This was begging for it in the worst way. Misery cloaked her nature as cosily as the serape hugged her body. She was trouble—born and bred—to herself if to no other. Addie Day watched the dance of mists upon the cliffs and winced at their frolic. This is a life. She thought this thing to herself and the notion struck her as vivid and precious and secret to her innermost self. This is a life. The thought enlivened the moment and Addie Day pranced down the boardwalk running with a bit of a skip and Caleb Farrow watching from the window deduced that her happiness had to do with him. As she came through the door he moved toward her to remind her of his presence and he noticed that a different notion ruled. Addie Day stood in the gloom of the doorway and Caleb Farrow observed her melancholy resume a careful observation of her affairs.

Caleb, she said.

Addie.

What do you want to do today?

There's nothing to do in a place like this. You know that.

We're just supposed to sit here?

That's what you wanted.

I thought we'd be together.

We're together.

So it seems.

She moved about the room and paused at the cistern and lifted a conikin from its nail and pushed the button to fill the cup and she drank and she drank again. What would you do on the gang if you weren't working on a day like today?

Work on a jigsaw puzzle. Or go hunting. Play cards.

We have cards. A cribbage board too someplace.

Indians play cribbage?

Wilf's been a miner. He's been a logger. He's been a fisherman on his own boats and he's worked on the draggers. He's done a little of everything. He's picked up a few whiteman's habits. Anyway, Indians play Bingo they must play cards.

Addie browsed a shelf boobytrapped by a collection of lures and fishing flies and she worked slowly to avoid being hooked. Amid the clutter she retrieved the handmade crib board with holes punched by hammering nails and rows that were somewhat irregular. She located the deck beneath the board.

Play? Addie asked.

Sure.

You any good?

I work on the railway.

They played. Caleb Farrow was lightning quick and Addie Day was ponderous in adding her points and choosing her cards to count. Maybe this isn't such a good idea, Farrow said. Cards I mean. We should have gone on the boat maybe.

Addie Day put down her hand. I'm sorry, Caleb.

It was fun while it lasted.

It's something I do. I don't mean to. I invent people. Places. Things. Circumstances. I imagine my life sometimes.

You invented me, Caleb Farrow said.

It's something I do sometimes.

Why couldn't you invent Van Loon instead? Why does it have to be me? Why do I have to be the figment of your imagination?

Van Loon is real somehow. That's how he is. He wouldn't let me invent him if I tried.

Caleb Farrow shrugged and a sadness expired across his chest. Do you want to finish this game or what?

Not really. I'll start lunch. I planned this big lunch so I might as well make it. We might as well enjoy ourselves.

I won't say no to food.

What's the use of a heavy romance if you can't get fed at least?

You bet.

Addie Day busily organized her luncheon and Caleb Farrow lay back on his pallet and breathed the mould and humidity of this place and wished that he could have a dry day—one dry day—to relieve his weariness of rain. He believed that she had loved him and that he had loved her and now he didn't know what to believe or whom to trust. He had betrayed his best friend when nothing more had been at stake than Addie's own lapse of reality. He could not trust himself. He had not actually betrayed Van Loon in the physical sense and Caleb Farrow agonized over that and realized that he felt better. Another person had shared a large corner of himself and that person had cared about him without judgment. He had given his difficulty licence to speak. He was wholly contained within himself no longer for now he did partially reside within the heart and life of another and Caleb Farrow realized that Addie Day had reinvented him in ways that she did not know.

They both heard the odd and displaced sounds at the same time. They looked at one another simultaneously. No voices belonged out here. Instinct made him crouch as Caleb Farrow moved to the window and Addie Day imitated his posture as fear bloomed inside her. She scrabbled to the window on her hands and knees and looked. Two men on the railway tracks who did not belong there searched around.

Shoot them, Caleb, Addie Day pleaded whispering. Shoot them, sweetheart, please now.

In the moment of her duress she had forgotten that she should not call him sweetheart.

You're forgetting something, Caleb Farrow said.

I'm sorry, Caleb.

I'm impotent. I don't shoot people.

For the first time she felt his wound and the festering of his rage. The terror constricted in her throat that now she was alone and abandoned and she watched Caleb Farrow to see what he would do and how he would betray her.

He smiled. Pass over the rifle, he said.

She moved on her hands and knees to the doorway and clutched the gun and brought it back to him keeping her head down. Farrow checked the clip and tested the bolt action and handed the weapon back to her.

She would not accept it. Shoot them, Caleb. Please. Don't take chances.

I don't know who they are. Do you?

The skinny one is Wart. He's brutal. The fat one is Hank. I don't know him that well. Shoot them, honey. Why do you think they're here?

I don't know but they're not here for me. I'll stall them. I'll convince them you don't live here.

Shoot them, Caleb.

Addie, I'm an excon and I'm not going back to jail for a lifetime for shooting two men without just cause.

Caleb—

Take the gun. He held it out to her and this time she received it into her hands. Slip out back. Go around by the trees. Make your way through to the cave. Stay there. Absolutely stay there. I'll come for you when the coast is clear. I'll go right up to the cave and call in to you. Don't shoot me by mistake. Don't shoot me by design either. But listen to me. Shoot anybody else who comes looking.

Caleb—

Do it, Addie.

Caleb—

Go now. Hurry.

She went then. She did not look back. He watched her slip out the back door and shut it quietly behind her. Caleb Farrow stood and moved to the front door. He threw on his plaid hunter's jacket. Outside he merged into the mizzle to greet his guests and he wore a smile.

THESE MEN WERE MEAN COUSINS, Caleb Farrow cautioned himself as he ambled up the boardwalk to the railway grade wearing a grin on his face and a frown upon his forehead intended to mollify. He chose to paint himself as simple and potentially idiotic—a threat to neither intruder nor foe. He strode along the boardwalk and he wondered why he had to be here in this place at this moment and in this circumstance and he contemplated again how that seemed to be his lot. Like clutching fast to stolen furs while the Winnipeg police picked through the coats to find the miscreant at the bottom of the pile or being in the prison barn as calves were led from their stalls for sexual misconduct. Why did he have to be the one on hand to greet these men alone? Why did he have to be the one to arise on this morning as Addie Day's friend and protector when clearly the result was bound to be unpleasant? The two men sauntered down from the tracks in their big boots clinking bits of unseen metal and they met Caleb Farrow at the grade's edge.

Morning, Caleb Farrow said.

We're looking for Addie Day, one of the men said.

This man was in his early twenties and bearded with an impressive girth to him and he bore himself along with a lassitude that suggested he had not been recruited from the hard labouring pool of a logging camp. His clothes fit badly and ill suited the rain—jeans and a denim jacket and Wellington boots and a black undershirt that did not cover the whole of his belly below. The second man was younger still and lean and unshaven with reddish eyes and a ruddy blemished nose and Caleb Farrow feared the wilder look to him and the untamed aspect to his malevolence.

Who? Farrow asked.

Where's she at? the big one wanted to know. Addie Day.

Caleb Farrow spread his arms apart in a kind of benediction and displayed for them the land and the river and the dismal sky and the smoke of one chimney. This is not such a big place that I don't know the people in it. There's no Addie Days here, he said.

The untidy and robust young man closest to him sniffled and wiped his upper lip on the shoulder of his coat. You're lying, he said. I'm about sure of that. God I hate it when folks lie to a fellow human being.

Caleb Farrow feigned offence. There's nobody here by that name. That's all I can tell you. I'm sorry. You're in the wrong place.

So you won't object in other words if we take a look for ourselves?

There's nothing here but open doors, Caleb Farrow told him.

The big man was smirking now and giving him a hostile grimace and Farrow knew from prison days to be wary of the gesture. A threat once implied could not easily be rescinded. He stepped back. The fat man reached out to him and gently rubbed the lapels of Farrow's coat between his thumb and fingers. Is that right? the fat man said.

Hey. Come on. I done time myself. There's nothing here for you.

Where'd you graduate?

Okalla Pen.

Kindergarten.

You been there?

Off and on. Not for awhile. I'm a free man now.

That's good. I'm a citizen myself.

Is that a fact? The man scratched under his beard. I'm not pleased you made me as a con, he said. I'm inclined to take that as an insult.

Caleb Farrow gestured with his arms and stepped back again. The man tugged more firmly on his lapel.

I want you to know you've got no problem here that's all.

The thin one repeatedly looked up and down the tracks like a hungry man in search of a morsel. He stared also at the windows of the cabin and traced the flight of chimney smoke as if that was a clue or the premonition of a clue. The first man turned his head back to the punk kid as though waiting for a command.

Do him, the thin punk kid said.

Hey come on, Caleb Farrow said and he was fearful below his immediate fright.

Don't walk away, the first one said. There is no place to go.

I've got no quarrel with you there pal, Caleb Farrow said.

I got no quarrel with you, the first man said.

So come on. Be cool.

He saw the knife that instant before it was embedded in his gut up to the hilt and both his hands clutched the hand of his killer while the gross man smiled. The intimacy of this union astonished him and he held the hand of his killer and glanced into his eyes and recoiled from the glower and lethargy there and Caleb Farrow stepped back once more and fell and tumbled and the pain struck home and he collapsed from the surprise of it and the woe. He landed on the boardwalk and fell again. His backside toppled onto the sodden fen while his feet rested on the boardwalk as though he had seated himself in a chair knocked backward. Caleb Farrow held his stomach and managed to look and he was dismayed not to find the knife there and merely the medallion of blood that graced his shirt now like a badge of honour from some foreign war.

Rainwater cleansed his face.

Caleb Farrow sensed the men observing him but they were beyond his purview now and beyond his just domain and he had no interest in their mere conceit. Against himself and beyond his own will and comprehension he groaned and clutched himself and groaned again.

He heard the footsteps of the two men travel on to the main house.

Caleb Farrow lay with his back in the swales of grass and water. He had longed for a dry place and now the water welcomed him and he felt himself afloat upon the strands. The sky was stippled with light and in the mirror of the silvery raindrops he watched himself grouse and falter and return to himself again and cry out. Rain bled upon his face and upon his wound and he held his hands fast to keep himself contained. Caleb Farrow dared not observe his wound again. His feet were above him on the boardwalk weighted in his boots and he tried but could not budge them. He lay in the water and felt himself grow liquid and believed to himself that this was the time of his reckoning. His life emerged as exorable to him—undaunted if tainted by the crimes of his hands and the sins of his feet and the failures of his will to refute the inbred mishaps of his wayward desire. One step after the other and hey there pal he was responsible and it was his life and his choice you bet he just never quite understood why he had chosen this or that route or why he had to be forever glued to his errors and why those base transgressions were so magnified now which even he could address in his age and suffering as the protracted whims of an ancient youth. He wanted to speak Addie's name. He wanted to hear the sound of it. He wanted to let her know that he thought of her at a time like this but he dared no further sound. Caleb Farrow saw her spotted amid the stippled light falling as rain upon his eyes.

The men returned.

Quit squirming. You're all right, sweetheart. You ain't had no real harm done to you.

That's what Addie had called him one time—sweetheart—but this was not her voice.

The slobby man stepped off the boardwalk and his big boots splashed down beside Caleb Farrow's brow. He bent low and put a hand under Farrow's head and held his ears above the water.

No harm done, Farrow whispered. In all this rain he had found dryness. His mouth and lungs felt parched and burnt from the inside out.

A needle and thread and you'll be a new man.

I'm bleeding real bad I think, Farrow told the man who placed one hand on his chest and kept the other below his scalp.

That ain't nothin but the rain, sunshine. There ain't no blood at all hardly. You're no bleeder. So tell me where she's at?

Who? Caleb Farrow asked him.

Don't mess with me, boy. Where's our Addie Day?

Farrow was still. He closed his eyes. He was not a man to pray but he requested of powers unseen a quickness to all that must unfold and the endurance to survive unto death.

The man hunched above him now. He tore Farrow's hands away from the wound then used his knife again—this time to rip his shirt.

Farrow opened his eyes. There's nobody here but me, he said very quietly and slowly, and I'm dying. I'm in a bad way. I'm hurting. I don't believe you about my gut. I'm bleeding bad you bet.

The man had things to say and threats to impose and Caleb Farrow was sheltered by a fond disinterest. The means of his dying was less curious to him now than the commotion of this hour. He stared up into the rain that fell upon him as lights with faces and lights with words and lights that soaked him in the moist glean of their reflection. The man quit on him and at the moment of Farrow's release the other boy the thin one pounced down and yelled out in a tongue that raged gibberish and his eyes bloated in the glee of it and the boy gutted his stomach in one swipe and another and Caleb Farrow was borne back into his life a moment and implored his hands to retrieve viscera and entrails that burst from their cavity and he held himself intact and did bay and with the dignity of his form restored he lay down in peace again to feel himself liquefy within a forlorn shape and become a trickle upon the stream of this day. Caleb Farrow let himself slide and he swam outward upon the ruddy flood to evaporate into the high clean air above the hills below the yonder sky.

ADDIE DAY LAY SEQUESTERED in the bleak damp dark of the cave where she had been dispatched by Caleb Farrow and she listened to the outcry of his travail and the distinct quiet of his death. Men so frequently diminished themselves in her sight. She raged at him for failing to open fire and for underestimating her enemies. She hugged the rifle against her chest with the stock butted against the stone between her feet as though it was her one lasting companion and she fought within herself not to weep just yet and not to succumb just yet to the eternal havoc of her remorse.

Addie Day prepared herself. She guided herself to breathe to guard against hyperventilation. The cave which the men so adored was a sticky foul place inhabited by mosses and soaked by the rains washing through the skin of rock. She wiped her eyes clear of tears and obliged herself to focus down the barrel of the gun. The men would come for her. Perhaps she was hidden. Perhaps not. Perhaps footprints in the grass and clay or the nostrils of these creatures would guide them to her hiding place and to the stench of her cavernous fear. Addie Day had learned a lesson in her harder life that now revisited her—no safe hiding place prevailed upon the face of this earth or below its rank crust. When the men arrived and if the men arrived she would be obliged to shoot first and work the bolt and fire again. No second chance. She must not miss. Unlike Caleb Farrow she would not oblige intruders with the time of day. She cleared her eyes and wiped them dry again.

Time expired. In the confines of the cave raw images more grim and agitating did vex her countenance and disfigure her resolve and Addie Day moved most cautiously to the open space. She lay upon her stomach and like a reptile crawled toward the wind. Her eyes adjusted to the brighter dimness of this grim wet day amid the depths of woods. She moved outward and became a twolegged creature again and stepped with great caution and the sound of her footfalls was concealed by the corresponding progress of the wind and rain. Toward the railway grade she saw the two men above walk the tracks. They scanned the forest on one side and on the other the river and she observed that they perused these quarters without expectation of locating her. Addie Day slowly raised her rifle and took aim. She could shoot. One man would fall if her shot was true and that would be a vindication and that would be an act of vengeance sweet enough and fine. The other man would easily be hidden before she fired again and at that instant she would become the hunted and the object of a vengeance more cruel and more cunning than her own.

Addie Day waited.

The men moved onto the bridge.

The opportunity moved as serum through her bloodstream. The second man had less chance to escape and no place to hide except behind the corpse or the wounded writhing body of his partner. Addie Day recalled the sight of Caleb Farrow shivering in his rain clothes and of Reed Kitchen's teeth chattering through his speech. A man being fired upon might easily assume the river to be a lesser evil and that alternate escape created the opportunity for her own demise.

Addie Day was determined not to err. She had no wish to be the author of her own execution here. Imbecilic fate she left to the Caleb

Farrows of this world. She did not shoot the men as they ambled across the bridge although they deserved and required her fire.

She heard the train. The men were alert as well. On the opposite side of the bridge they stepped off the tracks and Addie Day took cognizance that they were disposed on the river's side of the rails. She moved closer to the grade hunched down through the tall grasses and trees. The great train slowed for the bridge as she had known it was obliged to do and from its sound and bearing she determined that here was a train of rare length. The bellicose locomotive bawled by her. Rifle in one hand Addie Day scrabbled up the crushed stone grade. The boxcars rocked and creaked past her and she gave this escape a last rehearsal in her mind then ceased thinking. Her first attempt to catch the ladder on a boxcar failed. Desperate and menaced she slipped. She required both hands. She dropped the rifle and caught hold and pulled herself up onto the ladder and this train carried her towards a greater ardor. Passing the Indian cabins Addie Day looked back. Caleb Farrow lay dressed out upon the earth—his innards outpouring, his throat slit, his mouth yawning to receive the rain and his life awash in blood and damp. Addie Day waited for her erratic breathing to subside then moved to the ladder between cars and there she clasped her life and freedom. The train regained its speed as the caboose passed across the bridge behind and the rain and wind were biting and cold and Addie Day breathed across her fingers to secure her grip upon this frail existence.

She gazed upward at the veil of mists that enveloped mountains.

She looked downward at the blur of ties that passed between her feet.

Her hair and her bluegrey dress whipped behind her like the flags of other nations.

She held on tight and journeyed east.

AMID THE DEADHEADS THAT MARKED the route to the log boom the small and worthy tug guided its load with caution. On the bow Margaret used a cant hook to untie the boom and the tug fell off to port and the logs in its wake followed a straight line into the confining circle of the boom. Ferenc Van Loon eased the logs along with the aid of a peevee and watched them sail into the boom like cattle to a feed stall.

They moored the tug and launched the dinghy and Van Loon rowed.

They landed on the mucky shore and pulled the dinghy high above the tide mark and went on. They stepped over the rails and Margaret then stopped and Ferenc Van Loon went running. First he saw him on his back and believed that he had fallen. He saw the blood and gore and still he did not comprehend and considered accidents and common occurrence. Coming upon him Van Loon did then perceive a glimmer of the savagery his mind was able to behold. He went on running to the first main cabin then to the secondary house in search of Addie Day. He did not find her. He went on through the woods to the cave in tribute to the hour when he and Caleb Farrow had shown her that place and had spoken of the site as a refuge. Wilf came up behind him as Van Loon shouted into the mouth of the cave like a man bellowing down the larynx of God. There was darkness there and there was no sound. Van Loon went in. The walls were moist and there was no sound. He came out and carried on past Wilf and they went on together the short way to the tracks and at the top of the grade Ferenc Van Loon found the rifle.

This is Caleb's, he said.

Maybe you shouldn't touch it like that, Wilf said for Van Loon had bent down and retrieved the weapon. Wilf said, Fingerprints.

Van Loon looked at the rifle and moved it from one hand to the other and back again and imprinted the whole of his hand upon it and he pondered the nature of investigations and inquiry. The gun was loaded and he put the safety catch back on. It's my rifle now, Van Loon said and Wilf looked at him in wonderment and dismay although his face showed no sign.

Van Loon scanned the river. He looked behind him at the mountains concealed by mist and cloud and rain. He looked his companion in the eyes and he told him, They took Addie.

Wilf did not reply.

If she's alive it won't be for long.

Wilf did neither confirm nor deny what he did not know.

Come on, Van Loon instructed him. We've got someplace to go.

III

The
Fraternity
of
Fire

7

THE INFINITE FLAME AFLICKER at the base of the oil stove illuminated bunkcar reflections in the window above Reed Kitchen and repeated the images as etchings on the night air in the window across. He knew or somehow he could sense the train approach and what within him did so respond? Reed Kitchen possessed an uncanny awareness of trains—an anarchy of spirit that he had warned himself was a gift without application. He delegated the trait to a higher faculty that separated him from other men as clearly as obvious attributes separated other men from the wilder beasts. He was aware of trains. Reed Kitchen dug himself out from under the covers and climbed from his pallet and stretched and took his clothes from the empty bed at his feet and dressed and moved to the door to await the locomotive's swift passing.

This would be the snowplough coming.

This would be the train due in the early predawn.

In Prince Rupert in rain country the plough was turned at the roundhouse to face the opposite direction and the train went forth at great speeds to clear tracks east of Kwinitsa where snows commenced along the northern line as along a border to another geography. The plough was affixed to the head of a locomotive and this short train was fast and shoved only snow and pulled only a caboose and he could hear its rumble now and the force of wind and the screaming bellow of displaced air. Reed Kitchen opened the door to herald the train's hard passing. He heard the whistle blow and the light appeared and this train was bulletfast and blasting as it stormed the garrison of Tyee and the bunkcars shook and rollicked and the unlit lamps swayed and the roar put a rattle in the windows and the old lumber creaked and he felt the clout of air as the train rammed past him and Reed Kitchen watched the red lights of the caboose grow faint then vanish beyond a bend of outcropping and pine. Steep silences followed in the wake of a train—a harvest of serenity rich with thought and wonder and the fragments of worry. Reed Kitchen pulled the door shut at the complaint of a sleeper whose nostrils twitched in the cold air and he turned back inside. He lay down fully dressed upon his bed. He looked across the short aisle at the empty pallet there that had belonged to his friend Caleb Farrow and now was home to a ghost of that man's memory. Caleb Farrow was sadly dead. Ferenc Van Loon had vanished off the face of the known planet as had the woman each of them in their affection had dearly loved. Addie Day was gone. Ferenc Van Loon was gone. Caleb Farrow was dead and savage had been that passage. Reed Kitchen was left behind in the storm of their absence to ponder these events. He was wisely sad. On this night the force of the locomotive had proven deficient to awaken answers to his distress from their impenitent slumber.

THE MORNING EASTBOUND PASSENGER TRAIN out of Prince Rupert shuddered and slowed to make the stop at Tyee. Steam expelled from the brakes and the smell of brakeshoes rubbed raw and oil and grease blew upon the men of B & B Gang 4 who gathered by the mail car where it halted. Supplies had been dispatched for Ruby Lake's kitchen and the men took cognizance of what had been dispatched. They piled the supplies high by the side of the track. Reed Kitchen was the first to see a man get off well down the train and walk towards them. He carried a travelling bag. The man smoked and the locomotive belched a thicker pall and the train was underway and the men waited for it to clear before carting the groceries on up to the pantry under Ruby Lake's exacting regard. Reed Kitchen did not move. He concentrated on the man's approach.

Know him? Kai Jensen asked.

I do, Reed Kitchen said.

Who is he?

He'll tell you.

When the man came forward he held out his hand to Kai Jensen and Reed Kitchen stood beside his foreman ignoring the complaints of his fellow workers.

How do you do? the man asked of them.

Hello, Kai Jensen said. He wore his pixie grin and his smile was awonk with wariness.

Hello, Reed, the man said.

Reed Kitchen nodded.

The man told the foreman, My name is Don McBain. I suppose Reed has told you who I am.

I said nothing to nobody about that, Reed Kitchen said.

He's been a quiet man lately, Kai Jensen pointed out. Relatively speaking. He looked at the man and waited for him to explain himself.

Railway Police, the new arrival said.

That I figured, Kai Jensen said.

I'll be staying awhile.

I figured that too. I made a bed up.

I have a few questions.

You're bunking with me, McBain. Today's you're lucky day. We got two less mouths on the payroll so you might actually get fed.

That's reassuring, Don McBain said.

We had the real police out here more than once already, Reed Kitchen told him.

I'd like to talk to you first, Yellowhead Don McBain said.

Kai Jensen picked up the detective's tote and turned toward his bunkcar. I need him on the bridge, he said over his shoulder. You want to talk to him you got to come out to the bridge with the rest of us. I can't spare the loss of one more good man.

On the bridge Yellowhead Don McBain was a man out of place.

His trenchcoat afforded scant protection from the harder rains and
the wet seeped around his collar. His hat drooped. He walked with his
hands in his pockets and his shoulders hunched and he strolled from
one end of the bridge and back again as though he had arrived to
inspect the work and a few men believed it to be so. Reed Kitchen
laboured beneath the deck where he was free from inquisition. He sat
away from Yellowhead Don McBain on the speeder's trek back to
Tyee for lunch and while he was washing up the visitor pursued him
into his bunkcar to have a talk.

You've been avoiding me, Yellowhead Don McBain declared.

I been doing my job. You got a problem with that?

We have to talk.

That's where this got started. With you talking and me listening and
that is something that should not be. It's against the laws of nature.

Fine. You talk. I'll listen.

Caleb Farrow is a dead man.

That's not my fault.

Dino Pratolini pushed between them and departed the bunkcar for
lunch. He seemed anxious to get away as though what they had to
talk about might prove lethal.

Don't I get to eat? Reed Kitchen asked.

Let's talk first. You do the talking. Tell me what you know.

I know you put your nose where it does not rightfully belong and
now a friend of mine has journeyed to his grave.

Van Loon killed him.

I do not believe that.

The police believe it.

They believe wrong.

You have no quarrel with me, Reed. If you want the truth to be
known I'm the best hope you've got.

Maybe I have no hope at all. Now you want to solve great crimes of
passion or of vengeance or of cruelty. Why can't you do what you were
hired to do? Investigate pilfering and foul language on trains. Satisfy
yourself with that. I am sure that such investigations will accommodate
your expertise.

Very funny. Tell me where Van Loon is.

I do not know.

We know Van Loon and Farrow had a girl down at the Green River cabins. The Indians told us. We learned she slept with both of them. Did you know that?

That I did not know.

What didn't you know? That she was there or who she was sleeping with?

Her companions by night.

So you see? They had a lover's spat. Farrow is dead and Van Loon ran off with the woman. It's cut and dried as far as the Mounties are concerned. When they find them we'll know for sure.

I hope you do find them, Reed Kitchen said.

Do you?

Then we will know for sure they are alive.

Why wouldn't they be? McBain sat down on a empty bunk and tossed his sodden hat beside him.

The girl knows things. She knows things about The Sip.

How does she know things? What does she know?

Things I would not repeat she knows.

So there's another possibility.

There is. Yes. Always.

You believe The Sip was here. Or his men. You believe they killed Farrow—and the girl and Van Loon as well?

I do not want to believe this thing. But I will believe this thing before I believe that Van Loon killed his friend Caleb. I know and everybody here knows that such a thing is not possible. Even when we read it in the newspapers we still do not believe this thing.

With crimes of passion anything's possible.

If Van Loon killed Caleb why did he not leave with his own good truck? Why has he left his truck behind? Not to mention his clothes and his worldly possessions. They are still here or they were until the Mounties unjustly removed them. Still at the Indian cabins also are the clothes and the worldly possessions of the woman.

That's a good question.

Yes it is a good question.

What's your theory?

I'm hungry. I want to eat. That's my theory.

I have something to tell you, Reed.

Tell it fast.

Reed, Yellowhead Don McBain said and he picked up his mis-shapen hat again and turned it around in his hands. Something has been discovered. He looked up.

You have always been a beat-around-the-busher, Reed Kitchen complained.

Straight to the point then. Bones. We've found bones. They were located in the place where you grew up. The siding in North Ontario where you were raised. One set would be bad enough, Reed. Two sets is suspicious. We believe one set belongs to a man hit by a train. The force of the collision was immense. The other set belongs to a woman—also hit by a train but not at the same time or in the same year forensics tells us. Can you shed any light on the subject?

You did not just discover these bones.

Didn't we?

Why would you make me a spy upon this gang and a spy upon The Sip when you could have had Caleb Farrow—a fine young man who wanted to be a citizen and who would bring to the job an excellent criminal background? You had plenty on him. A man like you with your ambition would not waste a chance like that. You made him your spy and you made me a spy on him at the same time that he was made a spy on me.

McBain turned the hat around in his hands and thought about reaching for his cigarettes. You and Caleb talked about this?

In our way. So what I have said to Caleb Farrow about the death of my father and what he told you cannot be believed.

But the story exonerates you.

You cannot believe it. Because I knew when I was telling that story that I was speaking to you. It was not you I wanted to hear that story. It was Caleb Farrow. He was my friend. I wanted him to know that whatever lies you might have told him about me should not be given an ear. We have our lives and we have our work and you come to us and interfere with those good lives and our own good work. You are a cruel and unworthy man to take away the enjoyment of our lives for no other reason than to pretend to be a real policeman like the others. Go away from here, Yellowhead Don McBain. There is no work for you in a place like this. Let the real policemen hunt for killers without your help which surely they must call a hinderance.

Yellowhead Don McBain put on his hat and indicated that he was about to depart. He grimaced in his kindly fashion and practised a frown and momentarily he volunteered a smile. Nevertheless, he said. We are closing the case on you, Reed. Your father's death and your mother's will be recorded as separate accidents.

Something that they were not.

They weren't separate accidents?

They were separate. They weren't accidents.

That's the end of it. There will be no further investigation.

There will never be an end to it. It surely will not end because you say so.

Let's go to lunch, Reed. We still have a deal you and me. I hope you haven't forgotten. We still have our business to accomplish.

I have not forgotten. I look forward to that business. I have a grievance with The Sip that grows with each passing day.

Then let's eat. I'm hanging around awhile. I have other men to talk to besides you.

That's a shame, Yellowhead. Nothing at all good happens when you come around talking your sly talk among us.

RAIN SLUED FIERCE TO DRIZZLY DAYS IN days out as winter ascended to the equinox. Augmented with fresh recruits B & B Gang 4 persevered on the bridge and within the frame of the old the structure of the new grew apparent. Steel spans had been hauled in by freight train and deposited by the mainline and lay as a shock of orange along the riverbank. When tide and circumstance ordained the men carried their lunches with them to the bridge. Reed Kitchen chose to take his break in the Indian cabins with Wilf and Margaret.

The one thing I have always admired about Indians is their silence in the face of my speech. I am free to talk among many Indians and they have honoured me with the intensity of their disposition. It's almost like you're listening. Most people do not honour me in such a way. This is one time I wish you were not that way. This is one time I wish that you'd blow me down with chatter and I was the one obliged to sit here dumb and listening. What can I wish for in this land but the chance to see what happened on that fateful day and Wilf—I know you were out to sea—I know you were on the river and I must say that that is a good place to be when trouble erupts. Had you been here then you might not be here now to tell the story but you are here now and yet you are not telling the story. I guess that means you were not here then. What happened? That's all a poor boy would like to discern. What happened. It does vex me. It's a trouble I have not known in this lifetime—the loss of a friend and the accusation of another in the wrongdoing. How I wish you could've been a witness, Wilf. That you were able and also willing to relate to me exactly what occurred. But you were on the river gathering your logs so what can ever be known about this affair? This is what I find so vexing. I wish that you could speak to me, Wilf, in a trusting voice. I wish that you could shut me up with the force of your unbridled chatter. Instead you listen and while you listen I must flood that silence with my talk for the pain of the silence I must fill is too much for this faint heart to endure.

Wilf stared back into the eyes of Reed Kitchen and spoke not a word. The marks on his face and the maze of contours and lines weathered by rain and salt air and wind gazed back at Reed Kitchen with the impassivity of a river or a sky and in the dour folds of shadow within the cabin he did believe that he could be looking upon the darker more solemn mists that roved the high mountains. K'shian. The River of Mists. This man was Tsimshian—of a people named for their river.

What I most wonder about is this, Reed Kitchen said. You are not a talking man. And yet you have said to the Mounties that Caleb Farrow and Ferenc Van Loon both enjoyed the attentions of our Addie Day in the nights of their lives. I wonder why you would say this thing. You would say it because it was true but there are many things

that are true of which you say nothing at all. Why this thing? You
would say it because Caleb Farrow lay dead upon your walk and you
are obliged to account for yourself—but why point the finger at Van
Loon? Unless you know that that is where the finger most ought to be
pointed? Or because you have another reason. The reason you have
said this thing is more odd to me and more interesting than the thing
that you have actually said. Do you understand me, Wilf?

Wilf nodded to indicate his comprehension and gave his chin a
scratch and then his arthritic right hip.

Oh, Wilf, I do not know if you are my best listener or my worst.
Am I better off with those who beat me back with their acrimonious
verbiage or is your silence the excellent accommodation for my
excess? I do not know. Like many things I do not know. But I want
you to know this. I am aware of my obligations. What I wonder is this.
When my obligations have been discharged—will we talk then? Will
you tell me then what I do not know now? Wilf? Will you?

Wilf scratched. He chuckled to himself. He shook his head. He
told Reed Kitchen that he was the strangest white man he had known
and Reed Kitchen thanked him for that high praise and Wilf laughed
a whole lot more.

A pall as constant as the rains settled upon the men of B & B Gang
4 and upon their labours. They worked with efficiency and aggressively applied themselves to bolting a new superstructure and backfill-
ing the rebuilt dumpwalls and driving the rest of the piles and laying
the caprails upon them. Much of the labour became the obligation of
Reed Kitchen and Kai Jensen who performed the more skilled duties
and Kai was alert to the temper of his bridgeman knowing how necessary he had become.

You don't ever think about leaving here do you, Reed? Kai asked
him on the scaffolding under the deck of the bridge while they
awaited a train's progress across it. I don't know what I would do without you.

I have my obligations, Reed Kitchen said.

What are those? the foreman asked him but his best worker would
not reply directly.

Train, Reed Kitchen said and they waited and soon the freight travelled above their heads and they craned their necks to look up at the undercarriage and at the wheels and at the timbers that danced below the burden. They moved in unison to the promenade of the timbers and Kai Jensen and Reed Kitchen bobbed up and down.

I have my obligations was all that Reed Kitchen would ever intimate in reference to his plans and Kai Jensen could only hope that the constituency of his devotion included the construction of the Hardhearted River Bridge.

You gave this bridge the right name, Kai Jensen told him.

I did not want it to be a prophetic name, Reed Kitchen said. I did not desire that.

The discerning day would come and it was a more foul rain and wind that greeted them upon the bridge. The men waited for the crossing of the morning passenger train and from that moment the track was closed to the east and to the west and no train would travel and the Wellman Crane voyaged out from Tyee. They worked with alacrity and with disdain ripping apart the old bridge and cutting the timbers free and the crane fetched the old wood away from the bridge and piled it high betwixt the tracks and the river. Their work was boisterous and exultant and the crane continuously returned and cables were attached and the winches were wound and the timbers were wrenched from the wreck of the old trestle. Ancient pilings were cut at the knees and taken away. The old ribs and crossing braces and topping beams were harvested and threshed upon the side of the track. By late afternoon the old bridge had been gutted and the new looked insignificant so far below the level of the grade. They inserted and bolted home the cross braces they'd been unable to connect amid the timbers of the old bridge. Then the great steel spans were hoisted aloft and this was the moment of calamity or of grace to determine if they fit.

They fit. The spans settled upon the bridge that the men had constructed with their own bare hands and the spans fit one to the other snugly and new ties and new track were hauled and placed upon the bridge and they worked on into the dusk of that day with the lights of the Wellman Crane and the lights of the first freight that would ferry

across the new bridge illuminating their progress. In the swirl of rain
that whipped around his face Reed Kitchen looked up into the bright
eye beam of the next freight and he knew in his blood and moiling
that the time of an obligation had emerged and he went on down to
the Wellman Crane and directed it as he had been directing it all day
long and he moved the crane back to the pile of debris strewn and
stacked between the railway tracks and the Skeena. He raised an arm
high in the light of the stationary freight and he would appear to be
waving into the darkness there and Kai Jensen saw that movement
and did not consider the coincidence of a fishboat getting underway
at the same time. He ignored Reed Kitchen's arm. He turned back to
his own endeavours and then spun around at the sound of the ruckus
and uproar and Reed Kitchen was continuing to provide the circulat-
ing movement above his head to command the crane to continue lift-
ing. As the cables were pulled high the stack of timbers catapulted
into the Skeena River and soon they were upon that tide and Kai ran
in the ample dark to Reed Kitchen's side and cursed him out and told
him, I'm supposed to save those timbers.

We have built our bridge and that is your obligation and mine also.
The timbers have fallen by an accident caused by my weariness and
exhaustion into the Skeena River where a salvaging man has found
them. He has a licence. The falling of the timbers was an accident,
Kai. A mistake of mine. But it does fulfil an obligation that I made.

Talk plain English, Reed. What are you up to here?

Plain English? Plain English. All right. I'll try. The railroad in all
its wisdom and in all its avarice does not truly need those old timbers
except to sell as surplus.

That's not our lookout.

This man who is scrounging upon this river has the greater right. I
have a debt to him for his hospitality. We have a debt to him ourselves because he is the man beside the river and he will be here after
we are gone and if we are not to be forgotten then he must be the one
who remembers. Myself personally I made promises that perhaps I
should not have made but I do believe that definitely I should keep
them.

You made a deal with that old Indian.

Now that the deal has been fulfilled we will find out if anything will change.

Plain English, Reed.

If I told you in plain Danish you would not believe me.

They worked on into the later night—the men of B & B Gang 4 and the section crew from Tyee. They laboured and they tamped the ties leading onto the bridge and they studied their final result and the engineer climbed to his post and the freight headed slowly slowly slowly across the new bridge. The crane backed away before it and the freight kept coming and the men watched and the conductor of the train watched as the freight crossed in safety and in rhythm and the boxcars chased each other past him and he leapt aboard the moving caboose and waved to the men who did not cheer themselves but in their hearts they were well pleased amid the welter of their weariness. The speeder followed the train on into Tyee and the men disembarked and clambered into their bunkcars to prepare for a gracious meal.

They had built their bridge. They had completed their task. Now they would eat and after they were fed they would lie themselves down and they would sleep. Among them only Reed Kitchen would stay awake and flag down the first westbound freight and mollify the engineer and hitch a ride back to the bridge to walk upon it in the night under the wonder of a peekaboo moon and after he had walked his bridge and climbed amid the girders and beams and scaled the steel span to the deck he would stroll on back to the Indian cabins to have a heart to heart with Wilf who had done so well for himself that day beachcombing timbers.

AT BREAKFAST THE MOOD OF THE MEN had improved owing to the modest sun and a dryness to the air. The wind blew warm. Mists had vanished and clouds scuttled across the sky in flight from a braver front. Reed Kitchen stood above the jigsaw puzzle and gazed down upon it and he did not move a piece into its anointed place. Kai Jensen came through the door from his bunkcar. I didn't know you had an aunt, he said. You told us you were out of family.

I don't have an aunt, Reed Kitchen replied in glazed stupor. Wildflowers bloomed across the foreground of the meadow and trees in the distance flashed green. The gaping wound at the inner circle of the puzzle had steadily healed. Reed Kitchen studied the puzzle and said no word. He had not slept. He had walked down from the Green River cabins and coldshowered in the washcar and he was thinking afresh and he was pondering.

I got a call on the radio that says you do, Kai Jensen told him.

Reed Kitchen looked up. Unless she's dying, he said. Then I do. The only aunt I might have is the one who's dying.

That's what I was told, the foreman said. Your aunt's dying.

Then I have an aunt for sure.

What's going on here?

There is a time that's come, Reed Kitchen said.

I guess it happens to us all, Kai Jensen said.

Kitchen gazed at the puzzle. I wish I dwelled in a place like this where the sun shines daily and the flowers grow, he said. That would be a wonderment to me today.

REED KITCHEN SADDLED HIS FEAR with a leathery expectation and clutched fast to the reins of his resolve. The Sip had demanded more of him than Yellowhead Don McBain had foretold. Reed Kitchen stated that he had expected nothing less after his own hindsight had mulled things over.

What? Yellowhead Don McBain asked.

He wants me to have my knowledge of him, Reed Kitchen explained.

That makes no sense, McBain said.

He wants me to know things. So that I will fear him. That's his way.

We'll turn that quirk against him.

We will try.

The Sip insisted that Reed Kitchen not restrict himself to parleying the numbers of boxcars and arranging to have those cars removed to the east. He demanded that Kitchen participate fully in the transport of alien citizens. It's no crime to give a man the numbers for a couple of boxcars, The Sip had told Reed Kitchen.

That's right. There is no crime in that.

So I can't trust you. You want to work for me, sweetheart, you dirty your hands.

Then I will be an unclean criminal in good standing.

You could say that. Then we can trust each other.

You want to corrupt me, Reed Kitchen told him. That is your way.

The Sip had chortled and he had laughed and he had rubbed his nose with a knuckle. I want you on side, he said. That's all that counts with me.

Then I will cross that line, Reed Kitchen said, and be on that side.

You better believe it, The Sip said.

I do believe it, Reed Kitchen said. Because I do believe that I have no choice.

You're a smart man.

Thank you for your kindly courtesies.

Now shut your face. I'm sick of how you talk. I'm sick of the way you look.

I never told you I was a handsome man. I have not misrepresented myself to you. I never put down on my resume that I have good looks.

The Sip moved closer so that the hair that sprouted about his collar and neckline tickled the buttons on Reed Kitchen's shirt. He had a square head and a flat face and the physique of a bear that made his words credible in this circumstance. You shut up when I tell you to shut up or you won't be talking for long, he said.

I shall accept your remonstration as my wise counsel.

What?

I shall accept—

Shut up. Sit down. And be quiet.

I'll do that, Reed Kitchen said. I shall behave myself here today.

You always want the last word.

The first word and the last one and most of those in between, Reed Kitchen warned him. It's my way.

On the morning of his eventful day Reed Kitchen took a cab down to the floating colony at Port Edward where he was greeted by the man called Tiny who had named him Jabbermouth and who escorted him into an anteroom where he waited. He remained in that uncomfortable gloom and mustiness and rocked gently on the waves until a man he did not know fetched him out of there. This fellow was young but not youthful and his skin was blemished and his eyes had the glint of bone and he said to Reed Kitchen, Shake a leg. We're outta here.

Reed Kitchen boarded a vessel that was a converted tug of the style popular in these waters to combat the high seas of the Pacific Northwest in winter. I am not a seafaring man, Reed Kitchen told his mates and they ignored him and he said, I do not have what I have heard are called sealegs. I am not an octopus man. I have my good balance on bridges and trains but upon the waves that is a different thing. I believe a man can walk upon the water but I lose my faith when I am asked to believe that a man can walk upon a stormtossed sea and not get sick.

Get on, the fierce young fellow said and Reed Kitchen was not willing to disobey him for long. He clambered aboard and other men worked the docklines and other men guided the vessel and Reed Kitchen stepped inside the cabin where The Sip turned in his swivel seat and told him, Get outta here. You stay on deck, Jabber.

What has been done cannot be undone. What cannot be undone will be done. What will be done will be done. I will be done with you.

If he says another word, The Sip said to his companions, shoot him.

Reed Kitchen remained on the afterdeck in the skelter of the rain and the wind untethered by trees and mountains and they departed the land and dwelled upon the sea which rolled and lifted and subsided. The hours passed. In the rain and under the mists and in the emerging fog the small vessel encountered a large dragger and Reed Kitchen was transferred onto a liferaft and he gripped the gunwales with the whole of his strength in fear and grave destitution. For this is the place where I have come and it is like no place at all but a lifeline the fates may slice or splice at their whim. The liferaft was hauled aboard the dragger and Reed Kitchen and The Sip and the young hellion were winging in the air above the tempest of the seas and the liferaft banged against the topsides of the ship and aboard the larger vessel that rolled and bounded in the waves Reed Kitchen staggered to the rail and leaned across it to deliver his innards upon an abiding sea. The other men laughed. They were amused by his jaundiced skin.

He slumped upon that deck beneath the intricate and rusting tackle and he remained outside the wheelhouse on this ship also like a dog dispatched from the company of humans. Reed Kitchen wondered if this was a day that he might survive or if this was a day that had been visited upon Caleb Farrow and visited upon the young girl Addie had told about who had been set adrift upon the ice only to shimmy off that ice in her shame and loathing and abject pain into the sure and final sanctity of the sea. He could well believe that here he was a witness and if he was a witness to this criminal detail The Sip might choose to jettison him as easily as he had himself cast his meal upon the gruel of the waters. His illness made him ache and his head spun and the sickness churned Reed Kitchen into a besotted and wretched fester of malaise. The pitch of the deck rose up to the ashen sky with stress and straining and collapsed against the black of the sea in a clamouring ferment and his innards heaved in sympathetic rhythm and moments abounded and longer spells endured when death for Reed Kitchen seemed a merciful solution.

In the long afternoon of that day the dragger agitated onward through high seas and the great bow rammed waves and the spray flayed the deck and Reed Kitchen upon it and the bow raised itself upward to the clouds and sallied forth toward waters more grim forever onward and ahead. Out of that woeful disposition a ship emerged and Reed Kitchen hung himself on a suspended net and held himself upright to observe the ship's approach. Men were in movement on the deck now and he observed the ship and the two boats bopped in proximity one to the other and Reed Kitchen could see the people amass upon the deck. I have come to the ends of the earth, he told a deckhand near him, and what is it that I find? There are people here off the end of that earth scrambling to climb back upon it. What is

the end to me is the beginning to these poor souls and I'm sorely confused and afraid standing here today.

Shut your face, the deckhand said and he described him as a body
part and would say no more.

Reed Kitchen spoke instead to the alien people as they came
aboard. Their lifeboats were lashed to a line between the two vessels
and he helped these frail creatures climb aboard and he welcomed
them with formality and consideration. For we are not lost at sea or
lost upon the waters of our rebuke—for we are friends who are among
friends who will carry us back to shore. There lies waiting there a train
of high regard to bear you across this land. I envy you that journey by
train—a train fuelled by the spirit of your suffering and bound for the
glory of your days and I do wish you well along the journey of your way.

The men and the women and the children held his hand as they
came aboard and listened to his speechmaking and they were relieved
and refreshed by the bark of belligerent voices that interpreted his
greeting and commanded them to squat upon the deck with their
heads down and the boat was fully loaded now with a human catch
and the dragger turned and slid upon the waters to be borne ashore by
the contentious disposition of its diesels and the driving rain and a
lofty wind.

After nightfall they were met again by the small tug which had ini-
tially carried them forth and Reed Kitchen was set to move from one
boat to the other when The Sip ordered him to stay put and he
remained with the refugees upon the high sea and upchucked unceasingly over the aft rail and the travellers reproved him for he was soiled
and he was sodden and he was as impoverished as they and he was
also abandoned to the rain and to the wind and to the flail of spindrift
in flight across his face.

He stayed on through the night sick and woeful was his discourse
through the darker hours. His voice was wretched in the swirl of chatter and he thought poorly of himself and of their chances and those
who observed him assumed that his panegyrical raving was the pre-
liminary sign of a man who had lost an ability to be sane. Yet Reed
Kitchen was the first among them to notice the darker ridge of the

night which would be the mountain range of the continent and he was the first to announce that the waters were more quiet which would be the river basin and he was the first to pick out the coded flash of lights ashore which would be the message to land at a secret spit and embark upon their next brave journey. The dragger did indeed make for shore and moor and small boats ferried the survivors of this ordeal to a hidden dock and Reed Kitchen was among those who rowed. The Sip greeted him carrying a flashlight and a rifle as the people were herded into the enclosed box of a truck.

You're a mess, The Sip said.

I do believe that you wanted me this way. I am a wretched creature here today and I do hope no one who knows me will catch sight of me in such disrepair.

Get in, The Sip said.

In back? Reed Kitchen felt dismay.

Stink like you don't ride with me.

I did have my hopes at one time. But they are dashed now that's true.

The rear door was shut and bolted behind them and they lived in blackness now with the sounds of their whispers and their sighs their only company and they breathed the air one another expelled and one man lit a match and the faces around the flame did glower like spirits from beyond this realm. The blackness was a fearful thing for children and the truck jounced on an unpaved road and the springs of the rear wheels screaked as did the voices of their own apprehensive hearts. Reed Kitchen spoke his words into that moving dark and at times the welter of human shadow moved away from him and at times it was attracted and conversation in opposing tongues swelled amid the bedlam. His words were intended to transpose the temper of their fret and vilify their transgressors and marshall their morale in line with their evident courage. Reed Kitchen's words were less meaningful than his tone and his tone travailed against the grisly excursion of this darkness and its proprietary fear.

To cross the sea you had to cross a line in your mind and in your judgment and my friend Van Loon is a man like that. He has crossed seas and now he wants to cross a line from which there is no return.

He is a man come back to the wild whose heart is brave and virtuous and his suffering grievous. I wish to cross a line also. Into the human realm. For it is there that I wish to abide but those who would have me would corrupt me and that has always been so. That is my dismay.

They travelled on by truck and it did stop and the back door was shunted upward and the dawn blossomed on their day. The skies had brightened. The rain had ceased and the cloudcover lifted to a higher plateau and the darkeyed men and women looked about them and Reed Kitchen also felt glad and forgiven to have his feet upon this steadfast earth.

He walked with The Sip toward the place where the boxcars waited and the horde of refugees gathered in behind them worried and expectant and Reed Kitchen said beyond his comprehension why, Train, he said, Train, and when the shot rang out he walked on with his head rotated in the direction of the fire and only when he heard the commotion and panic of the throng behind him did he turn to comprehend that The Sip had fallen. The man who had walked beside him knelt in sad rebuke upon the ground shocked by a bullet through his right arm.

There was outcry and there was ferment and the boy who was often with The Sip who had a blemished nose and a rancorous spirit squatted low beside his boss and withdrew his pistol and searched in the direction where the sound had echoed and decayed. Reed Kitchen walked back the four steps and he did not duck as all others had done and he stood beside The Sip and gazed sorely upon him.

What did you do to Addie Day? Reed Kitchen asked the man who had dropped his head to examine the wound's boil. He shot a wild glance up at him and this was the look of a man not mindful of his pain.

You bastard. Shoot him, Wart. Shoot the runt shit.

In the midst of the melee Wart looked around wildeyed as the aliens huddled and no more shots were fired but he was disinclined to shoot Reed Kitchen before this field of witnesses like shrubs wild and attentive in their dread.

What did you do to Addie Day? Is she walking among us or is she dead?

Shoot him, you—!

The Sip's other shoulder jolted back and twisted to the ground and the pain on his face was instantaneous and surfeit and the bark of the shot followed. His torso rebounded from the coil and recoil of the second wound and now two red badges had been pinned upon him. The Sip remained in a slump upon his knees. The boy called Wart had run and with him the throng did suddenly disperse. In every direction the people scattered and clasped their children and bundles to their sides convinced that the first and the second shots of many had been fired and convinced that they had arrived here to drown in their own blood upon this soil. The men and women and children fled in haphazard directions where men with guns appeared and the people turned like birds in flight and ran off at another tangent until that way too presented a barricade. The people in their flight realized that every access to freedom and release was blocked and the human tide around them arose like the sea.

The Sip was breathing rapidly and his lips were flared and he crossed his arms in deference to his wounds and through his teeth he declared, She's whale food. We cut the bitch and drowned her.

The forehead of The Sip fractured and whipped and bone and brain spit from the back of his head and a small black crater marked the moment of his dying before blood issued to fill that cavity and he toppled over to one side and down.

Reed Kitchen stood above the prone body of The Sip and he said to that body, This should keep, and the blood of the wound seeped outward at his feet. He said to the corpse, Caleb Farrow—he was a friend of mine.

The refugees were encircled and ensnared and most were caught in the same web as the men who worked for The Sip who had mysteriously disarmed themselves and claimed no involvement in wayward migrations. Yellowhead Don McBain shouted above the throng of aliens and policemen, Who fired the shots? Who shot? and no officer of the Railway Police or of the Mounted Police would step forward to receive his merit. One Mountie claimed that the shot had come from the hills behind and this was confirmed by others and they concluded after cursory inspection of weapons that no police bullet had been fired although many had been aimed. McBain pushed through the melee to reach Reed Kitchen and said, Maybe we can exonerate him for Caleb Farrow but this is something we don't let pass. Hear me? We don't let this pass.

You are jumping to a conclusion here, Reed Kitchen warned him. I would not just say that you are jumping. I would say that you are leaping across a great divide with both feet forward.

Don't bullshit me. I'm not in the mood. I don't give a damn who the victim is—no way in this world will your buddy get off. Of all the stupid bullshit things to do. Tell me something, Reed—don't give me none of your crap. How'd he know The Sip would be here this morning? You had to be in on this, Reed. Tell me you sonofabitch. You were in on this. You're an accessory.

Reed Kitchen examined the far hill where he had heard the weapon fire and he looked again upon the lump of death at his feet and he said to Yellowhead Don McBain in a voice that was both plaintive and wise, This is the thing that has been done.

What?

I do believe that you may have heard me. This is the thing that has been done here today.

Yellowhead Don McBain nodded and flexed the muscles of his neck and under his chin. Let me tell you something, Reed. I'm not done with you yet. You and me—we're not finished.

That I don't believe, Reed Kitchen said. He looked into the eyes of his mentor and his archenemy and he said, I do believe that we are done. I do believe that this is finished here. I do believe that this is the thing that has been done and it cannot be undone by you or by me for all the sorrowfulness in this land.

I'll have your balls for breakfast.

You used to be a friendly man, Yellowhead Don. I do not like you but I shall miss our courteous conversations.

The two men turned as their attention was drawn to the plaintive outcry of a refugee. The woman bawled and her man held her and the people fixed their attention upon Reed Kitchen. They waited for him to resolve this dispute. They waited for him to greet them now that they were ensconced upon hard land. They gazed upon him as the one who had administered the last rites to the man responsible for their wellbeing and who now stood among these others as neither a man arrested and in cuffs nor a man of authority with a weapon. Reed Kitchen moved among them. He spoke in a language they did not comprehend and in a voice that confounded those who did possess knowledge of his tongue. They accepted his tone. The sound of his voice calmed them and bequeathed expectation. The sound of his voice was a music amid the rancour of their arrival that the mettle of the police could not dispatch. He moved among them and at once— miraculously—they conversed. Welcome, he said, to the hour of your great despair. For you have been delivered from the hands of evil into the grip of authority—out of the frying pan and into the fire—and never has a gentle saying contained more truth. Welcome. Welcome. Welcome. To the day of your sad reckoning. Welcome, people, to the ends of your earth. Look around you. This is where you are.

The alien citizens raised themselves up and invigorated themselves with a blessed gale of chatter in another voice and in another tongue.

8

THE JIGSAW PUZZLE ARRAYED at the far end of the table showed splotches of wildflowers and a bridge of grassland and the bark of trees proliferate and disconnected within the maze. Spurred on by cigarettes and coffee Kai Jensen persevered and endeavoured to position a tatter of greenery under the coaloil light. Ruby Lake sat on the bench beside him at the weary end of her day and smoked as well and drank less coffee and catalogued mild complaints. Summer had come but the pall of winter had yet to be forsaken.

Kai found the place for the jigsaw piece and attached it to a limb right under his nose. Eureka, he said.

Ruby Lake arose from the table and carried her mug to the sink and absently rinsed it out and placed it on the dishrack. Catching the eye of her reflection in the window Ruby reached up under her chin and stretched the skin of her neck taut then ran the hand through her hair. She touched the shoulder that ached. She gazed in the window at the melancholy of her days and wondered where her children had travelled and did they think of her often or at all. Her husband had died too young. She rubbed her cheeks and lifted her chin and Ruby Lake did not recognize the texture of her skin under the touch of her own fingers. The one thing she had always thought she would hate more than growing old and alone without a home was growing old and alone and foolish besides. She was thinking differently now. She was hating foolishness less now.

Okay, she said. She looked at Kai Jensen and the diminutive Dane was pensive and eager and bent over the puzzle and there had been an era in her life when she had had a cleaning lady in the house and three yappy kids and this time she spoke louder. Okay.

Kai did not look up and moved his body as if feinting with his own shadow that stretched across the table diminishing his view. He said, What's okay?

Okay, she said quietly without emphasis.

Kai looked at her where she stood by the stove. Okay what?

Okay okay.

Kai Jensen put down the pieces of the puzzle he had palmed and lifted his legs out from the bench. He moved towards her and butted his cigarette in an ashtray at the near end of the table. He reached her and placed both hands on her shoulders and he smiled with that pixie wonky grin of his and feeling as old as the Coastal Mountains she placed her ancient hands around the small of his back and they embraced and he was so tiny in her arms and solid as a titan—a wee weary titan—and she whispered to him, Go back.

What? Kai whispered in return and his breath was on her ear.

Turn out the lights.

She watched him go to the far end of the car and lift a coaloil lamp free from its holder and cup one hand against the back of the glass rim and blow hard and that light was out and she watched him do it again and that light was out and he returned to her from the darkness and Ruby Lake lifted the globe of the lamp above the sink and she blew once—hard—and the world was ever dark and a shape emerged from that black rivery zone to cradle her in his arms and she turned with him toward the pantry where they moved through an invisible buffer with only the flames of the kerosene fridges burning at their ankles and they stepped beyond the scents of flour and lard and fragrant potatoes into the place where she slept and Ruby Lake undressed in the graciousness of that omnipotent dark and she listened to him undressing and his skin was suddenly light and tingly against hers and much of this was the shock of recognition and much of this was company and old loss and much of this was memory on a night where sadnesses rained with intermittent velocities upon the windows of her room.

Later they lay entangled and he roused her with the fret of his sleep.

What's wrong? She soothed his brow.

He sighed.

You've been muttering to yourself all night.

Again he sighed. They're coming for Reed in the morning.

What do you mean—coming for Reed?

It was bound to happen. I put them off as long as I needed him. But the bridge is built. I wouldn't do their dirty work I said. If they want him canned they got to come here and do it themselves.

They're firing Reed?

They've got some gripe against him.

She was on her knees and shoving Kai Jensen out of bed. Go, she said. Tell him now.

Kai bounced off the floor. There's nothing he can do about it, Ruby. It's the middle of the night.

He can damn well quit. He can damn well deny them the satisfaction.

Her words were stern and somehow victorious as Kai stood on one leg and pulled on a sock. He had not wanted to be the one to break Reed Kitchen's heart but he had already agreed that this might be the better way.

Go, Ruby said. Now.

ON THE MAIN STREET OF PRINCE GEORGE Reed Kitchen swung his gunnysack down upon the planked sidewalk and observed the dusty moil of human congestion. He had spent the night in a cheap hotel and that had been a time. Wayfarers had tried the knob on his door in the wee hours and he had been awake to detect their failed entry. Women sold their pleasures on the streets and in the beer parlours and hordes of men who worked in camps and mills ardently subscribed. Fistfights and knifefights were as common as spilt drink and a wild lad with whom he had peaceably been chatting informed him that his name was Boog and for no apparent reason smashed a beer bottle against the wall and held the jagged edge to Kitchen's cheek and demanded that he shut up.

You got to break that bottle hitting the end straight on, Reed Kitchen tutored his assailant. Hitting crossways like that as you can plainly see cuts your hand.

The youth dribbled blood onto the floor of the beer parlour.

I want your money, the young man snarled and it was a snarl worthy of the wilder beasts—rabid and badtoothed and sourbreathed.

We have that in common, Reed Kitchen said.

What? What?

I want my money too.

Bouncers hauled the youth out of his seat by the hair and pummelled him briefly and Reed Kitchen saw him thrown back into the night more bloody than he had arrived. He finished his beer and the time seemed right to head up to his room and lie down in the shelter there but the night had not declared itself as one for sleeping. Fights verbal and physical blustered in the corridor and songs from drunken choristers were deafened by trumpets of complaint. Men brayed in this realm and women wailed and laughed. Lovers rode their beds hard against the walls and Reed Kitchen stayed awake smoking. Sometimes he spoke to each of the four walls and to the portly dresser. The bridge is built, he said. Wilf has his logs. Van Loon has read in the newspapers of his guilt but I must tell him that he is not accused. Wilf will swear under oath that Van Loon is a man of innocence and this will then be known. He could not say this thing before. He pointed the finger at Van Loon because that is where Van Loon wanted that finger pointed. He wanted that finger pointed upon himself and not upon his friend Wilf who was doing him a favour one more time.

A neighbour pounded on the adjoining wall to silence him.

The most persistent of nocturnal thieves obliged him to rise from his chair and beat the door to chase the fellow on his way.

Reed Kitchen scanned the congress of working men and transient men and displaced men on the streets of Prince George and he looked for Van Loon there. This was a place for the disinherited and the criminal to congregate. This was a place for the hungry and the rough and the lost and those who were discarded by a swerve of fate. This was a place for honest men to gamble on a quest for fortune. He was lost and this was a place for a man like Van Loon to lose himself also. Caleb Farrow had journeyed here following his release from prison and Reed Kitchen knew that Van Loon would remember those stories. Addie Day had worked these streets in another time. Van Loon would come here he believed because it was on his way and once he had come here he would stay for this was a place to hide. This was a place for the located to be expelled and for the missing to find themselves lost and not be found.

Reed Kitchen picked up his gunnysack and slung it over his shoulder and went off to look for shelter for the night to come. He had chosen his first lodging poorly and the next required greater intent. He spoke to those who would listen briefly and learned that the place he sought was a covert house unknown to the citizens of the common domain. The house was a secret preserved among thieves. He had first to locate a thief and be directed to that house and in the evening of that dusty buginfested sunbleached day he was accompanied further on down the block away from the heart of town to the house for exconvicts where Caleb Farrow had one time stayed and there he rapped upon the door.

He was let in and told whom to see.

This is the place to where I have come halfway, Reed Kitchen told the nightshift manager.

Pardon me?

This is a halfway house I am given to understand and I am halfway in myself.

The man extracted a form from his desk. Name? he asked.

Reed Kitchen.

Where're you in from? the fellow asked.

Isn't it where I'm out from that counts?

Same difference, the man said.

Okalla Pen. I have had my share of friends there.

They might be here. Sign, the man said and pointed, here.
Reed Kitchen signed. Am I in all the way? he asked.
You bet. I'll take you down to your bunk in the basement.
You bet. That's what my friend would say. You bet.
The man led him though the house and showed him the kitchen
and the diningroom and he parleyed the rules and he led him upstairs
to the common room and Reed Kitchen said, This is a place set aside
for speech and talking. I like this place. The manager led him down to
the basement and selected an available cot and men sat around on
bunks smoking and gazing at newspapers.
This is the place to where I've come, he announced to those who
had gathered. It's great to be all the way in halfway especially when I
just got out.
None of his new companions appeared to be talkative types. None
of them gave him a nod or indicated they were listening. A voice did
finally reply, I remember you. Prince Rupert. I tried to take a piss in
the can in a beer parlour and you stood around gabbing the whole
time. I hope you don't plan to shoot your mouth off like that around
here.
Reed Kitchen shucked his gunnysack under his bed and flopped
down on top. He tucked the pillow beneath his neck and closed his
eyes. My reputation has preceded me, he announced aloud. He
endeavoured not to grieve and addressed himself to sleep for he had
not known a moment's slumber in a great long while.

UPON THE IMMACULATE SERENITY of impassioned dreams men snored
and sputtered in their fitful rest. Alone among them Reed Kitchen
awoke to steps creaking down the basement stairs. He breathed the
scent of men asleep and the rank sweat of their days ambient in the
cool redemption of the night. He did sense the trespass of strangers
here amid the strangers asleep and waited for what could possibly
unfold. Reed Kitchen turned as though asleep to surreptitiously peer
upon the intruders and he counted three and his heart stirred with
affliction and with grief. Under the illumination of a protuberant

moon afloat upon the sky streetlamps shone through high windows into the basement dim below.

Intruders sought a bed particular to their quest and discovered it and flailed the carcass there and the waking man shouted out once and his mouth was gagged by an attacker and his body cudgelled by the others and Reed Kitchen sat up upon his bed. This won't turn out right, he said. Other sleeping men now awake sat upon their beds and watched or lay with their backs turned against this transgression. One man gagged the thrashing man and another man whupped him where he had fallen on the floor. The third man showed his blade to the room and the light did contribute to its sheen. Stop this now, Reed Kitchen said and he placed his feet upon the floor.

The pummelled man was past bawling out and he was kicked and thwarted upon the floor and two men conferred his demise. Reed Kitchen stood upon his feet and said, That's enough. This thing is done here now tonight. The man with the knife moved towards him. I have my tricks, Reed Kitchen advised and the knife did flash and he eluded that advance but he was felled for the man had tricks of his own devising and the hand of the man upon his chin forced open his mouth and the blade of the knife was inserted within.

The blade of the knife forced his tongue down and the sharp tip nipped his palate and the pressure on the tongue did make him gag. He gasped for his proper breath and his tongue fought against the mendacity of this probe and injured itself so doing and the far side of the room emitted the muffled sounds of the battering and the beating and the breathing of the intruders. Reed Kitchen waited for the instrument upon his tongue to be removed and gazed into the eyes of his attacker and swallowed with exasperation his own blood and listened to the sounds of the beating and the crack of bone and the expirations of the quarry and the grunts of the hunters by night. They were done. The two backed away and the steel blade was removed from the cavity of Reed Kitchen's mouth and his stomach did heave and upon the tide of his offal his own blood flowed freely and without cessation.

The sleepers in the basement dorm roused themselves from their

beds like ghosts and lifted the beaten man upon his cot and they
assisted Reed Kitchen to sit slumped upon his bed with his mouth
faced downward and his spirits downtrodden and the blood streamed
between his lips and they shushed him and he could not properly
complain. One man returned on tiptoes silently walking with a mop
and bucket and Reed Kitchen's discharge and the blood of both men
was scoured off the floor.

Reed Kitchen sat upon his bed not sleeping and he did mourn this
trespass to his life. He bled into a bucket and endeavoured to quietly
moan to preserve the harmony of this catacomb and the peace of
those who dwelled within.

In the morning the beaten man was removed to a hospital. While
he was being lifted away the stretcherbearers were stopped and the
man was informed of his expulsion from the house for fighting and
Reed Kitchen did mind his own token peace. He had his breakfast
and drank his own blood with his coffee and splurged ketchup upon
his eggs to camouflage the drips about his mouth. When the men
were done with eating and they had cleaned the dishes Reed Kitchen
was quietly escorted by his new companions outside and taken to a
hospital where he sat amid the casualties of the night until the roof of
his mouth and the top of his tongue could be amply sewn. He spoke
after that in a comical voice that made all men laugh and even he did
smile with the sound of himself although smiling was hurtful to him.

There was peace the second night.

On the morning of the next day the men were informed that they
had been hired. The carnival had landed in town and the excons
were dispatched to erect the tents and rides and Reed Kitchen landed
on the fairgrounds and volunteered for a particular task. I wan ta buil
tha thain.

It's called a rollercoaster, he was informed.

I wan ta buil it.

He did build the rollercoaster and he was the best man on that job.
The others were men accustomed to their drink or they had not toiled
during a long absence from the world of work while ensconced in
winter prisons. They lent their muscle to the task and Reed Kitchen

worked facing the youth called Boog who had threatened him with a
bottle nights before and who seemed to possess no recollection of that
event. They held track above their heads to get the line started while
other men bolted the rails and braces and the youth's face went red
from his exertion. His pallor sunk to white before he fainted from the
weight and heat and the track collapsed held up in part upon the back
of Reed Kitchen. Boog's place was assumed by the young man who
had pinioned Kitchen's tongue within his mouth. He said his name
was Colby and he asked him how many stitches he had taken.

Theventheen, Reed Kitchen said and the man who had cut him
laughed hard enough to shake the minirollercoaster down its length.
His arms were raised like Kitchen's above his head and the muscles
flexed the imprints of dissolute ladies.

Come and see me when you want them out, he said. I'll cut them
out for you free.

Thangthoo, Reed Kitchen said and they constructed that rollercoaster in the high heat and billowing dust of the day.

At the end of their labours each man was paid a fivedollar bill and
they were driven back to the congestion of town feeling as solvent as
merchants. For this evening they would pass on evensong at the Salvation Army and instead draft glasses cluttered their tables in the
beer halls. Here was a festival of chat and story and Reed Kitchen did
his best to contribute although muted by the discomforts of his
tongue. He and many of the excons made their way homeward in
good time for curfew. Others were too involved in their drink and dispatch to observe that hour. At midnight the beer parlours closed and
the men who arrived late at the halfway were not admitted and in
their temper smashed as many windows as they could reach and all
the windows in a ring around the basement. Reed Kitchen's bed was
blanketed by shards of glass and he and the others moved their bunks
into the centre of the room and they endeavoured to sleep in tight
convoy beneath the prickly covers and the bedlam outside. Police
chased the vandals on their way but they returned in the deeper dark-
nesses to fling their own collected stools upon the men and they
pissed through the broken windows between the bars and the staff

watchman who ventured outside to intercede was pummelled upon his head with a garbage can and then his head was wrecked against the walls of the house and the men did flee again as the police returned. Reed Kitchen did wonder why another body had to be broken in this realm. The culprits reappeared again before dawn and garbage was emptied through to the basement and the youth called Boog snarled between the bars and flung bottles at the sleepers that smashed upon the floor and upon unfortunate heads and the young man whose name was Colby threatened them all with vivisection and other grim details.

It wasn't us who locked you out, a codger complained but those within approved of the segregation.

They survived until morning then walked out upon the streets.

So many men—so many migrants—so many travellers into and through this realm and Reed Kitchen maintained his faith that the man whom he sought would yet appear. This was most evidently the domain of the lost and the condemned among them and Kitchen believed that Van Loon would hide and abide here amid the conflagration.

The days were hot and arid and he appreciated drying out after his winter sojourn on the coast. His body perspired in the compulsive heat and dust coated his pores and dirt was streaked upon him and he was permitted a shower but once a week. Thith ith the plaith where I haf come, he told his friends at the halfway house. I am lotht. Thothe who art lotht thall find me.

What? his friends asked. Then they said, Never mind. We gotchu.

Thith ith the plaith where I haf come.

And on a day when they were weary of his particular remonstrations they returned him to the hospital to have his stitches prematurely removed.

Now I can speak, Reed Kitchen said, and my words are laced with the blood of my bleeding. He spat red globules of blood upon the dry and dusty earth.

After evensong at the Sally Ann he went down to the railway yards to listen to the boxcars shunted. The clamour in his ears raged as music to him as a lullaby of bedlam that sustained him through his night.

THEY BAKED UPON THE SURFACE of that town from the dawning of their days until the dusk. The heat segregated men into clumps of shade and one of their number filched beer for refreshment as their skins scorched red under the glare of that sarcophagic sun. More men converged upon the town at first for the promise of summer and more men came when timber companies ceased cutting due to an hereditary fear of fire. Men emerged from the woods monied in saturnalian mood and rambunctious was their revelry and the fighting was ribald and bloodied were their faces and women filled purses with the loot of a bountiful harvest. You are the halfway men, Reed Kitchen sermonized to his friends where they sat shaded upon the walk, for you look up the long legs of the ladies and dream of drink and scrap in secret places. But you do not love these women in your nights or in your days and you are not drunk enough to satisfy your thirst and you must temper your disputes according to the whims of parole officers and dayshift and nightshift managers. You are the halfway men, he told them, for you are halfway in one society and only halfway out of your prisons, and a voice shouted to him, Si'down! Si'down! the people in the back can't see, and merry was their laughter and the streets did wend before their eyes and the congestion upon them.

There was a storm and thunder and lightning and the men bathed themselves under the swath of rain. The storm passed on. The heat returned and the next day men who slept upon the streets were tossed into trucks and others were coaxed aboard and the halfwaymen retreated from this advance and returned to their home where soon they were placed under siege. Everybody out, the dayshift manager said. Leave your stuff behind. It'll be here when you get back.

Where're they taking us to? one of their number asked.

Forestfire, boys. Big one. You just got hired to fight it.

What if we don't go? another did inquire to satisfy his interest.

Why do you think you boys been held here uptill now? Why do you think you been fed and sheltered?

A voice amid the collected throng answered that question to his own satisfaction. We thought it was so we would not break any laws. We thought you wanted us off the streets and out of trouble. We thought it was so we can have half a chance to go straight.

You won't be breaking any laws in the woods, the dayshift manager told him. There won't be none to break. You'll be off the streets for sure. There is no place to go but straight once you're fighting that fire.

What if we don't fight that fire? somebody said and that man laughed. What if we just kinda spread it around?

Other men joined in the laughter and the dayshift manager waited for that noise to subside. You'll fight it, he said and this time he was the one man smiling. Or you'll burn. That's the choice you got.

Do we get paid?

Excons get paid one out of four hours at minimum wage. The other three hours you are happy to volunteer and for every four hours of work you are fed one meal.

Reed Kitchen asked him, Is this a fire to be fought only by criminals and last night's drunks?

Any man who moves without a job attached to him, the dayshift manager said, fights that fire. Plus everybody else connected to the forest industry.

Then I will fight that fire, Reed Kitchen said. I will be the first in line. I want to see who will be brought forth to fight that fire.

The dayshift manager said, That's good, Reed. That's good because you're the first man I want in line out of here.

The men did take what belongings they required and laced on their boots and catalogued what they were leaving behind. They lined up outside to board the truck. One more thing, boys, the dayshift manager told them. When you get that fire put out and you come back here to collect your stuff you will be paid—but understand that your beds will by then be taken. When you get back here you will be obliged to move on.

So that's how it goes, Reed Kitchen said.

Nobody can live here forever. We have to have our turnover.

And those of us here now are hereby turned over, Reed Kitchen observed. I have come back to the place where I have been and now I am turned over.

They stood upright on that dumptruck and the men watched forward and they gazed behind as the day ebbed and the sun was consumed bloody behind the hills and avast ahead of them loomed cloud as black as nightfall arising from the land to the sea of sky and that could only be smoke—that cloud could only be a sign of an ultimate destination.

THEY ARRIVED AT THE END OF THE DIRT ROAD on which the truck could carry them and other trucks and buses conscripted to the cause unloaded their human cargo and the stream of vehicles was continuous. They had to walk and they had to carry with them equipment and supplies and in the night they scrabbled over the rocks of the fire line and each man traced the path of the man in front in a cable human and serpentine and everlasting. They walked on through that night hungry and cold enough and the moon illuminated their passage and before the dawn of the sun they emerged upon a crest of hillock to behold the dawn of the fire blazing measureless across that horizon. They crabbed on. The men were banded into groups and Reed Kitchen walked together with his mates and they established camp by a pond where birds had fled and fox mewed in their visions and deer drank and crossed the parade of men and raccoon skittered. They erected poles and crossing beams and draped canvas over the supports to form tents and slept until motorized vehicles made it through with pumps. Hoses were attached and in groups they lugged hose deep into the woods and attached new hose and carried on and engaged the fire where it grazed contentedly in a grove of alder. They sprayed the woods and dug trenches on command and chopped trees back away from the line of fire and the flames were dormant and benign and this would seem a detail they could do. Men carting hoses slept on their feet. Men as exhausted as cadavers dug. The sun came up and there was a calm and the men heard a crackling deep within the breach of flame and on its back a guttural roar and the fire spotted them and swooped and turned on the wind and its voice was vernacular and foreboding and flame the height of watchtowers swished forward and shade trees glowed red in an instant of combustion and the sky blackened with the windshift and a blizzard of ash and sparks snowed upon them and the men conjoined with fear as they ran gathering their hoses behind.

Aircraft swept low through the soot above and exploded water upon that fury.

They retreated and they escaped.

They carried back what they had carried in and dropped what they could not hold and moved more quickly away than they had advanced. An intermingling of forces of men arriving and men in flight disrupted the systems of command and the migrations inter-sected and turned and were lost together. Men gathered where they believed they might be fed and Reed Kitchen and his halfway friends made camp again and collapsed onto the desolation of their remorse. A twohour sleep and in that interim marshalls contrived new plans and Reed Kitchen heard from the confines of his tent the suggestion that the cons be sent into the firehead to see—the man was saying—if we can't roast a few and there was laughter within that congress. They were sent back across a rocky shallow stream and scrabbled through the hills where the roar of flame spoke in a despot's voice and the heat of the flame scalded their skins and ash snowed down upon them and their faces were grey and black and grisly. The flames moved again and this time they fled running racing the thrash of fire aswish in the treetops and their own skins considered to explode and hoses were left and tools and they ran and made it down to the river-bank where marshalls insisted they entrench.

The fire sashayed down to the river in its arrogant wigglyassed con-ceit and they ran their pumps and sprayed the inferno with squirts of water that evaporated before reaching the flame. A senior marshall when he arrived raved against his juniors and had them turn to the opposite bank and dampen the unburned forest there and cut back trees to distance the woods from the fire and the fire waltzed along the riverside in mockery and disdain.

At night they were relieved and went back to where the camp was sheltered and food was prepared upon the open hearth. They ate beans and the eating was a pleasure and they drank the juice that was provided. They ate bread and Reed Kitchen's crew was fortunate to divide an apple pie baked by some disconsolate bride and brought in.

A boy sat down beside Reed Kitchen. His flinty eyes were fearsome in the hearthlight and his face smeared metallic by the dirt of this dominion. I know how I got away, he said and then he said, 'cause I crossed them up in the confusion. What I don't know is how you got out.

Reed Kitchen savoured the final portion of his beans. When that windshift hit I could've raced a bullet shot out of those woods, he said. I didn't stop to see if I had pants afire—I just presumed it to be so and ran with that conviction.

Hell, Jabber, I ain't talkin about no fire, the young man said and Reed Kitchen looked at him again and through the solder of dirt upon him.

Your name is Wart, he said. I remember you.

The last time I saw you you was talkin to The Sip while somebody in the hills took potshots at him. I took a hike. I was wonderin why you never ran. I was wonderin how you escaped without never tryin to.

I got lucky. Like you I crossed them up. Now I'm here. Like you. That tells you how lucky I got.

The young man nodded and he stood up. You can go on callin it luck if you want to. We'll see about that, he said and he walked off not looking behind.

Reed Kitchen listened to the thrumming of the distant fire. He was lost and he had been located. The one who had discovered him was not the one he would wish to have found him.

IN THE MIDDLE OF THEIR NIGHT the canker of the fire crossed the river and those who had been their relief came running. Reed Kitchen awoke stupefied and struggled up while his companions trammelled him underfoot. He emerged from the tent and gazed upon the glow behind the hill and in the light of the hill where men ran wild bulldozers had turned tail and also slouched their way.

All right men, a marshall of whom they were not fond was saying, gather up what you can and we'll get you out of here on the double.

Never mind that first part, a voice announced and Reed Kitchen could see in the light that the young man whose knife had bit his tongue had spoken. Colby stood beside Boog the fiendish youth and the boy named Wart and together they formed a trio of wraiths in this grim light impoverished and depleted—spirits evoked and brought forth by the combat of these days. Colby and Boog and Wart had not arrived with the halfwaymen. They had been loitering elsewhere and solicited and were now shepherded together to the dissatisfaction of a few. We'll just get on out of here, Colby said.

Maybe you mistook my meaning, the marshall said. You will gather up what you can and only when you are loaded down like some pack-mule will you move an inch. Now. Is that clear to you?

The only thing that's clear to me, Colby said, is that I'm leaving and I ain't carrying a damned thing with me.

Mister, you're free to go anytime you want.

Then I'm going.

Then go.

They waited.

Well you just point the way, Colby said.

The way behind you will do just fine, the marshall said. It's the shortest I do believe.

Colby looked to the woods aglow. He turned back to the marshall who was a robust logger and wore a hardhat and was more than a half-foot taller than him and sixty pounds heavier. He was twenty or more years older. You brought us in here. You got to take us out, Colby said.

Son, I don't have to do no such thing. You want to go you can go. We're a hundred miles or more from the nearest town and I don't recollect in all this confusion exactly where that is. Now you can walk through the fire or you can walk away from it—it's up to you. Nobody you meet will have the time or the patience or for that matter the inclination to take you by your girlie hand and lead you on out of here. So stay put. Or get lost. Or gather up all that you can and let's beat it. Those are your choices and I don't particularly care what you choose. But if you choose to come with us then you will be carrying supply—and if you're carrying supply then you had better shake your purrty little girl's ass before you get it burnt right off.

The young man who called himself Colby took out his knife and he moved it from one hand into the other. Loggers were coming down out of the hills chased by fire and they were coming and they moved in towards this litigation with their axes and with their spades. They formed a judicious circle of intent. Colby looked around at those eyes lit by the distant glow and he sheathed his knife and he chose to clump together tools and a water jug and he raised them up and walked on.

They all walked on weighted by their loads. Reed Kitchen carried hose jointly with another three and they went on asleep in their heads while their feet traversed the bullied earth. They would not set up a new camp so much as collapse and sleep where they lay and in the morning battle fire with shovels and axes and with their own hands and they retreated and the fire went on and the next day was the same. They ate and they slept almost never and they fought the fire unceasingly and retreated.

The fire would move on past them and the blessing was that it did not go through them and the excons and the other groundpounders were summoned to move to a new location. The fire was engaged by professional woodsmen and firefighters now and riffraff brigades were moved to the rear in a broad march. They walked behind the blaze and they fought it from behind with burnt out woods at their backs and they showered the charred trees with water which fizzled and bubbled and boiled on contact and they worked on. They set up camp by the ponds they pumped and lay upon the scorched earth and sopped the heat of the ground through their clothes and skins and believed in their clement hearts their bones were kindling.

In the morning they expected to move forward to battle the flames from behind but they were transferred further to the rear. The men received instruction to soak the charred earth again and they did so wearied and consumed and slept longer and ate better and stomped upon the blackened earth and soaked it down. A marshall told them,

The woods are smouldering underfoot. The fire underground's primed
to ignite again. In teams they soaked the ashcovered earth whose
stone and soil and inflamed roots nourished a fire within.

They chopped smoking trees and drenched the blackened wood.

The burnt air stank and they were ever covered in ash.

I would never have believed it, Reed Kitchen confessed, that the
day would come this year when I would pray for rain.

I want you to shut up, Jabber. I don't want to hear your noise.

Reed Kitchen moved away from those who would keep him silent
and they followed. They were three and he was one and the young
man called Colby liked to pick at his teeth with his knife and smile
upon him. Wart elected also to gaze upon him and without expression.
Boog grinned upon him badtoothed and salient in his ways. Reed
Kitchen sucked blood from his tongue and spat and talked to those
who would rather not be seen to know him. It has been promised, he
reminded them and foretold, after the flood the fire next time.

They moved in groups that fanned away from one another and
lugged their hoses deep into the tenebrous woods and under the heat
of the sun soaked the parched earth and turned the ash to mud and
flooded the lairs forsaken by the wilder beasts and coaxed seed within
the soil to be reborn. The meal bell pealed and bore them together
again and they ate their slop and this was a respite for sleep and conversation.

When I was a kid, Wart said, I used to take apart the bones of cats
and try to fix them back again.

Was those cats alive or deadens?

Wouldn't be no fun if they was dead. Mosttimes they ended up
dead but they never started out that way.

When I was a kid I shat my dump in my parents' bed, an excon
said.

How many times you do that?

Ever' chance I got. After awhile they got used to it.

So then you stopped.

No I never. In the pen I used my partner's bunk and he had to
clean it up day by day.

Then you must like it here where there is no place to shit except where you want.

I don't mind it so much.

When I was a kid I shot my dog.

When I was a kid I turned the electric stove to high and walked on the burners to see how tough I was.

How tough were you?

Not as tough as I believed. Burned my feet like anybody would. Bawled about it after that.

When I was a kid I robbed my grandma's house every Saturday and Tuesday. I did that for fourteen years and the last time they put me in jail and I never could figure out what made that one time any different from all the rest. I guess that's what you call injustice.

When I was a kid me and my buddies robbed beggars.

When I was a kid my daddy brought me down to the railway tracks and he held me there to stare down the bright eye beam of the train and he would say to me, This train—this train is gonna blow you from here to kingdom come, and I would shout at him as the train approached, Who am I, Daddy, who am I here today? And he would scream in my ear, You are a man! How do I know that, Daddy? How do I know I am a man? And he'd tell me, 'Cause you work upon the railway! He did not believe that I believed I was a son of his and he did want to convince me so. He wanted me to know that I was not one of the wilder beasts although I behaved rightfully the same and he wanted me to know that I was not born out of the thin air of my mother's dying like some spooky god made flesh and together we yelled out at the top of our lungs *Trrraaaiiinnn* as that engine approached and we leapt together on out of the way before we got ourselves kilt. Then we laughed and we had a good time lying there by the side of the railroad watching the train go by. Myself personally I had a wonderful youth.

So, Reed Kitchen finished and he spat blood, who else has a story from when they was kids?

Boog and Colby and Wart preferred to sleep more and work less and the marshall had to kick the soles of their boots to get them moving again. The marshall returned in the evening of a day and he walked in and gathered the groundpounders at their ease while the sun set beyond the burnt hills and a fence of leafless limbless trees stood in silhouette upon the high switchback like the stalks of gravesites. The fire we fought's still blazing, he said. We got fires at work throughout this province now, he said. It's a real dry spell and it's a question of manpower, he said. So we need some of you to stay on here and keep on doing what you're doing and we need the rest of you to come on back to the frontlines. I have prepared a list, he said, of those who are coming out.

Reed Kitchen learned that his name was not on that list. He would stay on here and soak the earth. Boog had his name read out from the list and he said, I ain't going.

Reed Kitchen said, I will take his place.

Colby said, I ain't goin noplace but right on out of here.

Wart told the marshall, Screw you.

I've told you in the past you have no choice except the choice to leave on your own recognizance.

Colby unsheathed his knife again. Maybe it's time you reconsidered, he said.

The men were standing now and they were wary and they were cautious here. The marshall did not have his logger friends on hand this time and they believed in the portent of this circumstance and omission.

Listen, girls, the marshall said, you're not worth the trouble to me. I'll tell you what I'll do for you. I'll take your names right off the list altogether. That means you ain't working no place. That means you were never here. That means you don't get a dime. Now you tell me what you want. Do you want me to stricken your name off the list or do you have a sudden inspiration that you'd like to get back to fighting fire like men and put an end to your sissified existence? The marshall looked directly at Wart. What'll it be, Alice? He looked at Boog. Give me your answer there, Betty. He looked at Colby who held his knife unsheathed and he said, What'll it be there, Annie Fanny? Do you want your name stricken or not?

Wart was the first one to move toward the marshall in a slow slump. Do you know what hurts the most? he asked him. The gut. Slice up the belly you get the most pain.

Reed Kitchen on the rim of the men who were observant of this episode commented, I had a friend who died that way.

Wart stopped in his advance and he tilted his head down to gaze upon Reed Kitchen. Did you? he asked him.

He was a friend of mine, Reed Kitchen said.

Was he? Wart smirked and moved on and he stepped up to the marshall who was standing with his hands on his hips and his clipboard poked out. The big man wore a green eiderdown vest glazed with oil and grime and he wore jeans and steeltoed boots like them all. Wart smiled and knocked off the man's hardhat.

You little shit. The marshall stooped to retrieve his hat and Wart kicked him in the mouth.

Now the man was down but he was not defeated. Boog released a yelp that echoed off the switchback hills and Colby hollered too and they both danced around the fallen logger and Wart waited still while the large man regained his composure.

This won't turn out right, Reed Kitchen said.

It'll be a fair fight, one of his number intimated and that man stepped forward and made the rules. One against one.

Colby turned with his knife and the man who had spoken slapped his own palm with the side of the blade of an axe. Colby blanched. Boog ceased his insane yelping. Wart smiled with a serenity unbefitting the occasion and as the logger lunged he kicked him in the teeth again and dislodged a few. The logger was counting his losses when Wart kicked him in the ear and the big man went down one more time. Wart jumped on his nose and jumped off him and he took a bow. The big logger scrabbled to his feet more quickly now and more warily and finally he dropped his clipboard and made a fist and walked backwards as he circled his foe. Wart let him walk. He let him circle round.

You can turn me dizzy if you want, he said. I'm still gonna ream your butt.

You dumb punk. He bled from his broken nose and ear. You don't know what you started.

Caleb Farrow was a friend of mine, Reed Kitchen said to the uncomprehending throng. He died with a knife to the belly. You watch your belly there, marshall. Don't you underestimate your foe.

First I do him, Jabber, then I do you, Wart said.

The logger did lunge at last but he was not possessed of fighting skills. Wart stayed away from him and skipped free. He could not do much without his initial advantage of surprise but the logger could do nothing more than walk around and look for an opening that was not there.

Now let us stop this business, Reed Kitchen said. Even those among us who would like to see a fight are bored out of our trees. You don't have to shake the other man's hand but it is time to stop this business.

The logger ceased walking. I ain't quitting till I kick his purrty girl's ass.

You have had your opportunity and you have not done it. Just give this one up and we'll go fight your fire.

That wild scream again awoke the mountains and Boog ran yelling upon the back of the logger who spun and tried to shake him off and Wart kicked him in the genitals and kicked him in the eyes where he fell and the man lay moaning and Colby grabbed a fistful of the marshall's hair and cut it off and held the swatch aloft and claimed, I scalped the sonofabitch. The man lay moaning and other men moved in upon the three with spades and axes and Boog said, Give me that thing, and he took the knife from Colby. I'll show you what a scalping is. He sat upon the logger who held his hands upon the pain of his eyes and Boog pinned his shoulders with his knees and he sawed down with the blade across the top of the logger's scalp. He came up clutching that bloody tuft of skin and hair and held his sodden trophy aloft. This is a goddamned scalp. This is what you call a scalp.

The men approaching paused in their alarm and the screams now were of the marshall upon his feet and skittering blind and bloody his head afire with the flame of his bleeding. The red sun shone upon him. The men in their halfcircle—a dozen or one less now and Reed

Kitchen among them—moved with purpose toward the three with their weapons upraised.

The man in the middle spun in a circle the halo of his scalp ashining and belligerent voice ecstatic and tongues of fire fluid upon his crown and dribbling down.

Eleven men moved upon the three and the three stood ground wild and manic in their regard. Boog snarled worthily and Colby reclaimed his knife and waved it upon those who would approach. Wart expressed no sign as though he had limited involvement here as though his fight had been concluded here and these ancillary events were none of his volition. Lo—Wart retrieved an axe from the ground and lifted it up and Wart stepped forward as though to make peace then stalled that effort with his smirk. Wart swept the axe upward cloudhigh where it flashed red in the circle of the sun and within the exhalation of a breath and grunt drove it down fullforce and splintered the marshall's skull.

The man fell upon his knees his face appalled his giant eyes imperiled the axe imbedded in the roof of his head the brain and blood outpouring.

Wart lifted the axe and with it the man rose up off his knees alive or dead his mouth ajar in loathing and dismay and his head clung to the shape of the axe and Wart rammed the axe down and the man down with it and the face split sideways apart and Wart shook the axe again and like splitting a timber wedged it down dividing the throat in two as was the face.

No voice was spoken among the men and the fight vanished from their veins as quickly as it had sprung. In a moment they stepped back where once they had stepped forward and the men gallantly retreated at a moment when their minds understood to advance. They moved backwards while they believed they actually trod forward and their eyes were upon the divided man and the axe that split him and upon Wart who even now did smirk.

Colby and Boog gazed upon the event and did not move and Wart kicked a boot into the back of the man and toppled him forward like a great tree ancient in the woods and now the axe alone did stand

upright in the air embedded in brain and bone and nostril and tho-
rax and they howled in evident elation like wolves in blessing upon
their kill.

Steps backward among those who had observed the death were
now long leaps and men turned upon their incomprehension and dis-
array to flee the scene as though by miracle of flight to deny this day.
Boog cackled in his wild incomprehensible way and stomped and
paused and showed restraint upon the signal of Wart's upraised arm.

Wart spoke into the gathering gloom of the burnt out hills where
the men fled as shadows upon the parched black earth, Where are
you, Jabber? Where do you think you can hide?

Reed Kitchen was not a man to quiet his tongue. Sootyskinned
himself in the clothing of this land he erred to speak his mind from
behind the charred black tree that concealed him. I have come to the
place where I been going and it is like a place where I have been.

I'm gonna shut you up, Jabber.

Worse'n you have tried, Reed Kitchen warned him.

REED KITCHEN MOVED BY THE polarized light of the moon upon a surface similar and broken. He crossed through regions of burnt woods
and a collapsed forest ploughed flat by earthmoving machines to cre-
ate fire lines that had not been sustained and he traversed clearcut
patches where felled trees had not been extracted in advance of the
firestorm and had burned where they lay. He moved shadowlike in
the soft illumination and his feet were swift and his footing steady.
Those who would pursue were outrun and slowed down by the debris
burnt and scattered across this lunar land and Reed Kitchen kept
them within his sight. He would stop. He would rest upon a prone
treetrunk the roots still hot to the touch and watch them skitter forth.
As they drew near to him he was compelled to speak.

There was a mob riled and fortuitous in their thinking. They hammered at the gate. They besieged the throne of power to hear them
out. Give us the crook! they cried. Give us the one who jimmies the
locks on our doors and pries our windows ajar. Give us the one who

carries a crowbar in his hip pocket. Give us the one who pilfers our hardearned cash and takes away our electronic equipment for sale on the black market. Give us the mugger who roughs us up and nips our wallets. Give us the filcher and the pursesnatcher and the villain who shimmies down chimneys in the deadfall of night and nicks our children for a ransom. Give us the crook! Allow the crook to prosper across the land in this time for all time. May crooks burgeon throughout eternity and we shall merrily suffer our losses and pay our higher rates of insurance with gladness. Give us the crook the murderer the thug the plunderer the blackguard—arm them all with knives and Saturday night specials and brass knuckles—give us anybody but do not give us the one who speaks when we don't want him to be heard. Keep the jabbermouth to your punishment ordained from the dawn of creation. Give us the crook! For we would rather have the thief among us nuisance that he is than the one that utters to us in a foreign tongue.

Reed Kitchen stood upon an immense fallen fir as the trio of wraiths scrabbled across the gristled earth and drew nigh to him and he spread his arms in benediction and said to them, Let thieves live— it's the talkers we want dead. As the three pursuers drew close Reed Kitchen turned and danced upon the burnt timber. He ran on as the others faltered gasping for a proper breath and they were pained and frustrated and enraged by the mockery of their prey.

His conditioning was superior and his heart more true and his strength more able for this contest and Reed Kitchen rested while his pursuers scrambled after him and wore themselves down and fled while they caught at their breath and hung their bodies in abject fatigue. He stayed ahead of them and pulled them along into the wilderness closer to the fire and he used his advantage to achieve a hill then hide below the fallen trees beyond. His attackers ran past him and loud was their breathing and remorseful the laments of their bodies. Reed Kitchen arose from his lair and said, Colby, here I am.

Colby stopped short and called to his cohorts. We got him. He's over here.

In six running strides Reed Kitchen was upon him now and the exhausted youth managed to unsheathe his knife and Reed Kitchen kicked it flying from his hand then skipped back upon a scabbled trunk. The wearied youth could but lean his hands upon his knees and breathe heavily awhile and wait for his strength to sponsor an attack. His compatriots came running and collapsed beside him spent as Reed Kitchen danced in flight across the pellmell earth and brittle was his chatter.

You are the finest of the friends that I have known. In my past people have had a tendency to want to get away from my company and elude my propensity for speech as though human discourse was something foreign to their bones. But you, friends! Romans! Countrymen! Buckeroos! I need not ask for the loan of your ears. You come running. You thirst for what I have to say. You do yourselves injury and endure the pain of hardbreathing all to be closer to my words. Yes! Come on, friends. Run on. I have so much to tell you. About the wonders that I have seen and the atrocities known also. For we live upon a world atrocious in its pain and fabulous in its spectacle. What grace is this to be words in such a story?

He ran on.

The phantom shades pursued him in their unrelenting folly.

They recited epitaphs upon the cool night air and swore that the blight of this land would be his tomb and their invective was shrill and churlish and foreboding in its promise. They denounced Reed Kitchen and censured his tirades with rants of their own wild invention and they bespoke his death and foretold his slow destruction and the unravelling of his alimentary canal and the damage to his limbs and digits and orifices and tongue and eyes and they volunteered the menu of his body they would oblige him to ingest and Reed Kitchen ran on.

He ran on. He ran on. He came upon a land of trees uprooted and displaced as though stacked upon this sand by tide and current invisible in time and upon his peril he ceased his travel and wedged himself below wood and stone and earth into the vacated lair of a wilder beast and there he snugged himself down upon the forest duff and closed his eyes for sleep. Above his scalp the wood glowed red. In time he heard the advance of his foes aware they had lost him now and they shouted his name as though he might again respond. Reed Kitchen had so much to say. He had so much to tell them and advise but now was a time to mind his peace and he quit his talk and turned himself to sleep. Above him on the black and moonlit earth the one who was known as Wart called out to him across the moor. We can wait you out, Jabber. You have to show yourself sometime. When you do we'll be ready for you.

That was a problem for the morning. In the interim Reed Kitchen would sleep—pursued yet safely cubbyholed within a bear's abode.

FULL AND CONSTANT IN ITS adoration the moon illumined the quake of crevices and upheavals shovelled upon the pillaged land. Boog mewled in his sleep and Wart would kick him where he lay and the youth slept devoured by his dreams and by the night above. Constellations and planets retreated as faint accords beyond the wash of light and Colby slept beneath their dim regard. Wart watched across that inert terrain his clairvoyant eyes affixed upon the scavenged night. His companions were wretched and mad he judged and had no purpose here save the balm of rage that eased the distemper of their souls. Wart had purpose. To split the skull of the marshall had been a pleasure he imposed on the necessity of his duty in this place. The Jabbermouth had pricked his guise. For that acuity a death was planned and he would await the morning.

ENGROSSED IN THE CONJECTURE of his dreams Reed Kitchen wiggled loose from his lair to stand tall in the light of the moon upon the seared ground. He hobbled along the parapet of the longer timbers and at his station Wart shook his friends awake. The three pursued bent low and hidden and Reed Kitchen walked in the fulsome debacle of his sleep and he did not awaken to the light of the moon and starry night or step beyond the quarry of those apparitions provoked by sleep. He was a sleepwalking man upon the crisp crust of this earth.

He jumped down and walked on and stepped high upon a smoking
timber and crossed over and those who did pursue moved with caution and quiet wary of an artful plan to compose their ruin.

He walked on—a solitary figure culled from the transmogrification
of this land to speak of destinies and ferment and to prophesy and
rant and to harangue the heavens and scold all those who dwelled
below and yet he kept his silent peace and lumbered on alone bereft
of counsel or of wisdom or of words. He walked on. Smoke arose from
the soil and from the fallen trees and he moved through that pall.
The burnt out forest yielded to a singed meadow where he stamped
his boots upon the path and the ash disturbed by his steps drifted after
him as aroused phantasm from the grave and the moon shone luminous upon him. Those who followed did fear his game and revere his
mettle in this commonwealth of desolation and they respected their
distance and followed hushed behind. He strode on.

Reed Kitchen in the realm of his sleep ascended a hillock where a
single resident tree stood still—charred and gnarled by the winds of
flame and leafless and spiritless upon this dire range. Reed Kitchen
stood in quarantine by that tree and ventured to gaze out upon the vista
from this height. The three could not move unseen across the open
land and they walked on and Reed Kitchen neither moved nor spoke as
they approached and they did not run but walked upright to him.

Now I got you, Wart said and Reed Kitchen was unresponding.

What's amatter with him? Boog inquired.

You think you can take us on all three? Colby asked him.

Wart alone did smirk. I'll be damned, he said.

What?

He's still asleep. Look at him. He doesn't even see us here.

I see you, Reed Kitchen said and they stepped back in dismay and
fear. Then stepped forward again. I see you here.

I thought you were walkin in your sleep, Wart said.

I like your horses, Reed Kitchen said. You gentlemen are riding fine
mounts.

The three looked one to the other and Boog did hoot and Wart
smirked in his particular way. Colby said, He dies.

Yes he does, Wart said.

I'll find a stick. We'll beat his head in, Boog suggested.

Don't leave us alone with him, Colby said. Then he had to explain himself forthwith. I don't trust this dude.

I wanna clobber him, Boog said. I wanna smash his skull. I wanna wallop every bone in his body.

Let's do it then. Let's get it done.

I'll get a stick.

We'll go with you, Wart said. Come on, Jabber. Let's go ridin along this ridge.

They laughed and they did marvel as Reed Kitchen rode alongside them away from the meadow's lone and stalwart tree as they gained upon the woods to fetch a weapon. They rode on and the first one to stop was the man pinioned between them.

Reed Kitchen hollered out. This is not right. This is not right that I go sleepwalking in my night.

Wakey wakey, Colby said. Boog and Wart clutched his arms and bent him down and Colby thwacked him upon his skull and Reed Kitchen twisted and bolted from their grip and fought them off. They could not hold him steady and he was too wild and tempestuous to hit. He kicked and thrashed and butted his head into the man who approached and Boog hung on him and was tossed about like a rider on a bronc and Wart was damaged and cut from his prisoner's moxie. They had the three of them to hold him down and that was not a facile duty. With three upon him no one remained to inflict the final damage. They dared not release him fearing his ability to flee and they could not send one of their number off to fetch a timber for two were insufficient restraint. They rolled and they struggled and they fought unbending upon the hill and where one tripped the others fell and that was the inspiration one required.

They had stumbled across a firehose abandoned in the flight from the advance of flames and Wart held a portion of it above the surface of the ground and he decreed, Boog. Colby. We'll hang him. Boog, he commanded of the one among them least able to subdue their captive, haul this hose back to the tree. We're gonna hang his ass.

This won't turn out right, Reed Kitchen warned them. Myself personally I wouldn't do this if I were you.

They fought on and twisted on the hill and rolled one body upon the other the soot and soil impregnating their skins so their eyes shone in the glow of the moon as lamps upon a distant shore. They battled on and Reed Kitchen was afflicted but he did persevere the strongest of these men and Boog returned to help drag him upward to the lone tree.

They dragged him up and Reed Kitchen spoke to them in his choler. You're lucky I am a sleepwalking man. If I was not a sleepwalking man you could never capture me. The likes of you in these woods—you are tiddlywinks to me. You have not outfoxed me. Don't let that ever be said. When you tell this story tell it right. You got lucky because it is my affliction to be a sleepwalking man throughout my days.

Boog smote him upon his mouth and endeavoured to reach within to extract the tongue. Shut your face! he hollered upon him and spat and Reed Kitchen was not inclined to be obliging.

Worse than you have asked me to be mute but that is not my duty in this realm. What do you say when you are being crude? Up yours. I say that to you now. Up yours. But know that these are not my words but your own which I reflect back upon you.

Dead men don't talk, Wart said. He'll be quiet soon enough. And they rounded him up beneath the tree.

Who can tie a noose? Colby asked and when neither of the others replied Reed Kitchen did.

I can. But I am not inclined to teach these skills of mine to you.

Boog smote him upon the brow and Reed Kitchen bent to the hurt of that blow.

You can't tie a noose in a firehose anyhow. Just knot it and string him up. Let him hang forever. Even if his neck don't break he'll starve in a month or two.

They did what they had promised and Reed Kitchen believed his final words were upon his lips and after they were spoken he would fall silent evermore. What to say? he said. What to say? The moon was descending upon the desolate hills. So many words and what should my last words be? The men wrapped the end of the hose around his neck and fought with it to tie and tighten the knot. Do I ask a question or give my final judgment upon life within this land? What to say? I yet have much to tell you. Questions I would ask. Rage I would dissipate. Comforts I would grant. You end my life to impede my speech and you can't fool me, Wart, it's what I have to say about you in particular that you cannot abide. All right then. End my life to impede my speech for my life is my speech and what I have to say will be said as long as I have breath. Within the cosmos of his probe he chose the most pressing of inquiries to impose upon those who would leave him dangling from a limb. Wart. What ever did happen to Addie Day?

Wart gazed upon him and he did reveal, I fed her to the whales.

That's what you told The Sip.

That's what I told him.

Colby climbed the tree and the hefty firehose was passed up and he scaled higher and hoisted the hose above a stout limb. They stiffened the hose and stretched Reed Kitchen's neck but they had no means to secure that line. Boog ran down to the woods and returned with a solid timber and begged to swat Reed Kitchen with it and he was granted permission but the wood was too heavy for momentous blows. They wrapped and knotted the hose to the timber and the three young men heaved on the timber to lift Reed Kitchen off the ground and he did yelp and clutch the knot about his throat. They heaved and he was lifted up and the three strained to wedge the timber between boulders in a cut gully and their strength evaporated and their grip was lost and Reed Kitchen collapsed like a raggedy doll upon the ground. You can stop this business right now, he said. Cease and desist. He yelped again as they heaved him up and he told them, This is against the law. It's been handed down from time immemorial that if you hang a man and he doesn't get hung you have to let him go. You boys have no respect for tradition. Listen up. You'll never make it—you don't have the strength. You're a pack of losers. And his goading inspired their strength and the timber was inserted into place and Reed Kitchen dangled above the earth forsaken.

He dangled and he swayed and flailed the naked air.

The three returned and hooted below him and did their dance although they had miscalculated his height above the ground. They were unable to bash him as they would have preferred and had to console themselves with the sight of him in agony above and their only torment was with words.

Keep talking, Reed Kitchen said. I enjoy the conversation.

He clutched the knot at his throat and with his great strength hoisted himself up awhile. This won't turn out right, he complained. They tried to swat at him to shut him up but he lifted his legs clear and frustrated their assault. Reed Kitchen thrashed in the light of the predawn and he warned them, You can't shut me up. You never could shut me up. You might kill me but that is all. When you tell this story get it right. I went on talking. I never was quiet for a second.

Wart said above his noise, You're gonna die real slow, Jabber, and that's okay with me.

I'll be waiting for you when you die, Reed Kitchen fought back. I'll have a few things to say to you then. I will be your personal hell—jabbering in your ear. There's no excuse for you. You're wretched. I will say these things until I speak no more. *I will let people know.*

Die slow, Wart told him. Die real slow. We'll be going on now.

Get me down from here, Reed Kitchen commanded. His legs bicycled through the smoky air. Get me down from here.

The three walked on. They did laugh and live again the sequences of that night and they walked on. Reed Kitchen swung in the gloam of the descending moon before the sun arose.

Come back here, Reed Kitchen commanded. Get me down from here.

The three walked on and vanished from his sight and hearing and their footsteps were mute on the meadow's soft down of soot and ash.

This won't turn out right, Reed Kitchen mused and fell silent.

The moon sunk below the awning of that desolated horizon.

The sun floated above the burnt hills and beams through the remnant stalks of birch shot upon his face and he thought he would be blinded. He thought he would ascend into the sky and into the light and Reed Kitchen squirmed at the end of his noose and jerked so hard he kicked a boot off. He thrashed and cried out and he began to speak in a savage voice in a language filled with rage and sorrow and fury and complaint and abject lamentation.

The sound of his words falling upon the thirsty earth gave him pleasure. He almost laughed—a dangerous thing. He could lose his concentration—his strength be sapped—his hands slip. He wanted to talk about this. He wanted to go back in time and tell his friends that he had seen the future and in that future he had died laughing. They would appreciate that sort of tale. Reed Kitchen began to speak—to tell the story—whether or not his friends could hear. Whether or not they'd listen.

In the burnt out meadow swinging at the end of a firehose Reed Kitchen dangled aloft and spoke to the rising sun as if to some old friend as if this was another beginning to a fine new day and he ought to savour the moment. This should keep, he told the rising sun. Surely this should keep.

9

THE ACRIDITY OF SCORCHED HUMUS wafted above the plane of the earth mingling with the stench of timber burn and yet his nostrils flared horselike as though alert to more telling scents upon the morning air. Ferenc Van Loon paused to sniff and to cock an ear and he was ever watchful along the fire line. He carried on. These had been valorous days and Van Loon was spent from the trauma of toil and devastation. He walked on. When the conflagration had passed this way he had stood amidst the tenements of flame and aimed his waterhose upon those afire. Men rescued one another as the forest was yet consumed and running for their lives had gained a high plateau where flame and smoke governed the woods around and firewinds blazed across that verdure so encompassed. He remembered the firewinds as beautiful—the way a swath of meadow would ignite—the crackle of air exhilarated above. Choppers fetched them out and those who had endured the worst were offered the least of jobs thereafter. Ferenc Van Loon declined. Bored with ease he volunteered for the frontlines again and yet again when that crew also would be routed. His third and final crew dispersed with their ranks ransacked by atomic billows of fire and men were afoot in sundry directions. He had been lost for days since to wander the burnt hills and feed himself upon the avails of an abandoned cache. This was wild country. For days he had pursued the fire and the flames had travelled on ahead and when he did

catch up no men battled there. He retreated and travelled the long
way around in search of others and grievous had been that sojourn.
He had met men bewildered by misery and dismay. He had met men
consumed by smoke and tended by companions on the shores of
ponds where they awaited discovery and salvation. He had stumbled
upon three corpses bound together by the fraternity of fire and roasted
in a heap. He had met men afflicted by other men and he had been
warned not to proceed and he did proceed as though scorched himself
and mentally disarrayed. He had listened to stories told and heard
mention of a talker. Heard one of the talker's tales repeated and that
curiosity provoked him. Tales were told also of a violent bunch. Van
Loon had walked on and he had found a man forsaken and his scalp
shattered by an axe. Van Loon extracted that axe from the fellow's
cranium to grant the corpse a dignity and he used the axe to excavate
the earth and marked the grave with stones and walked on now with
a weapon.

He followed human tracks upon the ash.

He met a youth blackened and grim on the morning of a day and
they were headed in opposite directions. Van Loon had been forewarned concerning his nature.

Hey there, Van Loon said and he sat upon a fallen trunk and his
position was alike a crouch from which he could quickly spring.

Hey, Wart said.

Which way you headed?

The way you been comin.

Not much down there.

Not much huh?

I'm headed for higher ground to see if a chopper don't find me.

That's an idea. Where'd you get that axe?

Found it. Why? You like this axe? What's so special about this axe?

It's all bloody.

So it is.

Where'd you get it?

Out of a fire marshall's skull. Does that surprise you at all?

Not the way they been behavin. Who're you anyhow?

Nobody. I been looking for a man I heard was hunted down by three crazy loons.

There's only one of me and I ain't a loon.

I am. That's my name. Van Loon.

I've heard that name before.

Yeah?

Some dude out around Prince Rupert named Van Loon. He's wanted for murder out there but I know he didn't do it.

How'd you know that?

'Cause I did it. But if he wants to take the credit then that's all right with me.

You killed somebody?

Boy named Farrow. You ever met him?

He was a friend of mine.

Then I guess you know The Jabbermouth all right, Wart said.

Where is he?

Jabber? Last I seen him he was hanging around the top of this hill. Looking for a chopper too I guess. Let me see that axe a minute.

I always figured my time as a jungle grunt would come in handy.

What's a jungle grunt? Wart asked.

A marine. Point is I can kill you with my bare hands but the axe'll do fine.

Think you can use it?

I know I can.

It's a messy job.

If I took it out of one man's skull I can plant it back in another.

You might think so but it's not the same.

Van Loon and the other man were quiet and waiting as though something between them remained to be decided or declared and Van Loon never took his eyes off him and the younger man said, I don't have no quarrel with you that I recall. I'm just a groundpounder walkin through the woods tryin to make it back to civilization.

That's your story?

I'm stickin to it.

So you don't want to start up?

Not when you're sittin there with that axe I don't.

So you're gonna walk on.

That's right.

Not come back this way.

If you don't want me to I won't. You're not inclined to friendliness much are you?

Why be friendly to the man I'm gonna kill?

You're not gonna try it.

Maybe I am.

You might think you're a shitfaced exmarine but you know this is what I do for a livin. You don't know for sure you can take me out just like I don't know for sure I can take you out. So I'm gonna walk on and you're gonna let me.

Is that right.

That's right. You know how I kill people so you don't want none of that handtohand stuff with me.

You know how I kill people, Van Loon said.

No I don't.

Yes you do.

I ain't seen you—

I should've shot you while I was at it. I could've easy when I shot The Sip.

For the first time the grimace on Wart's face indicated a measure of surprise by the turn in this conversation. Each man had confessed his sins one to the other and neither man forgave the other.

I guess we will meet again, Wart said.

Count on it.

I'll do more than count on it. I'll look forward to it.

Wart walked on downhill through the stand of braised timber.

Van Loon recrossed the ground Wart had previously traversed and followed his footprints in the soot and ash. Further along he found a body the head bashed in by rock. The bloodied corpse had been violated and the pants tugged down and when he turned him over the man's genitals were seen pulverised to alter the gender. Van Loon walked to higher ground distraught and his heart was as heavy as the boulders there and where the woods gave way to meadow a second corpse lay provident below stalks of burnt bush. This man had been punished more thoroughly and every aspect of his form assailed. He did not recognize the torso of either man and Van Loon walked on.

He reached the smoking fields and climbed onto a crop of hill and scaled the path beaten down by footprints up to the mountain meadow and upon the ridge there a lone tree pondered an expanse and from it swung a dangling friend. Van Loon went on and the man suspended against the sky was slack. Van Loon went on without haste. This was not a mission he would enjoy to bury the dead and mark their sacred ground. Van Loon came upon the end of the firehose and he chopped it away and the line broke and the body fell with a clamour and touching ground it yelped. Van Loon jumped then and ran toward the squirming cadaver that groaned upon the scorched earth. He knelt above the blackened fellow. You're alive, he told himself and told the man and turned him over gently and cradled his head and wiped blood from his murderous lips. He struggled to unravel the welt of hose around the strained neck. The man gurgled and coughed and his eyes and mouth went wide with recognition. In a voice made harsh by circumstance he managed to convey, Van Loon. Van Loon. You found me.

Van Loon knew already whom he would discover under the soot and blood but he cleaned him first with the inside of his grubby sleeve. He leaned above him and inquired, What are you doing here, Reed?

My reputation has preceded me, the hoarse voice whispered for Reed Kitchen had talked himself bone dry.

What?

This is the place to where we've come and now we're here.

Hoo boy, Van Loon said and his eyes scanned the raven woods where no sound and no sight emitted where even the breeze had departed with the fowl. I don't like this. He looked upon Reed Kitchen. I think we should get out of here, Reed. Can you walk?

Van Loon. Van Loon. I have so much to tell you. You have no idea. I have so much to say.

Hhohghdverdoma. What else is new? I didn't ask you if you could talk. I asked if you could walk. We got to travel.

I'm ready. You can count on me, he said although when Van Loon assisted him to his feet and then let go Reed Kitchen crumpled.

THEY DESCENDED THE MOUNTAIN TOGETHER and Reed Kitchen led the way the compass of his mind intact. Breathing was painful for him and his bones and muscles ached and the simple motion of walking required a fury of concentration. His endurance had been depleted and Van Loon supported him along the way. They walked on steadfast in tandem that first whole day and under the evening sky located a place to sprawl within the earth like gnarled tubers proportionately outcropped and embedded. Reed Kitchen chopped the rope of a long charred root. They walked on and waited for the ample dark and retraced their steps to that place again in silence with luminous decree and trekked through that incinerated copse where in the pitch of night they settled and rested still and listened.

Tie me up, Reed Kitchen said. He retrieved his root and knotted it about his waist and asked Van Loon to do the same. I'm a sleepwalking man and I do not wish to escape the comfort of my dreams.

Hhohghdverdoma, Van Loon stated.

How do you spell that? Reed Kitchen whispered in their subterranean sanctuary beneath a slide of rock.

G-o-d-d—

I knew it, Reed Kitchen said.

What do you know?

It's a religious remark in a foreign tongue.

I guess you could say that.

You could too. There are many things here for God to damn.

Are you going to talk all night or do we get some sleep?

Maybe both, Reed Kitchen said. We'll have to see. Don't let me walk in my sleep but maybe you should not let me talk neither.

The moon arose and through apertures in their parapet they viewed the devout night sky. They slept beneath the panoply of stars under that assembly of stone and awoke before the sun to travel on.

They walked on. Reed Kitchen employed the axe as a cane.

Stop looking behind us all the time, he said.

You know who I might see.

Maybe you will and maybe you won't. Maybe he'll be ahead of you by then and not behind. That's what you don't know.

Van Loon absorbed that advice and keenly observed the terrain in various directions. He told Reed Kitchen of the horrors that he had seen.

The kid you met was Wart. After him the first body was Boog.

How do you know that?

Because Colby is a criminal and a mean soul and not a psychopath like Boog. Colby would not beat Boog to death for the sport of it even if Wart incited him to do so and Wart would know that. But the other way around—yes. Boog and Wart together beat Colby first—the one you found last. Wart killed Boog soon after Colby was out of the way. Wart prefers witnesses to be dead so it was ordained that both men die. Wart's the one of the three and him alone who would dwell upon such things.

Other men saw him kill the marshall.

Other men saw an unidentified youth with an indistinguishable unrecognizable blackcovered face kill a marshall. They don't know who that was and that's one reason Wart was willing to do it. You and me are not blessed by the ignorance of those men. We know exactly what Wart looks like and we know about him.

So we have trouble.

To the ends of our days.

This is not a place I'd want to die.

It's not a place I expect to.

They journeyed on and they endeavoured to camouflage their tracks and they buried their faeces underground and in time they believed their path eluded all hunters in a land more vast and unbroken.

They traversed a gorge still smoking and flames licked upward to the sun like some vestigial remnant of creation's fire dormant and abiding in the darkest fold of earth's ancestral rock. They scrabbled down one side and clawed their way up the other and on the far crest rested upon a virtuous stone bluff.

Do you think he might be coming? Van Loon asked. What're the odds?

Depends how far he had to walk to find an axe of his own.

So that's it.

Wart weighs his chances first. He might come at you even steven but I doubt it. He wants the advantage before he does his deed. The best chance we got now is there's two of us and we got the axe.

Keep that axe, Van Loon said.

I mean to.

Are you all right? Van Loon asked.

Most of me hurts. My lungs my ribs my belly. My insides are clamouring with pain.

Can you keep moving?

As long as I got somebody to talk to I'll be fine.

God help me.

I agree with you there, Van Loon. I hope He helps me too. I hope He helps us both someday.

They walked on and Van Loon pestered Reed Kitchen as he often did regarding their direction and prospects.

When I first came to this country, Reed Kitchen said, I saw a map on the wall and railway tracks ran through Prince George east and west and north and south. We got picked up and carried out here to fight this fire and we stayed west of tracks while we were trucked a long way north. So we got one hope. That we didn't come so far north that we ran out of track. We're headed east and I do believe that somewhere we're bound to cross that mainline.

You know this way's east.

Any fool knows that.

So we're looking for the railroad.

We're looking for the railroad and a train upon the tracks.

All I see is trees. Burnt trees.

There are enough of those.

They walked on and their progress was slow with Reed Kitchen hobbled by affliction. They walked on wearily determined and Van Loon shared the last of his filched food that was a dried noodle soup they soaked in pond water within a bowl of rock. They walked on and Reed Kitchen spat blood and endured his lesser and greater pains and they advanced together. They crossed the last cremated weald and the mountains beyond were green again and the two lay down in a forest fragrant and thick and bountiful and unburnt. The next day they followed a riverbed mostly eastbound and Van Loon said, He can't trace us now. Our feet on the ash was like a map but he can't follow us now.

I hope he did follow us. Wart would die out here.

Maybe. I don't rate his chances any worse than our own.

I believe I know where I will die. It ain't here.

I'm counting on that.

In the river they cleansed themselves and washed their clothes and the water ran black away from their garments and flesh. They felt renewed and walked on and Reed Kitchen said, You wanted to live in the wilderness and now you are.

This is not what I had in mind.

You got anything against raw meat?

I'm Dutch. I eat raw meat for lunch.

Then give me back that axe.

What're you planning to do with it?

Chop deer.

Where do you see deer?

I don't. You expect me to walk up and bash a doe between the eyes when it's looking right at me?

No. Van Loon was laughing between his teeth.

You don't go hunting for what you see. You hunt for what is unseen. Deer travel down this knoll to drink and they ford the stream over there and they do it on a regular basis as anybody with eyes in his head can plainly see by looking down at his feet.

Van Loon pondered the evidence of droppings by the riverside.

Come on, Reed Kitchen said. I want you downwind with me.

They waited in their leafy downwind blind for deer to stroll by. Hungry and aggrieved and flush with water now their spirits had revived. They waited for deer and the land was dense with animals for the wilder beasts that had not burned had fled the rage of fire. They lay in their blind and Van Loon slept and Reed Kitchen tarried and affixed his heart with patience and his axe with the keen edge of awareness. He waited. The night was falling beyond the hills. He waited. He gripped his axe and watched. He waited and taunted himself awake. Across the bosk a timid prey stepped forth its nose in the air alert to a recondite scent. This was an age to mind his tongue and he was a mute hunter. He waited for the lunge of neck to pass him by. He swung the axe with the skill of a man who had hammered a thousand spikes home and true and he swung the axe with the strength of a man who had tamped ten thousand ties. He swung his axe and the neck of the beast split so gently now no resistance was aroused to obstruct the slaughter. The neck divided and the blood gushed forth as a geyser mysteriously bored in rock and the knees of the beast buckled and the animal went down and Van Loon was awakened by the pulpy sounds of carnage and jumped up and stared back into the doleful eyes of Wart sensate and surprised and overtaken with his head aflap upon the quarterneck and his blood abubble betwixt throat and shoulderstump and his eyes agog upon the verisimilitude of time's eternal guise.

Reed Kitchen extracted the axe and the boy toppled down as reticent and perplexed as any timber yet standing.

Deranged for breath Van Loon gasped with the might of his lungs. His eyes too were paramount in his head and Reed Kitchen turned behind him and lightly tucked the inside of his elbow over his friend's mouth and nose and Van Loon breathed through Kitchen's shirt until his rampage subsided.

They sat on the ground awhile with the head of the dead man between them. You call this deer? Van Loon asked Reed Kitchen.

You're right. He's too scrawny to eat.

How long have you known?

I'm aware of trains, Reed Kitchen said.

What's that supposed to mean?

I'm aware of trains.

Why didn't you tell me?

Myself personally I didn't need your help.

Why didn't you tell me, Reed?

I didn't want to scare you.

Why didn't you tell me?

You already killed one man in all this meanness. This one was my turn.

Van Loon nodded. He seemed satisfied. I guess you had a right. Getting hung.

No, Reed Kitchen said. I didn't have that right. But you already killed one man and this one was my turn.

I don't understand you.

Reed Kitchen released a gush of air. I don't feel like talking. You can quote me on that. Come on. Let's keep moving.

It'll be night soon.

We'll follow the moonlight on the river.

Ferenc Van Loon and Reed Kitchen got to their feet and Van Loon had to support his friend awhile until his pains were quelled.

Should we bury him? Van Loon asked.

Did he bury Caleb?

He didn't.

I didn't kill him for vengeance. But I will leave him here to rot and for the crows to eat and that will be my sweet revenge.

Why'd you kill him then?

Because I'm hungry and slow and weak and sore all over and I couldn't keep ahead of him much longer. That's why I killed him is that all right with you?

Okay, Van Loon said. Let's go.

Check his pockets first, Reed Kitchen said.

You want to rob him now?

I want to know if he's got food in his pockets. Something has kept him undaunted in pursuit.

I'm not going to eat his food.

You'd rather starve.

We'll do like you said. We'll bag a deer.

Anybody who thinks you can kill a deer with an axe has got to be the stupidest sod I've met yet. Are you the stupidest sod I've met yet, Van Loon?

Van Loon laughed lightly. That could be, he said.

You can't kill a deer with an axe.

Okay. I'll check his pockets.

Wart's pockets were found bare. Van Loon's skin shivered as he felt inside and he believed it was the warmth of the dead man's blood dispersing. Van Loon stood. Do we take the axe? he asked.

This is a wilderness, Reed Kitchen said. We take the axe.

They travelled down the lip of the knoll to the rocky stream and waded in. The night was darkening now and the sun was well set and they walked on slowly in the deadfall each man a prop to the other and together they managed to balance and progress. At first the moonglow and later the waning moon itself arose above the precipice and they staggered on along the riverbed. Stars resumed position and constellations aligned and planets drifted upon the cool clear air and they walked on through the night below the orbs of other deities and spoke one to the other and in the morning slept.

FERENC VAN LOON AWOKE TWITCHING and felt bugs acrawl upon his skin and determined through a rigid constituency of mind that mostly they were grass aquiver in the light. He sat up and saw that his companion had departed. Van Loon stood and peed away from where he had slept as if in deference to the next tenant of this patch and he crawled through shrub and made it out to the river to a brighter expanse of light. He called Reed Kitchen's name. He called again and he called again and he could not believe that he had been abandoned here. He walked on in the direction they had been travelling and stopped to shout at intervals and around a further riverbend discovered a bridge that spanned the gorge and upon that bridge squatted the bent figure of Reed Kitchen alone and still and intimately forsaken.

Ferenc Van Loon climbed the riverbank and scrabbled up the rock and dirt and wayward root and made it perspiring and fatigued to the crest. He walked out upon the railway bridge and Reed Kitchen did not monitor his approach and Van Loon sat between the rails facing his companion with the axe of infamy between them and they were quiet awhile and it was Van Loon who proved more eager to disrupt that silence. How did you ever get here, Reed?

Climbed up through the trestle. I have been a bridgeman. Shame on you ascending the bank like a goat and not like a man proud of his profession.

Van Loon said, I didn't mean how'd you get up on this bridge. What are you doing this far east? Why are you here fighting forest fires?

Reed Kitchen explored the hinter of his vest pocket and extracted a leaf and he asked Van Loon if he had a light. Van Loon did and Kitchen said, Good. He pinched tobacco in short supply from the base of his pocket where it had accumulated through the years. I figure we got a quarter smoke between us.

You got papers?

I got this leaf.

Reed Kitchen rolled his small smoke and they smoked it and that was like food to them and sufficient. I came to fight this fire because I expected to find you here. I was right about that.

Van Loon sat unspeaking and he did marvel rather than condemn Kitchen's folly in this land. I was surprised, he said, that day Wilf showed up in Port Essington to tell me that you had said where and when. I was surprised you even knew I was after The Sip but I guess Wilf told you that much. Maybe it was easy enough to guess. What surprised me most of all was looking down my gunsights at a choice of targets and seeing you one of them. Seeing you there walking side by side with The Sip. Walking so close together you could have been holding hands. What did you and The Sip have to do with each other, Reed? I want to hear that story.

You haven't asked me why I wanted to find you. I wanted to find you, Van Loon, to tell you of your innocence. No matter what you have read in the papers the police do not believe that you killed Caleb Farrow. They understand that now. They think you killed The Sip but they have no proof of what they must surmise. I'm here to say you're a free man.

Van Loon exhaled and passed the roach of cigarette back. I don't underestimate you, Reed. I respect you. But I got to say that for all your wisdom you are naive. If they can't convict me for the crime they know I committed they'll convict me for the crime I did not commit and think it's all the same.

Reed Kitchen appeared to mull this over as he smoked. I concur that I am not wise in the affairs of human people.

That may be. I'll tell you one thing. You're the first man I'd want by my side in a place like this.

That may be, Reed Kitchen said.

Or for that matter on a bridge.

We built that bridge, Reed Kitchen said and his eyes were luminous and for the first time that morning intent.

I don't know how to break this to you gently, Van Loon said. But I don't give a damn about that bridge.

That's a difference between us, Kitchen said.

What was between you and The Sip? Van Loon asked again.

The story was told then of his coercion and Van Loon complimented the genius of McBain's choice and lamented that Caleb Farrow had also been tied to a string and that neither man had confided in him.

That is a regret, Reed Kitchen said. And he said, I have something to say to you here today.

What's that?

The Sip told me before he died—in the interval between your shots—he told me with his dying breath that he fed Addie Day to the whales. Now when Wart strung me up and left me for dead I asked him about it and he wanted me to know with my dying breath that he had fed Addie Day to the whales. He said very much the same thing with the same words.

Van Loon sighed. No smoke remained worth smoking and he tossed the ember of the leaf into the river. I got no regrets, he said. None. The Sip and Wart can't be dead enough as far as I'm concerned.

They said they fed her to the whales, Reed Kitchen said. What does that say to you?

Van Loon shrugged. They drowned her.

It means they're lying, Reed Kitchen said. I don't only talk you know—I also listen to people. The Sip was not a man with a poetic inclination and Wart was not a man prone to vivid description. Wart told The Sip that he fed Addie Day to the whales because in fact he didn't and that was his best lie well spoken. The Sip repeated that lie to me upon his dying lips exactly as he had heard it because he did not believe it either.

Van Loon tried to unravel the thrust of Kitchen's remarks and failed. What are you saying?

I'm not saying anything that you don't want to hear, Van Loon. I'm just telling you that Addie Day's alive I do believe.

That's—How—? Where?

You were on the river that day. Did you not see a train go by?

Ferenc Van Loon canvassed his memory for the traffic of trains. Addie Day's alive?

I do believe that to be true. That is why I came here to fight this fire so that I could be in a place where you could find me. I didn't know you'd take your own sweet time.

Do you know how I found you? Van Loon asked him.

You followed the trail of bodies, Reed Kitchen surmised.

I heard people talking. I heard one of your stories repeated. That's how I knew you were here.

Yes, Reed Kitchen said. You followed the trail of stories. Stories travel in the company of men and that has always been my way.

Van Loon shook his head at such a revelation and levelled his regard. You don't know where she is, he said. Then we'll have to find her. Van Loon looked around as though Addie Day might be spotted strolling amid the lofty trees.

That's your job, Kitchen said. You will have to search among the affairs of men to find her. You know your way through the world of these places and I do not.

Van Loon considered Kitchen's remark and recognized the signal of farewell. Where will you go? Van Loon asked. What'll you do?

Reed Kitchen ineffably shrugged. Then he said, Train.

You're kidding, Van Loon said. His head perked up and he cocked an ear.

It's far off yet, Kitchen said and he added in a plaintive voice, Yesterday, Van Loon, under the eye of man and the brow of God I killed a man.

Van Loon nodded. It had to be done, Reed. Don't worry about it.

It's not the first time, Kitchen said.

What do you mean by that?

We all kill our fathers I do believe. Each in our own way. I killed mine just like mine had killed his father before him and I cannot attest to how many generations this has gone on.

What are you talking about now? Your old man tried to do you in. You defended yourself as you had to do. He was slow getting off the tracks and that's what killed him more than anything else. He put himself on those tracks and you with him so it's him who has to bear the consequences. The consequences don't fall on you. As he spoke Van Loon accepted his affection for this man and his sympathy for the pain he had endured. You told me that story, Reed.

I told you that story but that's not how it was. My father was not slow getting off those tracks. He would've gotten off those tracks but myself personally I slowed him down. I made that train run him down point of fact.

Van Loon did look to the sky and down the river gorge and his gaze rested upon the visage of Reed Kitchen. You killed him. Intentionally?

Intentionally and with meditation aforehand on the subject. That's who I am, Van Loon. To the ends of my days that's who I am.

You had to do it I guess. Just like you had to do it yesterday.

I didn't have to. I could've let one more train pass by and then another and so on through my days.

That's what I mean. You had no choice. Don't beat yourself up about this, Reed.

Train, Reed Kitchen said. And he said, You'd better get off this bridge.

What are you going to do? How're we going to stop this train?

It'll stop for you.

Let's get off. Van Loon stood. Reed? His companion showed no sign of moving. Reed—your father—that business had to be done.

Wart too. You might have had more than one choice but you made a choice and I don't see why you want to go on moaning about it now.

Moaning about it? What do you know about moaning? What do you know about raging in the night and wrestling with your own father for your own life and choosing your own life over his and why do I have this awareness of trains, Van Loon? Why do I have this awareness? Do you hear this train?

Van Loon listened silent on the bridge high above the river gorge in the midst of the forest's contented tintinnabulation. No, he said. He heard no train.

Train, Reed Kitchen said. Trrrraaaaiiiiinnnnnnn! I'm telling you. *Trrrraaaaiiiiinnnnnnn!* Believe me.

I believe you. I don't doubt you about these things.

Reed Kitchen pounded his own fist upon his chest square above the heart. I am a man because I have worked upon the railway, he declared.

Get a hold of yourself, Reed. Don't go nutty on me.

Get off this bridge, Van Loon. Or I will throw you off it.

You and what army?

Myself personally.

I'm only leaving if you do.

Then you will die here.

Then I'll die here. So what?

You got Addie Day to go find. You got something in your life. Go yourself and find her, Van Loon.

Van Loon gazed upon his seated incomprehensible friend. Why do you want to die here, Reed?

Why not here? This is a good place. I want to die upon the railway tracks of my life.

No kidding. But why now? Today?

If I had a son, Van Loon, do you know what he would do? He would kill me like my father tried before him.

Not necessarily.

He would truly kill me. Or maim me bad.

I don't understand you.

I don't work for the railway anymore. I quit before they got to fire me.

So that's it. Van Loon squatted down.

I gave you something didn't I?

What'd you give me, Reed?

You forgot already? You're an ingrate, Van Loon. I gave you back your life. I gave you back the knowledge of the life of Addie Day and now you have your purpose.

I'm not getting off this bridge without you. How much time do we have here, Reed?

You can't hear that train yet? Are you deaf? You can't hear that train?

Van Loon pried the day with his senses and he could detect no train. No I can't, Reed.

My daddy used to say to me when he was so inclined, This train—this train is gonna blow you to kingdom come, boy. I'm saying that to you now, Van Loon, and I want you to listen even though it is clear to me that you are a deaf man. This train, Van Loon, this train will demolish you here today.

Van Loon made a fist over the front of Kitchen's jacket and with one strong jerk raised him upon his feet. Reed Kitchen did not slump and remained standing and Van Loon appeared prepared to strike him down when he stopped and tilted his head.

What? Kitchen asked.

I heard it. He waited. I can hear it.

This train, Reed Kitchen whispered, this train is bound for glory. This train will rattle your bones. This train will blast your mind apart and ransack the empty hollow of your devoured soul. This train will blow you to kingdom come unless you get yourself off this bridge forthwith.

I'm taking you off with me if you're not coming.

I'm not coming.

Van Loon seized him up close then began to drag him.

Reed Kitchen said, I have my tricks.

Big deal. I'm an exmarine.

Well I'm an exrailroadingman and I was a better one than you everyday of the week and I could do many things that you could not do and I did all things better.

Says who? Van Loon asked and he kept dragging him along although Reed Kitchen resisted him now and each tie was hard won.

Ask anybody, Reed Kitchen dared him.

Then let's go ask them.

We'll ask them from beyond the grave me and you.

You're coming off this bridge, Reed. They wrestled and spun together with the river far below and progress was not made in either direction now.

They stood face to face and one man's exhalation was the other man's breath. Stand with me here, Van Loon.

What?

This should keep.

What does that mean? Van Loon demanded with anger and affliction in his voice.

What does that mean?

What does it mean?

What does it mean?

What does it mean?

This should keep. It means that this day and this moment and this incident will survive the harvest of your soul and it will be a part of you always no matter if you live or if you die or whether you come or go. They wrestled on the bridge and Reed Kitchen in his sorrow wailed, You have me at a disadvantage. My body is sore from outside in and inside out again.

Don't give me your excuses.

Well you get yourself hung! You get yourself hung and see how that feels. See how much you like it!

Van Loon locked Kitchen's head in his arms and pulled him along. Is that what's bothering you?

They hung me. They hung me, Van Loon. They hung me with a hose and if I had showed them how to tie the noose I'd be a dead man now.

They were wild men, Reed, Van Loon said and they stumbled on the bridge above the gorge and Van Loon fought and achieved his feet and pulled Reed Kitchen along.

Everybody hangs me, Reed Kitchen complained.

That's because you talk too much.

I don't talk too much, Van Loon. I don't talk enough as far as I'm concerned.

If only you would shut your yap once in awhile. Give it a rest.

Nose to nose each man was seized by the grip of the other and Van Loon gained advantage with every step and they battled and endured and Reed Kitchen forswore, It's only human to talk! It's only human!

Van Loon spoke with quietude on this morning. You overdo it a bit that's all.

I overdo it?

That's right.

I have a fault within me?

You could put it that way.

And for that fault within me I get hung?

Only by madmen, Reed.

I get hung by the whole damn world. You know it to be true. For me to live I have to ditch myself in the wilderness and be a wilderness man but that is never what I wish myself to be. I want to walk among people and enjoy multifarious conversations and if that means that from time to time I babble then let me babble on! At least if you ever get yourself hung it will be because you killed a man—with me it's because I'm gregarious. Where is the justice in that?

With a swift counter in lieu of a response Van Loon spun his opponent around and achieved the edge of the bridge. They stood bound in one another's grasp and saw the train approach at fair speed along the slight and long downgrade. Now we'll step off this track, Van Loon said and he heaved to no avail.

You step off. I gave you back your life.

I saved you once already.

You thought I was a corpse. You chopped me down to bury the dead.

They adjusted and spun again and no change to their position ensued.

Stand with me, Van Loon, Reed Kitchen said.

No.

Then let me go in peace and get away from my life.

No.

The train attained the other end of the bridge now and churned toward them blind in its progress and the men were unseen and unaccounted for in this wry and vacant land.

This should keep, Reed Kitchen said.

Yes. It should.

I gave you Addie Day to look for. I gave you back your life.

You did that but I will save yours anyhow.

Let me die in peace. I don't want any more of this. Let me die in peace and the son that I do not have will thank you for saving him the trouble.

You're a pain in the ass, Reed.

I don't speak that language but so are you. They struggled and the train approached and their heads conjoined and Reed Kitchen laughed at the sight of them on the quiet of this day with the engineer asleep at his throttle and all their lives consumed. Van Loon grunted and accelerated his fight and Reed Kitchen matched him and he cried, It's gonna blow you to kingdom come, Van Loon.

You just want me to die with you so you can talk my head off after we're dead.

That's occurred. Are you prepared to die, Van Loon?

I'm prepared.

Reed Kitchen pulled him up to him and the train was nigh upon them now and Van Loon turned to the light of the train and all that he was was shining in the light and he knew now that he had no time to disengage from Kitchen or disparage him further and he had no time to escape and he looked at Reed Kitchen at the moment of his death who was smiling now and who told him as the locomotive thundered down upon their lives, I have my tricks, and soon the axis of the world did shift and his life was spun away.

VAN LOON SKIDDED AND TUMBLED DOWN the steep stone grade and
abutted against a boulder painted with lichen. The train pounded past
him. A relatively short train—twenty or at the most thirty cars in
length. He scrabbled to his feet before the train was gone and clambered
back up the slope. He looked for Reed Kitchen on his own side of the
rails and he was not there and the train went past him and he looked for
Reed Kitchen on the other side and he was not located. He called his
name and received a mute response. His nerves were in riot and Van
Loon scanned the distance further off the tracks where the body might
have been thrown and peered over the edge of the bridge into the gorge
below. No Reed Kitchen. He did at last look upon the vanishing
cabooseless train and there upon the rooftop of the last car bent double
laughing was Reed Kitchen who was managing also to wave.

Van Loon sunk upon his knees and he was wracked by joy himself
and a paroxysm of laughter overcame him that he could not control.
He waved to the departing friend as though to a spirit ascending to
the sky and to the clouds no more to be known upon this plane. The
train became minute and the last Van Loon saw of Reed Kitchen his
friend was walking down the rooftops of the cars probably to arouse
the engineer for a chat.

Van Loon did not know if the train ever would stop for him as he
ambled down the tracks in faint pursuit. He had gone some twenty
paces when he halted and returned to the bridge to fetch the axe.
Reed Kitchen had forewarned him. This is a wilderness. We take the
axe. He retrieved the axe and in so doing believed that the train
would not be braking for him and it would not be braking because
Reed Kitchen would not ask this train to stop. He took the axe and
walked back the way the train had vanished. In the parabolic silence
cast off by the rampage of the locomotive Van Loon moved as
through a sphere unknown while all that was known to him and
clairvoyant lay outside a protective cocoon of still and calm and
opaque quiet.

He walked along the tracks and balanced on a rail and Van Loon
confessed that he had not felt this fine for miles. He had felt neither
this free nor this forgiving. The passage of the train had made him

giddy. This was straight track and dull track and he followed it down
and the track offered him direction in the wilderness of his life and
that was something extraordinary enough. He thought about Reed
Kitchen. He tried to conjure the permutations of mind that led Reed
Kitchen to abandon him here. He could not at first. As he walked and
the day wore on he delved more readily into the contours of Kitchen's
thinking and insinuations presented themselves and he mulled over
his divinations somewhat absent in his mind with fatigue and suddenly he knew as though the very axe he carried had chopped the
idea into his noggin why Reed Kitchen had been terrified by his
awareness of trains. Kitchen was not convinced that he actually did
hear the onslaught of a train before anyone else. Reed Kitchen feared
that he himself summoned trains out of the bedlam of the earth—that
he invoked their wrath and fury—and that he like any man possessed
innate within him the power and the inclination at times to awaken
the world from its fitful rest and blast through the dormant inhos-
pitable land with wickedness and affliction and pain and death and
that that power was inherent in his being to so invoke the infernal
wonders of this world and that was the power that he acknowledged
and feared and rode upon as he strode upon trains. Reed Kitchen
dreaded the god within him empowered by his own godlessness in a
savage land and Van Loon understood why this train would not stop
for him on this day. Reed Kitchen would not let him on board as his
final act of kindness and tutelage. He would not let him on board just
as he had chosen to bludgeon Wart himself to spare Van Loon the
ignominy and spare Van Loon the blood of another upon his soul for
Reed Kitchen believed that he had evoked Wart by the blood upon
his hands and the death thereunto and that he had evoked him as
surely and as decidedly as he had provoked the train to erupt from the
bowels of the earth's portent. For the world enslaves its citizens in the
mercy of their own devising and Reed Kitchen had delivered him
instead unto the clear wild spirit he had sought and he had abandoned him thereafter upon track and country ennobled and transformed. Van Loon surmised that he would need to catch the next
train travelling in unknown direction for the nature of Reed Kitchen's

grace was to spare his friend the affliction of this train and this world by taking it upon himself and Van Loon walked on brave and alone and destined to traverse those rails.

Van Loon walked on and he heard the voice in his head and upon his breathing that he likened to the voice of Reed Kitchen that babbling brook and knew then that his companion had been right—he had had so much to say and he had never actually been allowed to say it and Van Loon wished now that Reed Kitchen was here so he might be privileged to listen to him speak. Van Loon did not view himself as a man free at last as he had once desired himself to be. He wondered what it was he had now become. He wanted to identify his new and inhabited guise and the best that he could say to himself which did provoke a smile was that he now knew that he was a man because he had worked upon the railway. He walked on and in the constellation of his day his own star would yet rise and in the stoutness of his heart Van Loon observed the traffic of those trains and roar and thunder and their bedlam beseeched him and their divine rambunctious noise and he was persuaded as well that he could summon trains from their hibernation beneath the crust of this land and rock and forest from without the enmity of nations and from within the raucous unleashed disturbance of his heart he said, Train. Quietly. Softly. Aloud. He said, Train.

THE END